PLACEBO
JUNKIES

ALSO BY J. C. CARLESON

The Tyrant's Daughter

PLACEBO JUNKIES

J.C. CARLESON

ALFRED A. KNOPF
NEW YORK

Text copyright © 2015 by J. C. Carleson
Jacket photograph copyright © 2015 by Ray Shappell
Interior illustrations copyright © 2015 by Shutterstock

Visit us on the Web! randomhouseteens.com

Educators and librarians, for a variety of teaching tools, visit us at RHTeachersLibrarians.com

Library of Congress Cataloging-in-Publication Data
Carleson, J. C.
Placebo junkies / J.C. Carleson. — First edition.
pages   cm.
Summary: Teenaged Audie pushes her mind and body to the breaking point when she participates in a series of clinical drug trials for cash.
ISBN 978-0-553-49724-3 (trade) — ISBN 978-0-553-49725-0 (lib. bdg.) — ISBN 978-0-553-49726-7 (ebook)
[1. Drugs—Testing—Fiction. 2. Placebos (Medicine)—Fiction. 3. Medicine—Research—Fiction. 4. Mental illness—Fiction. 5. Love—Fiction.] I. Title.
PZ7.C21479Pl 2015
[Fic]—dc23
2014042559

The text of this book is set in 11.5-point Minion.

Printed in the United States of America
October 2015
10 9 8 7 6 5 4 3 2 1

First Edition

*For my boys, who are
both the cause of and the cure for
most of the craziness in my life*

PROLOGUE

Subject # 4 0 1 8 3 2 6 6 9 7
Male, DOB 4/15/1987
Allergies: none
Blood type: AB+
Immigration status: temporary (B-1/B-2)
Emergency contact: none

Check a box. Initial.

Check a box. Initial.

Waiver, waiver, sign and date.

Consent. Acknowledge.

Release.

It's money in your wallet, every little square. Check a box, ka-ching.
Check a box, ka-ching.

Fuck yes, consent.

You wake to a burning sensation.

It gets worse as you shove off your covers and stiff-leg limp down the hall, then sails way past critical and all the way to freaking *agony* as your urine stream rat-a-tats unevenly into the toilet bowl, and it's all you can do to stop it, hold in that razor-blade wetness long enough to find a cup, a bucket, anything to catch it, *dammit,* and you barely manage to stifle your scream of triumph as you find an empty Snapple bottle in the trash can and fill it with your beautiful, cloudy piss with its faint but unmistakable trace of blood.

You're mesmerized by the dancing sunset clouds of bacteria and protein, afraid to believe it at first, this pastel *screw you* note from your kidneys.

A verifiable side effect.

Ka-ching.

The other squatters see what's in your bottle as you walk out of the bathroom, and their faces go hard with envy.

It's money in your pocket, this cotton-candy piss. You hit the jackpot, you can see it in their eyes, those poor placebo motherfuckers.

You keep your bottle next to you while you scarf your breakfast, then you take it for a stroll. The lab doesn't open until nine and you never know what some of these people will do for money.

One more month. That's all you have to last.

One more month till you have enough. Then you can close up shop, say *sayonara* to the needles and the pills, and give your orifices a much-deserved rest. It's nothing, thirty days—a hop a skip and a hump. Could be even less if the burning turns out to be serious. They don't mess around with serious here. Bad for business. No faster way to get paid—here's your check, don't let the door hit you on your way out.

You knew it could happen when they sent you to the twelfth floor, but no pain, no gain (*pain pain pain*).

It's nothing that a little rest won't take care of, maybe a bowl of Mom's spicy beef soup. By then your appetite will surely reappear. Good old Mom will put the meat back on your bones. Your bones.

Your bones.

It's 9:00. Time to get to work.

CHAPTER 1

Charlotte comes back from her six-week protocol bloated and yellow. She takes one look at me, her gaze skipping over my patchy hair and scabby skin, and her jaundiced eyes fill with tears. "You lucky bitch. You're so skinny," she says.

"Don't worry," Jameson calls out from the other room. "They're starting psychostimulant trials on Four again, probably later this week. That shit'll knock the junk off your trunk in no time."

But Charlotte refuses to cheer up. "With my luck I'll just get a placebo."

She sounds so glum I wonder if whatever gave her a case of the oompa loompas also messed with her head. It happens sometimes. It's hard to know whether it's a side effect or just a bad mood these days. For any of us. Still, after six weeks in she should be happier—most of us would kill for that kind of stint. The longest I've ever gone in was eight days. It was heavenly. Premium cable channels and doctor's orders to do nothing but lie around drinking chalky weight-loss shakes. No exertion allowed except twice-daily weigh-ins—*aye aye, captain!* The shakes weren't bad, either. I wonder if they ever made it to market. You'd be surprised how many of these things never do.

Jameson does his little nervous-habit throat-clearing thing as he comes in with a glass of something for Charlotte. "Drink up. It's just water with a squeeze of lime. You need to flush out your system, lower your bilirubin levels if you want to get in on anything starting before the weekend."

They don't let us volunteer if they think we still have side effects from another study. It screws up their results. But there are ways to beat the system, and if anyone knows how to do it, it's Jameson, who's kind of like a highly anxious cross between an Eagle Scout and a drug dealer, if that makes any sense. I mean, he might supplement his income with a little under-the-table pill-transfer action, but it's not like he's selling crack to schoolkids, you know? He's actually really into the medical stuff—he has all sorts of pharmaceutical reference books lying around all the time, and he reads research journals, Annals of Dermo-Oto-Neuro-blah-blah Medicine, shit like that, for fun while the rest of us play Xbox or whatever. He always wants to know what we took, how we took it, what we felt, and depending on what it is, he'll sometimes buy it off us if we have any left over. He doesn't even blush when you tell him the embarrassing parts, like rectal suppositories or period stuff. Seriously, he knows more than most of the doctors I've met—he'd probably be the world's youngest brain surgeon by now if he'd turned left instead of right back at whatever fork in the road spit him out on the low-rent side of the tracks instead.

6

I sometimes wonder if he shouldn't be volunteering, a guy like him. I mean, not just because he's too smart for this shit, but also because he's gotta throw off the results with all the ways he's always gaming the system. *Anomalous response* they call it, when you don't react the way they expect you to, and they get pissed when it happens. Well, pissed in their quiet, lab-coat-y kind of way. They're pretty cool in general, the techs. Most of them, anyway. They know we're just there to do a job, same as them.

Dougie and Scratch show up with beer and a stack of dirty magazines Dougie got from some Viagra-lite kind of trial, and Charlotte and I snort and laugh our way through the pages because they're the cleanest porno mags you'll ever see—completely raunch-free. They're really not even sexy at all, like the photographer was standing behind the camera telling the models to think about good hygiene. Just the thought of some middle-aged lab administrator leafing through a catalog of medical-grade pornography and placing a bulk smut order cracks me up, and before long we're all relaxed and it starts to feel like a party, so I reach for one of the beers even though I'm not supposed to have any alcohol during the study I'm in now. I glance over at Jameson before I take a sip and he gives me a tiny nod. He knows about the restrictions and he'd warn me if the beer was going to show up in the morning blood work. With his blessing I tilt my head back and enjoy.

Even Charlotte chills out. She's talking about this guy she knows, swears he's the reason for the tattoos. "Yeah, so he got into an appendix study. A big one, huge cash. Like, lottery kind of cash, and all you had to do was let them take out your appendix. Like anyone's ever needed an appendix, right? He doesn't even know what they're testing. Some robot laser scalpel, or something—freaking sutures that play 'Ave Maria,' whatever. Doesn't matter. So my buddy goes through with it, gets his appendix removed and collects his check. But he's kind of a dumbass, see—I mean, he's a nice enough guy, just not the sharpest tool in the shed—and he goes out and blows all the money right away on something stupid. I don't even know how he possibly spent all the money as fast as he did, but he managed. So what does he do next?"

By now we're already laughing, having a good time, and my tolerance must be way down, probably from all the weight I lost last week, because my head is feeling spinny and light. We all know exactly where this story is going, but Charlotte's such a damn good storyteller, especially now that her funk seems to have worn off, that we're all hanging on her words anyway. Charlotte's a good egg. Lights up a room when she's in a good mood, you know? She already looks a little less jaundiced, too, though it might just be the dim lights. I notice Jameson scooching the beer out of her reach while she's distracted.

"Yeah, so he shaves off his goatee, combs his hair a little different, and goes right back to the same damn office. Says he lost his intake paperwork, but he still remembers his subject number."

Scratch calls bullshit here, but Charlotte cuts him off. "No, I'm telling you. He just took a wild guess, used his old number then added ten or something. And the intake tech totally buys it. The same one, by the way, who processed him in the first time around, but he doesn't suspect a thing. It's just another lab rat checking in, right? We all look the same to them—nothing but human petri dishes shuffling through the door. So anyway, my buddy's getting prepped for surgery, and the doc sees his scar from the first time and freaks out. I mean, it's not even a real scar yet, the goddamn sutures were barely out and it's right over his appendix, of course. But I swear to God, this guy is the best liar you'll ever meet. Even better than you, Scratch." She blows him a kiss before she continues.

"Even half dosed up on the twilight sedation stuff, or whatever it was they were using for anesthesia, he manages to convince the doc his scar has nothing to do with his appendix—no, he swears it's from a car accident the week before, just a nasty gash. And the doc's busy, he just wants to move the meat off his table, you know, so he says fine, signs the paperwork, and cuts my friend open again."

"Whoops," Dougie drawls out in a baritone.

"Yeah, whoops is right. No fucking appendix, and the doc is *pissed*! But he'd already signed off, already cut in, so they had no choice but to pay my buddy the full amount. *Again.*" She giggles, then wipes a tiny speck of blood from the corner of her mouth. "So thanks to him, now they do the tats."

We nod. We all have 'em. Little *x*'s or numbers, or sometimes initials. They're not tattoo artists, the techs and the nurses, so they don't try anything fancy. They just make whatever kind of quick mark they'll remember so they don't accidentally go in twice. There's this one nurse who does a tiny smiley face, though, which I kind of appreciate. I have a couple of those.

There's a lull in the conversation, so I check my watch. "Okay, y'all, it's getting late—I'm out." I yawn a good night to everyone, then bat my eyelashes at Charlotte and Jameson. "Can you guys boost your awesome roommate creds by making sure I don't oversleep tomorrow? Pretty please? Subject processing starts at 8:30."

"Sweet electric sheep dreams," Jameson calls after me as I close my bedroom door and turn out the light. He's a little weird, I know, but who isn't? They're like my family out there, those needle-tracked guinea pig fools.

CHAPTER 2

TODAY'S POST: GETTING STARTED
So, you think you want to be a professional volunteer?

First thing you should know is, not all clinical trials are created equal. General rule of thumb: the more it pays, the worse it's probably gonna hurt. More on that later. But assuming you can take it, that you're not some delicate fucking flower who can't stand the sight of blood or who gets all bent out of shape about things like radiation exposure, here are some tips for how to make a living as a human test subject:

Tip 1.
Have a pulse and at least one
vein that's not on the verge of collapse.

Ha ha. You think I'm kidding, but this is seriously enough to at least get you in the door. Though judging from some of the people you'll meet in the waiting room, the pulse part can be negotiable.

Tip 2.
Be healthy.

Be able to fake it, anyway. Hold it in, cover it up, tell the voices in your head to pipe down for a minute, whatever it takes. Do whatever you gotta do to stay upright long enough to at least get through the screening. Once you're on the books, you can let it all hang out—you'll still get at least a partial payment even if they show you the door the minute your TB test comes back dirty.

Tip 3.
Come from a healthy family.

I don't care if you come from the sickliest, dead-est family ever. When filling out the forms, no one in your family has ever died, *ever*, from anything except ripe old age. Healthy bastards, your forefathers, yes sirree bob! Absolutely no family history whatsoever of high blood pressure, bad cholesterol, or paranoid schizophrenia, no ma'am. Healthy as horses, every last (dead) one of 'em.

Tip 4.
Be at least 18 years
of age, or have parental consent.

Or, in my case, have a reasonably convincing fake ID. Don't worry, they never look too close. As long as you're a warm, willing body who meets their testing criteria, they really don't care if your driver's license has the name of the state spelled a teensy bit wrong. (For the record, yes, I DO know that Massachusetts has two *t*'s. Lesson learned: proofread forged documents before paying.)

Ready to channel your inner pincushion and get started now? Just follow my lead and then rinse, gargle, repeat. Happy testing, fellow guinea pigs!

CHAPTER 3

Damn. She's a Beagle, and it's too late to move.

I should've known. Should've seen the look on her face before I sat down, that *aren't I generous* set to the mouth, that martyr's twinkle in her eyes. But there's no changing seats once the needle's in, so now I'm stuck listening to her Humble Tales of Great Sacrifice and Small Thoughts About Life.

Kill me now.

There are five stations set up in the room. Deep reclining chairs covered in long strips of crinkly white paper. Bottles of juice and water within easy reach, two types of muffins. A fan going in the corner. Everything all alcohol-swabbed and vinyl-padded faint-proof. All is as it should be, if only Mother Teresa's second cousin on my left would pipe down. Yup, definitely a Beagle—a particularly annoying subtype of serial tester. Beagles are the people who act like volunteering for a drug study is some grand act of charity, like they're doing the world the biggest damn favor ever, and *by God,* we'd sure as heck better appreciate their sacrifice. She rummages around in her enormous quilted purse and pulls out knitting needles. Of course she does. Why do they all knit so much? Seriously, what can they possibly need with all that knotted-up yarn, these *just doing my part* little old ladies? Funny the way they never shut up about just how great it is, what they're doing, though, always wearing their Red Cross T-shirts and their I DONATED pins. They're gray-haired junkies in reverse, always wanting to pump shit out of their veins instead of in. And they Never. Stop. Talking.

This one's no exception. On and on and freaking *on*, about her favorite Crock-Pot recipes and her grandniece's birthday party, and isn't that Kelly Ripa just the sweetest thing ever, and most of all her son, her nice-boy CPA son who's almost certainly a deviant of some variety, I mean how could you not be, with a mother like this up in your grill all the time? I pick at my cuticles without saying a word, just waiting for her to mention a cat. There's always a cat. Or at the very least there's a cat-sized dog, a Shih Tzu or a Pomeranian. Something small enough for a goddamn knitted dog sweater.

Her knitting needles click-clack while she talks, making her IV line jiggle and sway, and on the opposite side of the room there's a talk show playing too loudly on the TV.

In other words, it's a typical day in the labs.

Today's an interaction study. Two drugs already on the market, already considered safe enough to use, just not necessarily together. It's not twice the money, but close. Interaction studies pay well.

This one's not complicated, but the nurse is obviously

brand-new and she keeps botching things up and having to start her checklist over. It's a double-blind study, and you can just see how that totally messes with her mind. Double-blind means, basically, nobody knows who's getting what. One pill and one IV drip per subject. *Is it real, or is it fake?* Neither the volunteers nor the nurse knows whether we're getting sugar and saline or some toxic chemical brew—an autoclaved version of Russian roulette.

As she checks us in, the nurse keeps asking everyone in this way-too-serious voice if we're absolutely *certain* that we understand the risks of the study. *Yeah, yeah,* we all say, and even the Beagle next to me looks a bit annoyed the fifth time we have to hear the same speech.

"She's awfully nervous; she must be new. It took her three tries to find my vein," the Beagle tsks, admiring the needle marks on her skin like they're freaking stigmata. "That never happens. I have great veins! Phlebotomists love me. They tell me so every time I come to donate. They say, Phyllis, you have amazing veins for your age. You're a dream donor. If only everyone had veins like yours, our job would be so much easier. . . ."

I tune her out by running numbers in my head, trying to figure out this month's likely cash flow. This business is hard to predict—lots of ups and downs. It's like a freaking game of Monopoly, except instead of landing on Park Place, you find out the FDA just tightened the screws on some product and all of a sudden Mama and Papa Pharma are willing to pay double, triple for as many volunteers as they can get through the door. Catch a cold, on the other hand, and it's the equivalent of pulling the GO TO JAIL card when you get the boot from the study that was supposed to pay the rent that month. *Womp-womp, Do not pass go, Do not collect $200.* Anyway, I'm mentally sorting the figures into little columns, working out best-case and worst-case scenarios—am I gonna bust or am I gonna boom?—so it takes me a minute to process the fact that the Beagle's voice is starting to sound weird.

I look over and her face, which was perfectly normal last time I noticed, is mottled with bright pink splotches now. She's still talking, hasn't even stopped to take a breath, which probably isn't helping matters, but her words are coming out funny— slurred, like her tongue is growing too big for her mouth all of a sudden. And then I think she realizes something's not right, because her eyebrows kind of pinch together and she finally shuts up for a second. She's looking puffier than I remember and I can hear from my seat, even over the noise of the fan and the TV, that she's making a whistling noise when she breathes. She cocks her head and stares at me with those big concerned eyes, and God help me, but she really *does* look like an actual beagle now—a thought I shove out of my head right away, because even I know how fucked up it is to be thinking it at this particular moment.

"Nurse?" I call out, but she doesn't hear me at first, because she's messing with someone else's IV. I look back at the old lady just in time to see the pink fade out of her face like someone flushed a toilet in her head and drained out the color, and then a pale blue shade starts to creep into her lips. It's pretty creepy, actually.

"Nurse! Hey! Somebody get over here quick!" I yell it this

time, and without even realizing I'm doing it, I yank the IV out of my hand and then step over and, more gently, pull the IV out of the Beagle's hand.

"What the hell are you doing?" the nurse asks as she finally gets her ass over to us, like I'm the one making the old lady twitch and wheeze.

"She's having a reaction or something. It happened all of a sudden—just now." I can't seem to get my words out fast enough, and for a second I worry that maybe I'm having a reaction, too, that it's slowing me down, taking over, but as the nurse races over to a phone on the wall and hits a couple of buttons, I realize I'm breathing just fine.

I take the old lady's hand while the nurse is on the other side of the room on the phone. She's definitely bluish and having trouble breathing, but she's conscious at least, still staring at me with those puppy dog eyes. "You'll be okay," I say to her. "They're getting help."

Paramedics burst into the room a minute later, one of the good things about being right next door to a major hospital, I guess, and I get shoved out of the way when they start CPR.

"There's blood! Where's she bleeding from?" one of the paramedics shouts as they move her onto a stretcher.

"No, that's my blood," I explain to him, holding out my shredded hand. I must've yanked the needle out the wrong direction—it's starting to sting. The nurse glares at me again, and then they're all out the door, still thrashing and pumping away at the old lady's chest.

I just stare at the door for a minute after they're gone. The whole thing seemed kind of violent and rushed, not at all like what you see on TV or in those perky "CPR Saves a Life!" instructional videos that make it look like getting CPR might even feel kind of good, just a particularly vigorous massage to work out some pesky cardiac tension.

I shake it off, look around, and the other three volunteers are just sitting there in silence. They're all eyeing their own IV lines nervously, but nobody moves.

"Do you think we'll still get paid if we pull it out?" one of them, a stubble-faced guy I've seen around before, finally asks.

Shit. That hadn't even occurred to me. "Shit." I say it out loud and sit back down in my chair, wondering if it's worth trying to get the damn butterfly needle back in. Probably not, even if I could manage it. The nurse already saw me moving around without it. There goes at least half my paycheck. They still have to pay you something, at least part of the fee, even if you drop out, but it won't come close to what I would have gotten if I'd kept my ass in my chair.

I close my eyes and subtract a chunk of money from my mental spreadsheet while I wait for the nurse to get back. Leaving test subjects unsupervised is a major no-no, but who's going to report it? Besides, she and everyone else even remotely associated with this study are already going to be up to their teeth in paperwork after what happened to the old lady. I kind of feel bad for everybody involved.

Better to just take whatever they'll pay and walk away from this one. There's bad juju here, and that shit's more contagious than anything else you'll run across in these halls.

CHAPTER 4

Back home I start telling Charlotte about what happened with the Beagle, but she stops me before I get very far. "Quit avoiding the subject, Audie," she says, and throws a handful of popcorn at me. "You still haven't given me an answer for Leonardo Di-Caprio. Before he got all jowly, obviously."

I have no strong feelings whatsoever about Leonardo Di-Caprio, pre- or post-jowls, but I make a stabbing motion just to mix things up. We're playing celebrity Marry, Fuck, Kill, but Charlotte never wants to kill anyone.

"I'm not a pacifist or anything," she says when I point it out to her. "I just have commitment issues. Killing's too permanent—with my luck I'd off somebody then realize two minutes later they were actually the love of my life. I prefer to keep my options open." She chews on a fingernail for a minute, until her face brightens with a solution. "There are plenty of guys I'd like to kick in the nuts."

We change the game to Marry, Fuck, Sack Tap, and that evens out our ratio considerably.

"There's something I want to talk to you about," Charlotte says once the popcorn bowl is empty. "A proposal."

"You're in no condition to be making any proposals," I say. "You just expressed your desire to marry the biggest douche bag in the history of reality television. Your judgment is obviously impaired."

"Not *that* kind of a proposal, smart-ass. Though any man would be lucky to call me his wife."

"That goes without saying." I roll my eyes, then duck as she swats at me.

"Shut up and hear me out," she says. "I'm being serious here. I think it's time for us to cash out. Or cash in. Whatever. I'm just sick of this place. I'm sick of being sick, you know? I can't take it anymore. I'm starting to feel like a prisoner."

I start to say something sarcastic about how no one's stopping her from getting up and leaving right this second, but then I notice the look on her face. For once, Charlotte is being completely serious.

She sits up straight, something else unusual for her, and explains her plan.

It's simple enough: She's going to sign up for everything. *Everything.* She's willing to consent to anything—she'll do any study that'll take her, until her pockets are bursting with cash, and then she's going to hit the road and never look back. It's a guinea pig marathon. A game of endurance. "Come on, Audie. It'll work even better if we partner up. I have a system all figured out."

Her system largely consists of binge-testing in staggered

shifts. She'll drag me home from my shifts, I'll prop her upright during hers. We'll run distraction for each other if the lab administrators ask too many questions, vouch for one another's unerring compliance, that kind of thing. We'll be the guinea pig equivalent of sober sisters.

I wait until she's done talking and then I tell her it sounds like suicide by experiment. "You should've seen the old lady this morning, Charlotte. The Beagle. She seriously looked like she was about two minutes away from Game Over. No one ever talks about it, but bad stuff does happen here sometimes."

Charlotte heaves a melodramatic sigh at me, and when she answers, it's in the slow voice she uses with people she thinks are stupid. "Duh, Audie. I'm not going to actually *take* all the shit they give me. I'm not an idiot. Don't tell me you actually swallow every pill they give you."

It's not a question, the way she says it. Ethics do not weigh heavily on Charlotte's mind.

Charlotte prefers to focus on survival.

"Here's how you do it." She starts telling me all the ways you can fake your way through studies. I've heard some of them, but she's turned the tricks people use around here into a science. I can't help but be impressed—Charlotte can be quite the little schemer when she wants to be.

Toss back a few caffeine pills and then chain-smoke three cigarettes just outside the doctor's office and your blood pressure goes sky-high, she says.

Fake a pregnancy with twenty bucks and a quick trip to the waiting room of the low-income clinic. There's always someone

22

willing to sell you a nice warm cup of piss brimming with all the right hormones.

Scarf a triple brownie sundae three hours before your glucose test.

"Fast when they say eat, and eat when they say fast," she says.

Load up on iron supplements and aspirin for five days before giving a stool sample. Mix metal shavings into Vaseline and rub it on your body before an MRI. "It'll fuck up their results enough they'll have to pay you to come back and do it all over again."

Drink enough Visine and you'll slip into a coma.

Charlotte has done a lot of homework. She closes her eyes and shows me the way she gasped and snorted her way into a diagnosis of obstructive sleep apnea just last week.

"What?" she asks when she opens her eyes and sees the way I'm looking at her. She knows people who've faked cancer. She knows someone serving a rough prison sentence who faked tuberculosis convincingly enough to ride out the rest of his time in a cozy isolation room. "Did you know you can order tapeworm larvae on the Internet?"

It's no big deal. Everybody does it, Charlotte says.

I happen to know she's right.

I remember the feel of a specimen cup shoved between my legs, my mother's voice hissing at me to *hurry up and tinkle, baby, you can do it, just hurry, goddamn it!* while the HR person waited outside. Back in the days when she occasionally held on to a job, dear old Mom could always come up with a reason for why I had to come into work with her on drug-testing days. My day care burned down, or maybe I'd just been sent home for lice—her lies rarely skimped on tragedy or humiliation.

So yeah, everybody does it, but that still doesn't make Charlotte's plan a good idea. Right now I do maybe two or three studies a week, on average. It doesn't sound like a lot, but once you factor in the paperwork, lab visits, hours and hours of observation time, and multiple appointments for each study, it's practically a full-time job.

And then you need to figure in the pain. The recovery time. The side effects. The blisters, the fevers, the days and days of knock-you-retching-to-the-ground nausea.

It's just not possible to keep up the kind of pace Charlotte's talking about. Besides, it's not so bad here. It really isn't. This is just one of Charlotte's funks talking.

And yet, I can see the appeal.

Her plan is completely unrealistic. It's crazy, really—stupid, dangerous crazy. But the money . . . the money would be nice.

I happen to have a great need for money at the moment. I haven't told Charlotte anything about it, but she's the kind of person who can sniff out that sort of thing. Charlotte's the kind of person who can smell weakness.

I don't mean that in a bad way. It's a useful skill in a place like this.

"I see that greedy little gleam in your eye," she says. "I can tell you're thinking about it. Hey, maybe we can even take off together when we're done. We'll be like Thelma and Louise, or something. I don't even care where we go. Just . . . away."

"You know what happened to Thelma and Louise, right? They died." But I can feel myself considering what the money would mean.

She shrugs. Grins. "Who cares? That movie was so good. Ooh, speaking of—vintage Brad Pitt: Marry, Fuck, or Sack Tap?"

I don't say anything. It's a ridiculous idea, not even worth talking about.

"Hello? Earth to Audie?" Charlotte nudges me with her foot.

"I'll think about it," I say.

I like to keep my options open, too.

CHAPTER 5

Sometime during the night I wake up, just barely, and Dylan is pressed against me.

This is a love story, after all. Are you surprised by that?

I don't remember hearing him come in, but we're in my bed, spooning. After the fiasco of a morning, I talked my way into a quickie procedure study and got nicked by a catheter wielded by some shaky-handed little shit of an intern, so I don't feel like fooling around. Did I tell Dylan about that already? I don't remember telling him, but my thoughts are all blurry, so who knows. Or maybe he can just tell.

The lab supervisor gave me a couple of Vicodin by way of apology, so I'm woozy on top of sore—maybe that's why I didn't hear him come in—but Dylan is awesome about stuff like that. He's been there, too. Not literally, obviously, though I'm sure guys can get their own version of catheter injuries. I just mean he's been sick enough that even the thought of sex is like someone rubbing sandpaper over a sunburn. Just . . . *no.* He gets it.

He's not a tester, though. Well, he is, but he isn't. I just mean it's not a career for him.

Testing saved his life.

Dylan's kind of a celebrity around the labs. He's an outlier. An anomaly. A six-foot-one, amber-eyed discrepancy. Usually that's a bad thing around here, but in his case it means that unlike the other thirty-odd people in his sample group, he's alive. A particularly nasty cancer, fast and mean—I picture his tumors in stained wifebeater tanks, muttering with my dad's bourbon scrape of a voice—and a violent brute of a treatment to match. Dylan somehow survived both. He alone still stands.

Rather, Dylan still lies. Here in bed. With me. His breath is warm against my bare shoulder.

He's my very own improbable outcome, if you're statistically minded. My very own miracle, if you're not. Either way works for me; I'm not one to pick apart something this good.

"I hate seeing you hurt. You should quit, Audie. This stuff'll kill you." He kisses my neck as he starts the conversation we've had a hundred times before. He doesn't push it, though. He just keeps kissing little feathery trails, letting the statement breathe on its own.

I love him.

I do—I love his mutant, scarred skin and his ninth-life mind. We fit together like two pieces of a waterlogged jigsaw puzzle, our damage swelling us tighter and closer. True, he doesn't like what I do, but that's because he still has one foot in Normal. High school, report cards, the whole bit, including a mom who gives him hell when she catches him sneaking out to stay with me. But he doesn't feel comfortable in his old life anymore, either. There, he's Cancer Boy. Here, he's a stud—a test-lab superhero. The Great Teenage Hope for a Cure. That, and I think it's pretty hard to give a shit about your senior prom after you've had nuclear waste injected into your gonads.

I met him in a waiting room, fooled around with him later that night, then again a few days later. I kept my low expectations, my no expectations, for a while. *Just hanging out. See ya when I see ya.* That's what people like us do, right? He's cute. He's tall. He makes me smile. It was plenty.

But it hit me *bam!* when he held the bucket. How long ago was that—two months? Six? It was a textbook's worth of side effects ago, and it's been obvious ever since: he loves me too. I knew it the moment he walked into the bathroom without knocking, sleeves already pushed up. "What can I do?" he asked, stepping in closer, undeterred by the foul liquid torrents pouring out of me, uncontrollably spraying out both ends at the same time—I was a two-sided fountain of sick. I couldn't say anything at all, I just heaved and retched, unbeautiful, untouchable, unwantable, and nearly savage with misery. But he stayed anyway, his eyes tactfully unfocused as he held my hair back for me, gently pulling it off my sweaty, vomit-crusted cheeks. It's a crystal-clear moment in a sea of muddy weeks, one I revisit often, whenever I can: I'm as sick as a freaking dog, pants around my ankles and oh my God the smell, and he walks in, keeps walking in even when he sees what's going on. *I'll hold the bucket,* he says in this gentle, deep voice, like it's nothing at all, and *yes,* I could see, I *can* see it through the tears, sense it through the stench, feel it through the cramps and the waves.

He loves me.

And since then, since that night, oh the fluids we've shared.

It's a special kind of intimacy, I think. All the usual puppy love and teenage sex, sure, but something stronger than that, too, something torn raw, then scarred over. I don't care if it grosses you out, I think it's romantic. He's seen me at my lowest, and he stayed. Stayed while I sprayed, puked, shat, dribbled, sobbed. And I've done the same for him. We've loved the worst of each other, so we get the best of each other.

"You're my blue moon," I whisper into his skin.

"Is everything okay?" He's half-asleep, still curled around me, but I can feel the question mark as clearly as I can hear it. "You're kind of a mystery lately."

I don't answer. We both know I'm keeping a secret from him—there's no use denying it.

It's getting harder, though. It's a big secret. The kind of secret that practically vibrates out of you, shimmering out of your pores—it's *that* good. I stuff it back down before I turn to kiss him good night, hoping he'll take the hint and go back to sleep. I'll tell him soon enough. In seven weeks, to be exact.

That's when Dylan, who should be dead, turns eighteen.

Dylan, who could still die—his is an IV tightrope walk of a survival—deserves to celebrate. But what do you buy someone for a birthday he was never supposed to see? A freaking sweater and some moo shu chicken from the takeout place down the street just isn't going to cut it.

I need to give him a gift worthy of the occasion.

A trip around the world was my first idea. I could do it, too. There's good money to be made on the testing circuit if you're smart about it. Picturing him in all those postcard places so foreign and far away they seem made up—the Eiffel Tower, Angkor Wat, Machu Picchu—just about brings tears to my goddamn eyes I want it so bad.

But Dylan can't travel. Not capital-T Travel, months at a time like that, anyway. His remission is still too shaky to untether so completely from his meds and his tests and his scans.

So I had to pick just one place. One place out of all the places he's never been. I'd been sweating it for a while, thinking, fuck it, I guess I'll just trust the masses and pick somewhere popular—we'll go see the Glockenspiel, or the Leaning Tower of Pisa or something. I've never been out of the country either, so what do I know? I was about to do it, to make reservations for some chumpy bus tour of Euroschlock, because I thought if I waited any longer we'd end up stuck at some divey Motel Six in Des Moines, since that's all that would be left if I didn't hurry up and make plans to go *somewhere*. But then that night we were watching the Discovery Channel, not even because we wanted to, but because neither of us had the energy to change the channel, and a program about Patagonia came on. They were showing this eco-resort called Castillo Finisterre, which the show's ambiguously accented (New Zealand? South Africa? Native-Born Reality TV?) host translated as "the castle at the end of the world." It's at the far tip of South America, perched on the edge of the continent, the very end of the inhabited world, with nothing else around except cliffs and glaciers and the occasional wandering puma. Some dude was paddling around icebergs in a kayak, and I'm not exaggerating in the least when I say it looked like something from a different planet. *Otherworldly*—that's the perfect word to describe it.

I was barely paying attention, to be honest—I'm not exactly a nature lover. I only happened to see the look on Dylan's face because I turned to ask him if he wanted to order pizza.

It gave me the chills, that look. Seriously, it just about broke my heart. He didn't say anything, but he didn't need to. I could tell exactly what he was thinking. Two thoughts at the same time, etched across his face like an acid splash:

1) I want to go there.
2) I'll never go there.

There should be a word for it, that simultaneous stab of desire and defeat—the knowledge that something is generally possible but personally impossible. It's like getting a giant middle finger from the universe, a great big *fuck you* of a dream turned inside out. All I could think while I watched that look spread across his face was, *Okay, here's where it all starts to go to shit.* It was like watching bitterness and regret take root inside Dylan in real time.

So right then and there I knew I had to do whatever it took to make Patagonia happen. I mean, come on—the castle at the fucking end of the world. It puts every other half-assed tourist spot to shame.

A secret like this one tends to leak through the cracks, though. Especially during moments like these, pressed skin to skin, his breath on my shoulder. But I can't let it slip yet. Not until the whole trip is planned, paid, and promised. And that's going to take some serious, vein-popping overtime—the place costs a damn fortune. But I've got a lot of skin, and a lot of blood. I'm going to give Dylan his impossible.

That's the thing someone like Dylan doesn't necessarily get about volunteering. For someone like him, it's a last resort. For someone like me, it's a starting line—the castle at the end of the world, and everything in between.

Unlike his, my version of normal sucks. I did the whole fast-food-restaurant job, GED, homeless-teen-in-the-system thing when I first left home. Foster parents, social workers, suburban-wasteland taco-chain night shifts so fourth-meal-seeking stoner assholes can come and eat their chalupas, giving me a hard time, leaning in and waggling their eyebrows for their friends while they ask me to squirt extra sour cream on their burritos *but do it sexy this time.* Making minimum wage except what the shitbag manager docks from my check because I called said fourth-meal asshole exactly what he was and squirted the sour cream all over his ugly face. And from there, couch-surfing, flophouses, shelters, alleys—barely managing to survive month to month, in the system, under the system, in spite of the system . . .

Dylan's not the only one saved by the experiments they do around here. My whole *life* was a fucking tumor.

So yeah, the side effects can be rough. But the money's

good, and the odds of survival are a hell of a lot better here than where I'm coming from. Think about it this way: the researchers and the drug companies have a vested interest in keeping you healthy. They *want* you to be okay. They'll let you know if your blood tests come back wonky, they'll patch up your sores, they feed you whenever you're in their labs more than an hour or two, tops—I'm talking organic stuff, feta cheese, that sort of thing. They don't want anyone dying on them—they need us healthy. They want us alive.

And that, my friends, is a whole lot better than anyone else has ever wanted for me. So sure, this life might kill me. But in my experience, real life kills you even faster.

I turn over and wrap myself even deeper into Dylan's arms, and I fall back to sleep knowing exactly what I'm going to say to Charlotte tomorrow.

I'm in.

CHAPTER 6

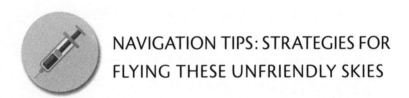

NAVIGATION TIPS: STRATEGIES FOR FLYING THESE UNFRIENDLY SKIES

Okay, Ladies and Specimens. You're really committed to doing this thing?

First, feel your skin.

Go on, do it. I bet it's nice and smooth. Pick your softest part. The skin on the inside of your forearm, or maybe that little patch just behind your ear. I don't care how hard you've been living, there's always somewhere that's still soft.

Now, imagine that nice, soft place of yours all blistered and poxed. Imagine peaks and crevices, rashes and boils. This life gives you a whole new topography—bumps and bruises, patterns and scars.

Your soft parts will never be the same.

Still ready to say goodbye to that pretty little complexion of yours? All righty, then. Here are some helpful tips on how to make a living in this crazy world:

1. Stock up.

The pay is lousy, but sign up for the right consumer-product studies and you'll never have to shop again. Deodorant, laundry soap, moisturizer, contact lens solution, hemorrhoid cream, tooth whitener. Get in on one of the big nutrition studies and you may even get your meals provided, or at least a few cases of diet soda with that new artificial sweetener that *probably* doesn't cause cancer, all just for agreeing to fill out a questionnaire or two. Sure, you might get hives now and then while they work out the kinks, but that's a small price to pay for a full cupboard, don't you think?

2. Pick your poison.

I've said it before—if you really want the big bucks, you're going to have to suffer. And generally speaking, there are two categories of suffering: deprivation and infliction of pain. But you learned that particular lesson long before you got here, didn't you? Still, know your limits before you sign up—do a little soul-searching, figure out just how far you're willing to go. For me, it's my eyes. I won't let anyone near 'em. Makes me break into a sweat just thinking about it. For my good friend Jameson, it's anything but his brain. His body is a temple, I guess, because the only labs he'll grace with his presence are the ones that do psych studies. Whatever. It all comes down to personal preference and pain tolerance, chickadees.

3. The foot bone's connected to the leg bone . . .

C'mon, don't roll your eyes when I sing. This little tip is the best one I have to offer. See, technically, you're supposed to wait weeks, or even months, between studies. But fortunately for us, the scientists who run these things aren't exactly social butterflies. They *never* talk to people working in the other labs. So, you lucky devil—this means you can hop from floor to floor, study to study, if you just play it cool and stay under the radar. You can even chain your studies together. Did you get burned during the laser hair-removal protocol, perhaps? They're testing an analgesic cream for that on Six. Are those funny new antidepressant pills giving you night terrors? Why not sign up for the sleep study just down the hall? Sure, you'll have to stay up for a couple of days, but what a great way to avoid those nasty dreams! It's actually sort of fun when you get the pieces to come together like this—kind of like a real-life Tetris game.

So work on your strategy and tune in next week, Warts Fans, for more helpful tips on how to survive and thrive in the Wild Wild West of human-subject testing!

CHAPTER 7

My midnight bravado fades a bit in the morning. Isn't that just how it goes? Moon swagger: everyone's a badass in the right light. Today I'm not so sure I want to do anything more physically or emotionally taxing than ordering takeout.

Reason number one for reconsidering Charlotte's test marathon: spite. Dylan was gone when I woke up—no note, no explanation. I'm not gonna lie, it stings. It wiped that little *he's worth it* glow right off my decision.

I'm sure he had a good reason. He's not a "love 'em and leave 'em" kind of guy—he's proven that much enough times to deserve a pass . . . maybe. Just this once.

And sitting here on the couch with Jameson, my favorite coffee mug in hand and music playing on a stereo that I neither had to pay for or steal, I'm working hard to keep it in perspective. Or at least to keep the sulking to a minimum.

But that just brings up reason number two for having second thoughts about Charlotte's plan: inertia. I mean, I've already managed to save up a decent chunk of money doing things my way, and Charlotte's system is, at a minimum, going to get us blacklisted around the labs once they catch on. Which they will.

And maybe it's just me being lazy, but I really don't hate it here. I'm comfortable. Plus, our apartment is the nicest place I've ever lived. Granted, that doesn't say much, but trust me, it's nice. Homey and clean, with actual curtains, and doors that have never been kicked in. Swirly-patterned carpeting that first strikes you as hideous, but ends up being sort of pleasantly mesmerizing once you get used to looking at it.

I'm sofa-soothed. Bathroom-tile-tranquilized. I'm not ashamed to admit it.

Okay, maybe a little.

I was nervous as hell when I first moved in. I felt like such a kid, just some punk trying to impress a bunch of people who seemed so adult at first—so inaccessibly stable. Not that Jameson is even that much older than me. He's somewhere in his midtwenties, I'd guess, and Charlotte's the same age as me—she just seems older because she's been on her own basically forever. But here were two people with a fixed address and all these grown-up accessories—things like two couches that actually match each other, hand towels, a freaking food processor. It took me a while to get comfortable.

We get along great now. We're all a lot alike—even Jameson, once you get to know him. I know he didn't have it easy the way he grew up—he swears his mom named him for the whiskey she was drinking when she went into labor, though I'm pretty sure that's just part of his *me and my brain against the world* shtick. But you can see all the little signs of a hardscrabble start if you know what to look for, like the way he gets really anxious around anyone who could remotely be considered an authority figure. His weird little throat-clearing thing goes into hyperdrive until it's just us in the room again, and then he's fine. He's happiest when he feels like King of the Castle, I think, even if the so-called kingdom is populated almost entirely by freaks and weirdos (present company included, of course). You almost never see Jameson sitting in a room by himself. Which is fine, really, because he's a useful guy to have around.

Charlotte, on the other hand, I call the Queen of the Fuck Off—a title she adores, incidentally. She's a ranter and a door slammer and a loud talker, but also a hell of a lot of fun, and it's completely impossible to stay mad at her. You'll try—she'll pull one of her tantrums or flake out on whatever you had planned, and you tell yourself you're completely done putting up with her shit, and then two minutes later she's worked her evil-bleached-pixie magic and she has you laughing so hard you have tears streaming down your face and you can't remember why you were ever mad in the first place.

It's funny. For as close as we are now, for as much time as we hang out—how we genuinely *like* each other—we don't talk much about our pasts. It's a common theme among guinea pigs. You don't exactly get here aboard the Yuppie Express, you know? If you're willing to sell your skin here, chances are you probably sold it in some other way, in some other place, too. Boo freakin' hoo, I know. Yours, mine, and everybody else's sob story. I'm just saying we're not the types to sit around and wax poetic about what used to be.

We talk, though. About a lot of things. Just usually in the present tense.

Like now. Jameson's trying to pry me out of my bad mood this morning, conspicuously avoiding all reference to Dylan. He'd rather talk about work, anyway.

He frowns when I get around to telling him about the Beagle, though, especially when I tell him the part about the nurse leaving the rest of us alone. You can always tell what he's thinking when he hears about stuff like that—that it would never happen if *he* ran the place. Like I said, he should've been a doctor, and I think it burns him up sometimes that he isn't. Jameson is the picture of thwarted ambition.

I, on the other hand, am the picture of comforter-wrapped complacency. I burrow deeper into the couch, pull the blanket up to my chin, and make up my mind to officially forgive Dylan. Nothing decided while feeling this cozy can be wrong, can it?

"Are you still writing?" That's Jameson changing the subject, just like Charlotte did when I tried to tell her about what happened. I told you—people around here don't like talking about bad outcomes. It's a superstitious thing, I guess. You don't call out the boogeyman's name. You don't rattle locked cages.

I shrug. "Kind of. When I find the time."

We both know it's a lame excuse. It's not like I'm trying to write the next Great American Novel or anything—it's just a blog for people who want to learn about drug testing. It was originally Charlotte's idea—she thought we might even be able to make some money out of it somehow from the newbies who come wandering in with questions about how this stuff works, or how much that hurts, or whatever. We're supposed to be doing it together, but she's hard to pin down sometimes when it comes to anything resembling actual work. Charlotte tends to be all spark, no fire.

It doesn't matter; I like working on it myself. It makes me feel halfway useful, since everyone's nervous when they first show up here. But you find your niche, I tell them. Your comfy little hidey-hole. And soon enough you wonder what all the fuss was for. So that's what I write about.

A lot of people here have gigs on the side—there's a whole underground economy. One lady runs a kind of travel agency for medical trials all over the country. She'll get you signed up, book your tickets, maybe even charter a bus if there's a big enough group going. Another guy walks dogs and waters plants, that kind of thing, for people doing inpatient studies. He'll also run errands for you, pick up medicine, whatever, if you're really hurting and can't fend for yourself for a while. All for a small fee, of course. Jameson keeps a whole damn pharmacy in the spare room in our apartment. He buys up our unused meds for next to nothing, then sells them for a ridiculous amount of money on the side. But like I said, it's not as bad as it sounds—it's not like he's running a meth lab or anything. He's just selling medicine that hasn't been officially approved, or maybe just isn't available yet, to people who don't have time to wait for all the boxes to be checked. Occasionally some walking skeleton of a person we've never seen before will show up, go back to the extra room with Jameson, and come out ten minutes later in a big rush to leave.

I don't ask any questions. You do what you gotta do, right?

"You're a good writer. And you let your personality come out more on paper. It's like you, only . . . more sparkly."

I stick my tongue out at him. "Are you saying I don't usually sparkle?"

"Oh, you sparkle all right. You sparkle like a horny teenage vampire," Jameson says. "I'm just saying that you can be a bit reserved in person, and I like the way you let yourself out of your head cage a bit when you write. You should keep it up, maybe take some classes." He turns up the stereo to drown out the sound of Charlotte having sex with Scratch in the next room.

"Yeah, right. Harvard keeps calling, asking me when I'm going to accept my full ride, but I just haven't gotten around to it yet." I yawn and then make a show of burrowing even further into my blanket nest, but Jameson doesn't take the hint.

"I'm serious, Audie. You're smart, and you should be in school. Not high school, you're already way past that. Maybe a class or two at the community college, though, or something online."

I shoot him a dirty look. He's doing what Charlotte and I call his Den Mother Thing. For someone who can't be much more than five years older than me, he can be a preachy bastard sometimes. "Gee, thanks, Dad. And if I don't, are you going to send me to my room?" I know he means well, but I hate it when people treat me like a kid. I may be young, but I pay my share of the rent and manage my life just fine, thank you very much. "Besides, I don't see you applying to med schools."

"Maybe not, but I've already memorized more textbooks

than I'd ever have to read in medical school. *I'm* pursuing my interests. Unlike you."

He's about a centimeter from the border between irritating me and seriously pissing me off. "Yeah, well, there's a reason you've never met a self-taught heart surgeon, don't you think?" I can hear my voice turning sharp.

"Easy there, Audie." Charlotte's still buttoning her pants as she comes out of her room. "The fine Dr. Jameson has hooked me up with many a cure. He's a hell of a lot more reliable than most of the quacks working around here." She hands me a pill and then sits down on the couch, practically on top of me. We both started a birth-control study last week and we're trying to help each other remember to take our pills. Mine are little beige ovals, hers are yellow octagons—it's anyone's guess which are the real deal. I'm usually the one to remember first, but sex with Scratch is probably an excellent reminder to take preventive measures ASAP.

They're both giving me that look, basically accusing *me* of being the jerk, and I can tell from the way Jameson starts clearing his throat with little *heh heh heh* noises that I actually might have hurt his feelings. "Sorry, J. You can operate on me any day."

Jameson winks away my apology, and we fall into one of those awkward silences. Charlotte shifts in her seat and I can tell by the semipredatory expression that spreads across her face that she's about to bring up her plan. She did a psych study once where she had to sit through assertiveness training, which is pretty funny, because Charlotte isn't exactly a shrinking violet. She kind of got off on the stuff they taught her, and she'll occasionally throw around some of the techniques she learned. I can tell I'm looking at a few of them right now: *Position yourself directly in front of your conversational opponent. Maintain steady eye contact. Always be the one to initiate a change of subject. Match your opponent's breathing pattern.*

Personally, I would've called it Manipulative Asshole Training, but that's just me.

After her training session, they sat Charlotte in front of a big red button and told her that each time she pushed it someone in another room would get a shock. It's one of those bullshit things they always tell you in psych studies, like anyone would actually be stupid enough to believe that was really what was going on, that some poor asshole on the other side of the wall was really going to sit there wired up to a bunch of cables and let himself get juiced over and over just because someone in a white coat said not to move.

Charlotte didn't press the button a single time. Instead, she used the little pocketknife she used to carry around with her to pry the whole damn button out of its casing, and refused to give it back until the researchers paid her in full for participating in the study. "I didn't want them to think I hadn't been listening," she said. "I mean, what's more assertive than that?"

But maybe I am still a little raw about Dylan's disappearing act, because I'm just not in the mood to be on the receiving end of Charlotte's Psych 101 bullshit techniques this morning. I start untangling myself from the blanket so that I can leave before she starts pressing me for a commitment.

I'm not totally lacking in self-awareness—I'll probably say

yes to her plan soon enough. I mean, we both know she'll talk me into it eventually. I can be sort of susceptible to certain types of people. And Charlotte, for all her flaws, just has this way of making her version of events seem so much *better* than anything I could ever come up with. It's like being best friends with a cult leader, sometimes.

Sooner or later I'll drink the Kool-Aid, but sometimes you have to show some resistance, put up a little fight, just to remind yourself that you can.

Fortunately, Scratch comes out of Charlotte's room and drags a chair over to join us just in time to distract Charlotte from pouncing on me.

Scratch. Poor, revolting Scratch. True to his nickname, he's got a rash. Scratch always has a rash. He's allergic to damn near everything. You so much as eat something for lunch that ever sat next to a tree nut and he'll sprout hives if you breathe on him three hours later. He's the peely-est, sniffly-est dude I've ever met, and as much as I've gotten used to finding his eczema shrapnel dusting our cushions and hearing him hawking up lung butter in our bathroom, he still makes my skin crawl at times like this, idly fingering the yellow-helmeted battalion of pustules marching up his neck. I would think he'd give the techs a heart attack whenever he walked into a lab, but he's carved out a nice little niche for himself volunteering in skin and allergy studies; he'll smear damn near anything on his flesh. I'm pretty sure Charlotte only fools around with him now and then because she feels sorry for him.

As usual, he bears news. Scratch is the human equivalent

of a tabloid magazine—all things conspiratorial and scandal-adjacent will find themselves embellished by his fuzzy tongue. Today is no different, and he's practically panting to get it out.

"Yo, guess who's back in town?" he says, dabbing at a bleeder on his neck with the collar of his T-shirt. "The Professor. I ran into him last night. He says he'll be getting back to work this morning."

Jameson groans. "God, I was hoping he'd disappeared for good."

Charlotte, on the other hand, cackles and then rubs her hands together. "This," she says, sinking back into the couch next to me, "is gonna be fun."

CHAPTER 8

By the time I get dressed and head over to the labs, everyone else has already left, presumably to entertain themselves by messing with the Professor en masse.

Back when I was a kid, I don't know, maybe eleven? Anyway, I had this friend, Krissy. I liked hanging out at Krissy's house because she lived with just her dad, who was one of those benignly negligent parents who just sort of assumed Krissy'd let him know if she needed anything, but otherwise left her alone. There was never any food in her house, but her dad was good about leaving cash. Whenever we got hungry, we'd walk over to the neighborhood convenience store and load up on all the junk food we could carry. That's one of the great things when you're a kid—you can stuff your face full of ten pounds of Pop-Tarts and licorice and whatever other high-fructose un-food you can find on the shelf that's never come within a hundred miles of any naturally occurring substance, and you never even get sick. You just stuff that processed shit in your face until you can't, and then you lie in a stupid, happy little sugar coma until it's breakfast time the next day, and then you just start it all over again, but this time with syrup on top. It's awesome to be a kid sometimes. Or at least it was awesome to be a kid at Krissy's house.

Anyway, we used to take a shortcut to the convenience store, because otherwise it was a really long walk. We'd crawl under this chain-link fence someone had cut through at the bottom, jump over a muddy ditch full of used condoms and empty beer cans, and then walk along the railroad tracks for about a quarter mile until we got to the rear of the store. This one time we were heading back right around dusk, and as usual we weren't paying attention to much of anything, when all of a sudden we heard a guy's voice calling out to us, *hey, girls,* or something generic like that.

We turned around, and there was a man standing there on the tracks behind us with a weird smile on his face—not threatening or anything, just more like he was waiting for us to hurry up and get the joke. I remember I was staring at him, trying to figure out what he wanted, when he started moving a tiny bit—not walking toward us, but just sort of fidgeting where he stood—and part of my brain started to catch on that something wasn't right. I kept staring at him, but another few seconds ticked by before my attention finally zoomed off of that weird smile on his face and panned out enough to realize exactly what it was that was strange about him. It was his pants. His pants were off, or at least unzipped, and he was grabbing at himself, tugging and jerking a little, and then a lot.

I was still young enough that I didn't even really have the words to go along with what I was seeing. I mean, I *knew* what he was doing, but I'd never seen it actually happening right in front of me. So I was staring, Krissy's staring, and the guy was grinning back at us, jerking himself off even faster, and it was like we were in some weird time warp for what felt like hours, until finally I snapped out of it. I grabbed Krissy by the arm, and ran like hell.

We ran as fast as we could, at least I thought we did at the time, but maybe not, because when we got back to Krissy's house, she still had the two-liter bottle of Hawaiian Punch tucked under her arm, and I still had the Cool Ranch Doritos and the Double Stuf Oreos. I mean, you can't exactly say we were running for our lives if we managed to hang on to the precious goddamn snacks, can you? We shrieked about it for a couple of minutes, *oh my God, did you see his* thing? *Soooo disgusting.* But then our TV show came on, and we just sort of forgot about it. And the funniest thing is, I don't think it even occurred to us to tell anyone about it, not even Krissy's dad when he got home a few hours later. It was like it never happened. The guy must not have put up much of a chase, since he obviously didn't catch us, but still—you'd think we would have locked the doors to the house or called the cops or something instead of shrugging it off to watch some stupid sitcom. Maybe we just instinctively calculated that the guy wasn't a real threat, and discarded all thoughts of him without getting hung up on all the *could'ves* and *might'ves* and *almosts* that start following you around once you grow up a bit.

Or maybe we were just too young and too fucking stupid to get it—our brain waves temporarily shorted out from our turkey jerky and Top Ramen diet plan. To this day, I can't decide.

Anyway, I think I feel about the Professor the same way I did about the wanker on the train tracks. My brain tells me there's something vaguely threatening about him, but I just can't get worked up enough about it to drop my munchies. I mean, how much harm could he possibly do? He's about the least menacing person you've ever seen, too. He's shorter than me, probably five four, tops, and with his ridiculous white beard he looks, no shit, exactly like a garden gnome.

But I still keep my eye on him. And I understand why Jameson hates him so much. The way he always lurks around, listening in on everyone's conversations, makes you feel like you're under surveillance. Every so often you'll hear a rumor that he's some kind of undercover something or other. A DEA agent, maybe. Or, more likely, a private investigator for the pharmaceutical companies, digging up dirt on the competition. Jameson, who can be a little paranoid sometimes, swears the Professor keeps a file on him.

I sort of like the idea of someone keeping a dossier on me. It's like outsourcing your own diary. Let someone else do the writing while I focus on the living. Genius, right?

But the real story isn't all that interesting. The guy's nothing but a wannabe academic—some pseudo-legit branch of sociology, I think—and rumor has it he's been working on his bottomless pit of a research paper for so long now that his university sponsors forgot he exists. He mostly just hangs out and watches us, constantly scratching little notes. He's a male Jane Goodall, observing his subjects in their natural habitat.

Which I suppose makes us his chimpanzees.

Which is probably why Charlotte fucks with him so much.

"Hey, Professor," she'll say. "Have I got a story for you."

He falls for it every time. It's almost sad how desperate he is to cannibalize our lives, to live vicariously through our stories. He's the ultimate outsider. The consummate wallflower, never invited to dance. So whenever Charlotte offers him a little nugget, his eyes light up and he copies down every word out of her mouth, scribbling so fast he occasionally has to shake cramps out of his writing hand.

"Yesterday one of the doctors invited me into his office and told me he was developing a new breast-exam technique and he needed a woman's opinion. He told me to take off my shirt and bra first, so I did." Charlotte feels herself up as she tells him the story, running her hands all over her chest, tracing slow, lewd circles around her nipples.

The Professor nods rhythmically as he writes everything down.

All the stories Charlotte shares with the Professor are about sex. All her stories are about being watched. She's convinced he's a perv like that. They're completely ridiculous, her stories—I mean, way over the top. Her whole goal in life is to rattle him enough so he either blushes or at least stops writing. But so far none of her stories have ever worked. So far, he's never blushed. And he never stops writing.

"They're testing sex toys in room 342," she tells him. "The

marketing people stand behind a two-way mirror and watch people masturbate. Today they're giving out gift certificates as a bonus, dinner for two at some steakhouse if you come up with a new way to use their vibrators that they can show in their promotional materials."

This one might actually be true. You never know around here. Someone, somewhere has almost certainly been paid to test dildos.

"There's a peephole cut into the wall of the proctology lab. Someone set up a camera and they're live-streaming colorectal exams for subscribers in Asia who pay twenty-nine dollars a month."

The Professor never cracks a smile, never stops writing. No matter how crazy Charlotte's stories get.

It drives her nuts. She storms around in a pissed-off mood for hours every time she fails. She thinks there's something wrong with him, that it's not normal to be so detached.

I don't feel as strongly as Charlotte or Jameson, but I still keep my distance. I stand back and watch the Professor watching us. Which is why it freaks me out when I run into him on my way into work and he calls me by name.

"Audie," he says. "We should talk."

CHAPTER 9

"No! I swear, I have no idea what he wants. I don't even know how he knows my name." I'm trying to cut through my chicken marsala while I tell Dylan about my run-in with the Professor, but it's not going well. "He creeps me out."

Dylan loves hearing my guinea pig stories. It's like the world's grossest soap opera, he says. He can never keep anyone's name straight, though. "Wait, remind me," he'll say. "Is Jameson the one with the mutant cold sore covering half his face?"

"No, doofus," I'll say back. "That's Scratch. Seriously, how can you forget that? I mean, his name is freaking Scratch, for God's sake. There's your clue right there."

"I beg your pardon," he'll say, usually in a goofy British accent or something. Dylan does awesome accents and impressions. He can be funny as hell when he's not in pain.

The pain is why he's so lousy with names. He never says anything about it, typical guy, but it's obvious that it gets pretty bad sometimes. I can always tell. It's like someone unrolls a blanket of fog over him, and his voice and even his eyes just kind of go fuzzy. I love how he still shows up, though—how he still makes an effort, even when it hurts. I love that we still always manage to connect, even through that terrible haze.

Luckily, Dylan's having a good day today—no sign of fog.

"What did that poor chicken ever do to you?" He shakes his head at the mess on my plate, then before I can stop him he leans over and plucks two black olives off my salad and holds them up to his eyes. "Why, Audie," he says in a Hannibal Lecter voice. "You're looking positively scrumptious. *We should talk.*"

He yelps as I kick him under the table, and the waiter glares at us again. He seems to be making a point of not clearing our dishes or refilling our water glasses.

We're used to it.

It's a dinner date. Italian. I'm letting Dylan make up for his disappearing act earlier, and I have to say, he's doing a fine job of it. His apology was a little vague on details, but that's okay. Real gentlemen don't make flimsy excuses—they just make things right. And right we are.

Besides, I don't think it's even possible to stay mad at a guy with an actual, real-life chin cleft. I mean, his eyes freaking *twinkle* when he reaches over to tuck a piece of hair behind my ear, I swear to God. It's hilariously unreal.

Aren't we so suh-weet you could just puke? Yeah, we're kissy-face and crostini, a fucking lasagna baked for two—all except for Dylan's grayscale chemo-sheen and med-alert bracelet, that is. And then there are my hands, shaking so hard I keep rattling the fork against the plate and fumbling my knife, which makes the waiter harrumph behind me and look pointedly at the line of fresh needle tracks marching up my inner arm.

We probably should have stuck to the hospital cafeteria, but screw it. I'm a sucker for a good plate of pasta.

"Are you okay?" Dylan reaches over and gently takes my knife and fork, cuts my meat into little bites.

"Yeah, I'm fine. I'm just starving. Are you going to eat the last piece of bread?" I grab it and shove half of it in my mouth before he answers. Medically induced hypoglycemic state equals Very Hungry Audie. My stomach feels like an empty pit, a monster growling for prey.

I feed the monster. Fill the pit. *Have a cookie,* I tell the beast. *Un biscotto.*

I'm more than fine. I'm *happy*. Italian with Dylan, and I added a nice chunk to the trip fund today. "This is nice," I say, making sure my smile doesn't run away from me and expose the two chipped teeth on the left. Gotta get those fixed one of these days.

He smiles back at me, but he's barely touched his food. He moves penne around with his fork, makes figure eights in the pesto sauce. I try not to let him catch me staring at his plate, but now that I've noticed, I can't see anything else. I'm pigging out, shoveling carbs into my face like I haven't been fed in a week, and he's just sitting there, poking at the ice in his water glass now, playing with the pepper shaker next. Why isn't he eating?

My mind starts to grind with low-blood-sugar angst. Is he upset about something? Is he getting sick again? He hates it when I hover over him about his health, but he does seem a little thinner than usual, and with his history . . .

Stop, Audie, I tell myself. *Don't go off the cliff.* I do that sometimes, I know I do. I get so much as a splinter of a bad thought in my head and it just starts burrowing in, deeper and deeper, until the only thing I can think about is the worst thing ever. I swear, I can go Zero to Catastrophe in seconds flat. I try to keep it to myself most of the time, hysteria not exactly being considered a redeeming quality in girlfriends these days.

I match Dylan's chewing pace until my heart stops pounding. *Chill the fuck out,* I tell my brain cells. *Just enjoy the evening.*

"Can we get more bread over here when you have a chance?" Dylan calls out to the waiter, who slow-raises one sullen eyebrow in response.

Ten minutes later the waiter comes back—the scent of his cigarette break wafting across our table as he tosses down a basket filled with crumbs and mangled crusts. "Never mind," Dylan laughs. "Can you just get us our check, please?"

I love that about him, how he doesn't get worked up over stupid things. How, as far as he's concerned, the past is truly the past. Dylan never brings up yesterday's argument. Dylan never loses sleep over last week's bullshit. The serenity of the almost-dead, he calls it, cancer being the ultimate *don't sweat the small stuff* lesson, I guess.

I, on the other hand, don't have a terminal illness, so I tear open sweetener packets and spill-spell *twat* in swirly cursive letters across the table, and then grab every last mint from the bowl on the hostess stand as we walk out.

I still have my health, so I am permitted to embrace petty grudges and commit small acts of cheerful revenge.

"*Audie,*" Dylan says as he opens the door for me, but he's kind of laughing, and I can tell he's glad I did it. I pop a mint into my mouth, then one into his, and then toss the rest over my shoulder as I stand on my tiptoes to kiss him. "God, you're awful," he says, and then sweeps me up off my feet, spinning me around in a bear hug.

I force myself not to notice the new sharpness of his shoulder blades. I shift my embrace slightly to help me ignore the prominence of his ribs.

I focus, instead, on how effortlessly he lifts me into the air. I move my hands to less worrisome terrain. His chest. His biceps. His ass.

"Like what you find?" he asks, grinning, and then pulls me even closer.

He's strong. Solid.

Nothing to worry about at all.

You hear that?

CHAPTER 10

So Castillo Finisterre, being the most awesome place on the planet, has this amazing spa. The website lists all sorts of crazy stuff they can slather you in, rub you with, and strip you of. I'm talking an entire catalog of muds, oils, lotions, potions, and I don't even know what else—tantric lava rocks and wax infused with emerald dust and the blood of virgins, probably. Serious rich-person voodoo shit. I'm not describing it well—I don't exactly speak fluent *spa*—but the bottom line is that they appear to be pretty damn proficient at turning you into something poreless, hairless, and tension-free. A pampered, wild-verbena-scented invertebrate. Again, that might not sound so appealing—there's a reason no one's hiring me to write advertising copy for luxury resorts. But believe me when I say that I mean this all in the best possible way. It's like platinum-card witchcraft or something—you look at the website and you *want* to be slathered in their moon-harvested Arctic lake mud; all of a sudden you *need* one of their goddamn green-tea and

Jurassic-algae wraps before your parched and unexfoliated flesh shrivels up and suffocates you in a permanent skin sarcophagus.

Anyway, one of the pictures shows a couple getting a side-by-side massage. They're lying on their stomachs on tables a few inches apart in a room with floor-to-ceiling windows showing the end-of-the-world views the place is famous for, all ice and water and crisp utopian nothingness. They're stripped naked to the waist, and tended to by dark-haired women in pristine white uniforms, and their heads are turned so they're facing each other, staring into one another's eyes with expressions so blissed-out and tenderized that they almost look drugged.

Here, this morning, Charlotte and I are also half naked and lying side by side on tables, but other than that, everything else is pretty much the exact opposite of the image from the website.

We're lying on our backs, for starters, and unlike the blissfully invertebrate spa couple, we're undressed from the waist *down*. The stirrups are cold against my ankles, my own fault for not keeping my socks on, and instead of ocean-kissed sunlight prism-ing in through bay windows, the fluorescent lights flickering overhead are so bright they're making my eyes water.

Not that I'm complaining, since today's first gig is an easy one: medical modeling. We're pretend patients for doctors and nurses in training. If I had a business card, it would read: *Because sometimes a cadaver just won't do.* Occasionally it's fun— you get to follow a script, moaning and weeping about fictitious symptoms until the flustered students come up with the right diagnosis. I am particularly good at feigning migraines—I can even work myself up to a fluttering little eye tic on command.

For today's assignment we're little more than spread-eagled mannequins, though—unspeaking orifices (orifii?) for rent—and right now six medical students are staring wide-eyed at my cervix. Today's class: Gynecological Exams for Dummies.

It's a welcome breather, actually, since the schedule Charlotte created has otherwise been skewing heavily toward the testing of ingestibles and injectables, some of which are doing quite a number on my digestive system.

I said yes to the plan. Of course I did. We all knew I would, right?

Dylan's ribs clinched the deal. That, and seeing him round a corner in the hospital at a time of day when he should have been in AP Chemistry. He was with his mom and I didn't want to make a scene, so I ducked into a restroom and locked myself in a stall until I was sure they were long gone. While I was in there, I tallied up the clues: long periods of not returning calls, conflicting stories about his whereabouts, an ever-changing patchwork of bruises shifting across his body.

Dylan's sick again.

It seems sort of obvious now, so maybe some part of me didn't want to know.

But now I do know. I know, because he would've told me if it was no big deal. He would've said something if it was just a routine checkup. We spoke on the phone for twenty minutes that morning, and he didn't say a word about coming to the hospital.

I'm not going to confront him about it; he'll tell me when he's ready. But now I know that time is running out faster than I realized, and that Castillo Finisterre is rapidly becoming a Now or Never.

I choose Now.

So Charlotte and I are officially co-conspirators. She runs the show, really—I've taken a subordinate role. I sign my name to whatever papers I'm handed, do as I'm told, and then hold out my hand for payment. We're milking the system, doubling down, raising the stakes, going all or nothing. However you want to describe it, we're doing it. We're going to squeeze every possible cent out of the human-subject testing system, which of course is also to say that we're going to squeeze every possible cent out of our own flesh.

We're almost a week in, and things are going surprisingly well . . . with exceptions, of course.

The female students who gather round us this morning are matter-of-fact. Two of the three men look terrified. Like, full-blown, ready-to-bolt-from-the-room terrified. They're fidgety, plucking at their latex gloves, and I'm fairly certain they would rather do anything right now, anything at all, than stick their fingers in my vagina, but it's part of the med school curriculum, so they have no choice in the matter. *Welcome to my pelvis, boys!* Another winning slogan.

It's the third man—if you can call a skinny, oily-faced twenty-three-year-old medical student a man—who's getting to me. He's standing there, arms crossed high on his chest, upper lip curled in disgust, looking for all the world like he's being asked to dive into an open sewer. His narrowed eyes stare at my crotch like it's the enemy, and I can tell he isn't hearing a word the instructor is saying, not even pretending to listen to how to drape the patient in such a way to preserve dignity, or how to communicate the steps of the process to the patient to minimize surprise and discomfort. My body is horrific to him, this scowling MD-to-be, and I'm not surprised when he positions himself to be the last in the group to take his turn, like he's hoping to be saved by the bell from performing this loathsome task.

The lecturer finishes up and tells the group of students to divide themselves between the two "patients." I brace myself and let my thoughts start drifting up into the buzzing fluorescent lights. This ain't my first time to this particular rodeo, and you'd be amazed by just how many ways a nervous student can fuck up a Pap smear.

My third exam is almost finished when young Dr. Misogyny finally takes his place on the stool at the end of Charlotte's table. I'm selfishly relieved that it's not me. Charlotte and I turn and give each other a look—she obviously caught a whiff of his sadistic asshole vibe, too—and for a second, lying side by side and staring into one another's eyes like that, we actually *do* look a little like the couple in the spa picture. But then the student picks up the speculum and gets started without so much as a single word of warning. Charlotte winces, hissing her discomfort, and the instructor snaps at the guy, which only makes him look more angry and disgusted than before.

I notice two of the female students watching him with razor-sharp eyes. They don't like him, either.

"You're going to have to get in closer. You need to visualize the anatomy," the instructor warns him again. Junior-doctor Dickface makes a sour face, then scoots his stool forward between Charlotte's knees, and I can practically feel him twisting the metal instrument as he leans closer to what he apparently thinks of as her gaping hellhole.

Charlotte's eyes go wide, then narrow, and I'm pretty sure she's about to kick him in his shitty, smug face, and who could blame her, but then she smiles and lies back, suspiciously relaxed considering what's being done to her.

Now, I happen to know that Charlotte is on day four of a weight-loss testing protocol she enrolled in long before we teamed up. It's working—she can't stop crowing about the pounds melting off—but the side effects aren't pleasant. *Oily flatulence. Abdominal discomfort.* She doesn't care—Charlotte's willing to suffer for beauty. But now it appears that someone else is going to suffer along with her.

Everyone in the room hears it.

It's a loud, bitonal triumph. A jaw-dropping, gassy explosion that sounds as if a hole is being ripped through time and space—a righteous blast if ever there was one. The student leaps back so fast he bumps against a metal tray table, falling over and knocking sterile instruments to the floor with a clatter. His face is purple and contorted, and no one in the room can keep a straight face except Charlotte, who looks positively angelic. And very relaxed.

"Damn it!" the student yells out from the floor.

The other students are howling. The instructor is trying not to laugh, but she's not hiding it very well, and you can tell that even she knows what a jackass the guy is.

One of the female students takes a few steps over to Charlotte's table and pulls the paper blanket over her legs, covering her up. "Nicely done," I hear her say to Charlotte in a low voice. "And thank you on behalf of all womankind, since that'll hopefully keep him away from obstetrics forever."

"My pleasure," Charlotte says sweetly. She stays reclined on the table until the class filters out. Dickface never looks back.

She checks her watch once everyone is gone. "Speaking of staying away from obstetrics, wanna go pee in a cup next?"

I nod, so we get dressed and head down the hall to the contraceptive study, still snickering about Charlotte's vigilante fart. The research office is already crowded (who doesn't want free birth control?), so we join the line for the single-stall restroom. One by one, brimming specimen cups in hand, women prove their un-pregnancies, making the research sponsors very, very happy. Empty-bladdered study participants filter out of the office with smiles on their faces, thrilled to be twenty-five dollars richer for doing what they were going to do anyway. Win-win. It almost goes to your head a bit, when the money is this easy. Like, you're so damn valuable that even your piss is worth something to someone. Almost makes you start believing crazy things.

The line moves fast and I go first. I flick the lock on the stall door, do my thing, and step out, moving slowly because I filled my cup a little higher than I meant to and I don't want to spill piss on my shoes. I'm holding the stall door open with my elbow, focusing on my too-full cup and thinking that I should probably be drinking more water since my pee is kind of a funky orangish color and I read somewhere that that's a sign of dehydration. "Your turn," I say to Charlotte after a second, starting to get impatient.

"Charlotte?" I look up at the same time that I let the stall door slam shut, and a few drops of pee slosh over the edge of the cup and splash on the floor between us. Charlotte doesn't notice, though, because she's gone.

I don't mean *physically* gone, since she's still standing there, right in front of me, but there's no other way to describe it. Her face is slack and disturbingly expressionless, and her eyes have a flat, unfocused quality as she stares, unblinking, at nothing in particular. It's like someone somehow sucked the Charlotte out of Charlotte.

"Hey, are you okay?" I poke her shoulder with my free hand, kind of hard, actually, since I'm pretty sure she's just fucking with me—it's totally something she would do. I'm expecting her to snap out of it with a *gotcha* grin on her face, but she doesn't even seem to hear me, and she just keeps standing there, staring straight ahead.

The next person in line, a girl in a Hooters uniform, shoves between us and into the stall, already wrestling down those weird suntan-colored tights they wear under their butt-hugger shorts. "Sorry," she calls out as she slams the door shut. "But if you're not gonna go, I will. I gotta pee like a racehorse—I've been holding it for way too long."

I step to the side to let her through, and when I look back, Charlotte is coming around, squinting at me like *I'm* the one acting weird. "I thought they weren't allowed to wear their uniforms outside of work," she mumbles in a strange, spit-strangled voice. Her head is tilted to the right, and she rocks slowly on her feet a few times, almost like she's sleepwalking.

I'm relieved to hear her say anything at all—there was something seriously messed up about that *there/not there* look on her face. "Let's go home," I say, ignoring the stinkeye I get from the next person in line as I drop my full cup of pee in the trash can. "There goes twenty-five bucks' worth of liquid gold. You owe me," I say, hoping to get some sort of response out of her, but Charlotte is silent and passive as I lead her out of the lab.

CHAPTER 11

It takes a few minutes, but once Charlotte snaps out of whatever was wrong with her, she does it so abruptly that I start to think she really was just fucking with me back there. We're not even out of the building when it's like someone plugged her back in, and she goes from foot-dragging zombie chick to Energizer Bunny on speed. By the time we're outside, she's rambling on about how hungry she is and what she wants for lunch, babbling out words so fast I can barely understand what she's saying.

"Let's go get takeout somewhere and eat it in the park. I don't even care what as long as it's spicy. The spicier the better. I know—let's do Thai. The newish place on the corner. No, never mind. Not Thai. Last time we ate there I itched for three days. I think I'm developing an allergy to lemongrass. Is that even possible? Whatever, let's get Indian instead."

She starts singing a stupid song she makes up as she goes along, *Vindaloo, for me and you,* and doing this stupid little hula dance move as we walk. She's gone from catatonic to manic in about ninety seconds flat, and as far as I can tell, she doesn't even realize that she shut down completely for a few minutes.

"We can get whatever you want, as long as you're paying," I tell her. "Since you cost me twenty-five bucks back there."

She gives me a one-eyebrow-up look that could be interpreted as either puzzled or annoyed, but then throws her hands in the air and shrugs flamboyantly. "Whatever, cheapskate. I'll pay, but I'm gonna tell them to make it so hot it's gonna burn just as much coming out as it does going in." She takes off skipping—seriously, *skipping*—down the block, and doesn't look back. *Holla, holla, tikka masala!* I can hear her singing at the top of her lungs.

"What. The. Fuck," I whisper. Then, louder, "I'm not going to *skip* after you, Charlotte!" I curse myself under my breath as I speed up into a trot.

By the time I catch up to her at the restaurant, she's already ordering. "Ex*cuse* me?" the man behind the cash register is saying. I've been here a few times with Charlotte, and I've never seen the guy be anything other than friendly, but he doesn't look so friendly now.

"I *said*, five-alarm ass-fire spicy," Charlotte says in a voice too loud for the room. The other customers all look up from their food to stare.

"Jesus, Charlotte," I say behind her. "Can you chill out a little?"

The restaurant guy's face goes hard, and without saying another word he scrawls something on the order slip and then hands it back through the window into the kitchen, where I can see another man cooking in a small, crowded space. It wouldn't surprise me a bit if he'd written instructions to put some choice ingredient *other* than spices in our food. I probably would've, anyway.

I convince Charlotte to wait with me outside the restaurant. Make that: *I* wait, she paces. Once our food is ready, handed over in thin-lipped silence by the guy behind the counter, we commandeer one of the two benches in the tiny park across the street.

"Holy fuck, this is spicy," I say after a few bites. I can feel beads of sweat forming on my upper lip, and my tongue feels like it's being attacked by fire ants. Charlotte doesn't even seem to notice—she's eating her way through one of the takeout containers like she hasn't seen food in a month.

I blow my nose into a napkin and wish I'd ordered something to drink—anything to quench the fire in my mouth. "Dylan loves spicy food, too; I should bring him here. But I think I'll have to limit myself to two- or three-alarm ass-fire spicy. I can't handle it *this* hot." I say it as a joke—I'm just trying to fit into Charlotte's manic, silly mood—but something dark flashes across her face and she tosses her half-full container of food in the general direction of a garbage can and misses by a mile.

"Yeah, you do that," she says, all the bounce gone from her voice as fast as it came. "You go right on ahead and bring Dylan here for your next little date."

I bite my lip and stop talking. I can't keep up with her mood swings. But I also probably should've known better than to bring up Dylan. Charlotte's always been a little weird about him. Like, she'll be perfectly nice to his face most of the time, but then she'll occasionally get all huffy and prickly when he stays the night, practically treating him like a home invader if she happens to run into him in the morning. "Geez, I hope no one ever gives that chick a real weapon," I remember Dylan saying once after she threw a fork at him because she claimed he sneaked up on her. "Is she the morality police around here, or what?"

And once at the hospital I saw her walk right by him in the hallway—she didn't even acknowledge him, like he wasn't even worth the effort of a freaking single-syllable greeting. She didn't know I was walking right behind her, or she probably wouldn't have been such a blatant bitch to him—fork-throwing aside, her snubs are usually a little more subtle than that. I never said anything to her about it, but it still bugs me. Dylan doesn't deserve to be treated like that.

I don't know if it's a jealousy thing, or what, the way she is about him. This isn't the time to ask her about it, obviously. Not when she's acting this weird about *everything*.

I'm about to take off—I'm not going to sit there and listen to her start trashing Dylan—when she apologizes. "I'm sorry, Audie, don't be mad. I've just got such a raging headache right now I can't even think straight."

She moans a little and bends over at the waist, cupping her head in her hands. She lets out a few more groans, like she's being tortured, and after a minute she peeks over at me to make sure I'm paying attention. When she sees that I see her checking, she grins like a Cheshire cat.

"Okay, drama queen," I say. "You can knock off the phony misery show. I forgive you."

She sits up and shakes her head from side to side a few times, the way you do when you have water in your ears. "No show; I really do feel weird." She opens her eyes extra wide at me, bats her eyelashes a few times. "Audie, can you do me the hugest favor ever? Pretty please?"

She wants me to take her two o'clock appointment. It's the third in a series of four clinic visits, and she doesn't want to get kicked out before she gets paid. "Please, Audie?" she whines. "I feel like hell. My head is seriously killing me right now."

She does look pale and shaky. And even if she's 95 percent full of shit, I know she'd do it for me if I asked. That's what friends are for, right? Not to mention the fact that we're supposed to be business partners now, in a manner of speaking.

"I'll split the money with you fifty-fifty," she says. "I'm pretty sure it's just a blood draw at this visit. If you were a real friend, you'd do it for free."

"Make it seventy-five/twenty-five," I say, and when she agrees immediately, I know I could've bargained even harder. Still, money is money.

"Just tell me where to go," I sigh.

CHAPTER 12

I make it about ten paces before the obvious problem occurs to me and I turn back. "I can't just walk in and say that I'm you—they already know what you look like."

Charlotte isn't worried, though. "Don't flatter yourself. You of all people should have figured out by now that we're all interchangeable. Besides, it's a bunch of interns and research fellows and third-world immigrant doctors who can't land a real hospital job here. I've never seen the same person twice. They don't know and they don't care who shows up, as long as their paperwork's in order."

But I'm still hesitant, so she rolls her eyes at me and then rummages around the scabby leather sack she uses for a purse. She pulls out her driver's license and flings it at me. "Here. On the zero percent chance they even bother asking for ID, give them this." She perks up as a new tactic occurs to her. "In fact, want to make a wager? Double or nothing says they don't ask for identification. Come on, just for fun."

"No, I don't want to bet on it." I glance at the license. "I don't look even remotely like you in this picture."

Charlotte snorts. "*I* don't look even remotely like me in that picture."

She has a point. The photo must have been taken a few hair color changes and a few piercings ago, because Charlotte looks almost wholesome in it, or at least a whole lot less bleach-y and spike-y and rage-y than she looks these days.

I'm still wavering when my phone starts to ring, and I know it's probably Dylan. I make it a point not to even peek, since Charlotte's being so weird about him, but it doesn't make a difference. "Go ahead, answer it," she says in a quiet voice. "Wouldn't want to miss a call from Mr. Perfect."

I shove her driver's license in my pocket and walk away, partly because I don't want to argue with her anymore, but mostly because she's right—I don't want to miss his call.

At least *I'm* consistent.

CHAPTER 13

 MATH FOR GUINEA PIGS.
OR: SHOW ME THE MONEY!

I'm no math whiz. Ask me to divide by anything over ten and you're gonna have to pass me a calculator. But these things are pretty straight-forward once you accept that this whole "volunteer" gig is actually a business. A mutually beneficial, pain-based economy, if you will. Here are a few equations you should know:

Supply = You

You are the commodity. The guns and the butter. You are the sum of your fluids, your pressures, your lymphocyte counts, your cells. Your value lies in your blood, your waste, and your mitochondrial minutiae. Don't fool yourself into thinking you're part of a research team—you're renting out your body the same way a back-alley hooker rents out her snatch. Really, the only difference is that you're turning *your* tricks at the cellular level.

Demand = Profits ÷ Volunteers

Hoo boy, but you can smell pharma-greed from a mile away. Want to know where the deep-pocket studies are? Look for the glossy recruitment ads and promises of free crap. (If I had a nickel for every ugly-ass canvas tote bag with a pharmaceutical logo on it . . .) It's simple: the more money the corporate man behind the curtain stands to make from a safe-enough pill, the more money you can make for being the first one dumb enough to swallow it.

Reward = Risk × Pain

Oh yeah, you're a tough one all right. A genuine badass. *Bring on the needles*, you say. *Take your pound of flesh!* Well, guess what, tough guy? Patience. Sometimes the real pain only comes knocking a whole lot later, and that's a different set of equations altogether.

Word Problem: How many X-rays and CT scans now equal one walnut-sized tumor a decade down the road?

Word Problem: How many years until the doctors find out those pesky little green pills have been silently chip-chip-chipping away at your kidney function and you end up aboard the Dialysis Express?

Word Problem: How long before that itsy-bitsy spider of a blood clot ambles out of its hidey-hole in the crook of your vein and creeps its way to your lungs or your brain?

Aw, frowny face. Our fourth-grade teachers lied to us, boys and girls. Math *isn't* always fun, is it?

If X, then Y . . .

No cutting in line! The order of things matters a great deal in the testing world, so queue up accordingly. The first tests are done on animals, of course—*monkeys and rabbits and rats, oh my.* If enough fuzzy-wuzzy bunnies make it through round one alive and kicking, the grim reapers of research move on, setting their sights on the junkies, the indigents, and the professional guinea pigs for round two. (Ahem. This is where we come in.) Next come the college students. Then come the ailing minimum-wagers—legit sick people whose crappy, barely-there health plans and stretched-to-broke budgets don't have room for things like "proven" cures. Only then, at long, long last and hopefully not too many testing *oopsies* later, will anything ever be tried on the upstanding citizens from Planet Properly Insured. Everyone eventually gets their turn, as long as they're not dying of impatience (see what I did there?).

So, it may not be fun, but I told you math for guinea pigs was simple. And now, what better way to conclude than with a few lines from Kenny Rogers, the patron saint of gambling fools:

> *Every gambler knows*
> *That the secret to survivin'*
> *Is knowin' what to throw away*
> *And knowin' what to keep*
> *'Cause every hand's a winner*
> *And every hand's a loser*
> *And the best that you can hope for*
> *Is to die in your sleep*

Gamble on, guinea pigs!

CHAPTER 14

The thing about testing is that you have to get used to overriding a lot of normal reactions.

Imagine a burly guy coming at you, a large-bore needle in his hand. I'm not talking about one of those harmless little slivers they use when you get a tetanus booster, either. No, the thing in this guy's hand looks like the goddamn Excalibur of syringes. Assuming you haven't bolted from the room yet, maybe you also start to have a few concerns about the guy's hygiene. Like, as he gets closer, maybe you see that he has orange Cheetos dust from lunch still staining his fingers. Maybe he's got greasy spatters on his scrubs, and his breath smells like a dog's ass. You take a close look at his face and maybe his eyes are a little bloodshot, and he's obviously on autopilot, not even paying attention to what he's doing with that needle in one hand as he kneads your limbs with the other, searching for a nice, meaty spot to violate. Maybe he's not even looking as he presses that sharp, silver tip against your flesh, because he's too busy bitching to his coworker on the other side of the room about how they're cutting lab-tech hours again, and how's he supposed to make his car payment without overtime?

Normal reaction: run the other direction as fast as your goddamn feet'll carry you. It's a no-brainer, right?

Or, let's say some lady hands you a cream. She tells you it's definitely going to sting, most likely going to burn, and quite possibly going to leave you badly scarred, maybe even disfigured for life. She hands you a clipboard with a ten-point scale on it, tells you to circle a number every five minutes to indicate how much pain you're experiencing. *Leave it on for as long as you can stand it,* she tells you. She'll just be working in the next room over. *Don't worry,* she says, *I'll hear you if you scream.*

Normal reaction? Shit-can the stuff, tell the lady to go fuck herself.

It's survival instinct. Fight or flight, lizard-brain stuff. Fear is the gift that keeps on giving—an anniversary present from the slithering and slope-skulled creatures we evolved from. The willingness to say *fuck this scene* and run is what kept your Neanderthal ancestors off the sharp end of a woolly mammoth tusk.

But guinea pigs have to turn it all off, ignore all those millions of years of hard-knock-life lessons. *Hey, Great-great-great-great-great-great-great-great-grandma, awesome job outrunning all those saber-toothed tigers, but I got this under control now.* And that's hard to do at first. You have to figure out ways to psych yourself up, to walk *toward* the tiger. It takes a while, sometimes, to be able to do that.

And that's how I met Jameson.

I was in the hallway, leaning against a wall while I waited

for the shaking to stop, and for my stomach to stop heaving and lurching like two sea monsters humping. I was trying, but not succeeding, to talk myself into going back into the room I'd just fled. I was not in a happy place.

I may have been yelling something about sadistic bastards and torture chambers. It's kind of a blur.

To my left was a door. Behind the door were a doctor, a nurse, and a human skid mark of a lab administrator, all waiting for me to override my fear, my disgust, my pride, and my last vestiges of self-preservation, and walk back in to submit to the rest of their program.

I was trying, I really was. Just maybe not hard enough. "You can tell Dr. Jekyll in there I'm not swallowing any more of his poison!" I may have yelled. "Fucking barbarians!" I wasn't really in the right state of mind for this kind of thing yet.

It's that mind-body connection people are always yapping about. Your body won't consent until your mind signs off on the plan.

Anyway, Jameson, who I'd never even seen before, walked over, parked himself next to me, and offered me a stick of gum, which I did not accept. Candy from strangers and all that. "You're only making it harder on yourself," he said. "They get paid either way. You, on the other hand, do not."

"Yeah? Well, I wouldn't go back in there for all the money in the world." I remember spitting on the floor, just missing his feet. "Someone needs to tell Nurse Stalin in there to go back to her gulag." I raised my voice and turned my head to yell at the closed door. "Go find some puppies to drown!"

I was going through kind of a rough patch then—not exactly feeling friendly.

But Jameson grinned. "Well, aren't you feisty? Let me guess. You're new around here."

I didn't say anything.

"Look," he said. "Do what you need to do, but I've been hanging around this place longer than pretty much anyone here, including the doctors. It may not seem like it, but you can actually make a pretty decent life for yourself here if you figure out how the system works. I can walk you around, show you the ropes a little, if you want."

Looking back, now I know that was just Jameson doing his den-mother, right-in-the-middle-of-everything thing. At the time, though, he made me nervous. I couldn't figure out his game. "Why?" I asked him. "What do you want from me?"

He shrugged. "I don't know. You seem interesting, I guess— you've got that whole feral, waifish thing working for you. And you curse like a champion. I always admire people who swear well." He unwrapped a piece of gum and stuffed it in his mouth. "Besides, look around. This neighborhood is starting to go downhill. Like I said, I'm an old-timer here, so maybe I just have a vested interest in welcoming the right kind of people."

I followed his glance and looked around. He had my attention, if only because it had never even occurred to me that anyone did this sort of thing on a repeat basis, made a life out of it. Not that the idea appealed to me in the least, but it was interesting on a theoretical level. Completely batshit insane, obviously, but still interesting.

I looked around for all of a few seconds. It's not a place you need to spend much time in to form an opinion. We were in an overlit hallway with Crayola-bright posters hung in compulsively precise intervals. Last decade's food pyramid. Jaunty retirees power-walking with denture-perfect smiles on their faces. Boldfaced exclamatory reminders to floss! Buckle your seat belts! Know the warning signs of heart disease! Prevent diabetes! Wash your hands!

And in the chairs beneath the posters sat exactly the types of pathetic fucks you expect to see selling plasma and/or queuing up for an experimental methadone program at 10:00 a.m. on a random Tuesday. Present company included, since I may have been a little worse for the wear. It was a linoleum-tiled skid row. We were definitely not a flossing, seat-belt-buckling, hand-washing crowd.

"Ironic choice for wall art, isn't it? The contrast makes for a nice visual." He stuck out his hand. "I'm Jameson, by the way."

I studied him for a minute before I took him up on the handshake. "I'm Audie," I said finally.

The closed door cracked open and a uniformed woman with wide eyes slowly turtled her head out.

"Fuck off!" I yelled, and sort of pretend-lunged at the nurse until she retreated again. "Keep your money—you people are sociopaths!"

I couldn't help it. I hadn't learned to shut off my instincts yet.

Jameson threw back his head and laughed. "Yeah, you're definitely feisty. Come on. I want to introduce you to some people. See if maybe we can get you set up with something a little more appealing."

NeverWhere

A brief crack in the darkness appears, and I wake to find myself in four-point cuffs. I take careful inventory:

> *Point 1: Left hand, tightly fisted.*
> *Point 2: Right hand, two broken nails.*
> *Point 3: Left foot, twitching.*
> *Point 4: Right foot, numb.*

My captors are clearly fools, though. They forgot the most dangerous parts.

Next to me a nurse bustles. She's squat and home-permed, all no-nonsense and bifocals.

"Can you . . . ?" I lift a hand as high as the restraints allow and try to look pitiful and harmless. My voice sounds hoarse, like I've either been screaming for hours or silent for days.

She turns to me with a bright smile on her grandmotherly face, then leans in close to answer. "No chance of that, you nasty little bitch. You're crazy. The old-fashioned kind of crazy. You're exactly where you should be."

She hums as she tugs at the buckles on the restraints, her coral-lipsticked mouth pinched smug and superior as she double-, triple-checks, and then turns around and makes a big show of inspecting and rearranging a series of filled syringes.

I go quiet and stare at the back of her head until she gets nervous and turns around to look at me. "I'm going to cut you into a million pieces," I say in a loud whisper.

I don't really mean it. Jesus, I was smiling and everything as I said it to her, but I guess she can't take a joke because something steely drops across her eyes and she doesn't turn her back on me again.

"Look, here comes the doctor," she says, sweet as sugar, sounding like an entirely different person, as she hears footsteps coming down the hall. "He'll fix you right up."

CHAPTER 15

I've come a long way since those early days. I know my limits now. I do my homework. And I don't like to brag, but I've gotten pretty good at working the system, picking and choosing the studies that pay the most and hurt the least.

But sometimes I pick wrong. Sometimes it can't be helped.

Or sometimes someone steers you wrong. Someone you trusted.

Like today.

Because now, everything is dark and everything hurts.

And even before I open my eyes, I know things.

I have been here before, oh yes I have.

I have been facedown on cold asphalt. (Welcome home!) I know the taste of gravel mixed with blood. (Earthy, metallic.) I know scrapes, and I know bruises, so even though I don't know exactly what has happened to me or precisely where I am, the one thing I *don't* feel right now is surprise.

I know betrayal.

Charlotte was right about the people running the study. No one gave me so much as a lingering glance when I checked in using her name. No one doubted me for a second. And no one saw the need to warn me about what was coming.

I coax my pain-squeezed eyes open and the daylight nudges the knot of pain that is my left temple to the next level. My *where* is clear enough—I'm sprawled on the ground behind the hospital, in the alley used to whisk away all manner of garbage and biohazards and contaminated materials. The *how* and *when,* on the other hand, are murky. The last thing I remember is swallowing something chalky and then sliding into an MRI machine—just another day in the salt mines.

I try to pull more detail out of the throbbing darkness, but there's little else there. Even without remembering anything else, though, I remember very clearly that this was supposed to be Charlotte's gig. I remember how she practically begged me to take her appointment.

I remember how she set me up.

The flare of anger that comes with this realization is almost immediately extinguished by icy dread, however, as I notice my backpack lying open on the ground next to me. A quick grope confirms my fear: the money is gone. All of it. A blockbuster week's worth of earnings, a nauseatingly significant portion of my (previously) growing nest egg, replaced by nothing but a rapidly growing lump on my head.

It occurs to me that I should check for blood, but the effort seems painful and pointless, so I give up. Right now the loss of the money feels far more vital than the loss of any amount of blood.

No money means no trip. No trip means no goal. No goal means no hope.

No postcards. No corny souvenirs. No holding hands during a bumpy takeoff, no room-service breakfast. No happy ending. No future photo album version of Us.

No future Us at all.

This and only this is clear in my mind—everything else a hopeless smear of jumbled images and fuzzy thoughts. (*Fuck you.* Just *fuck you* if you're going to lecture me about carrying that much cash on me. Where's an underage vein grifter like me gonna get a checking account, genius?)

"Fuck!" I scream it to the wind.

Somewhere behind me I hear a door open and then slam shut. "Are you okay?" someone asks.

It's the Professor, creeping around and watching like always. Of course he's here—back-alley academic that he is. Except he's changed. He's huge now, the size of an elephant, and my brain scrambles to understand why everything around me looks supersized. The Dumpster on my right is the size of a building, and the bricks in the wall are the size of car windshields.

Pieces of conversation return to me in jagged bursts, and I remember. Something about the study—*Charlotte's* study— went wrong. Lilliputian effect. Just a minor hallucination, boys and girls, nothing to worry about. A few synapses crossed, a few neural pathways scrambled. The scene reassembles itself in my aching brain: the lab tech going practically giddy as I described what was happening to me in a whimper that didn't even sound like my voice. *"I'm shrinking, why am I shrinking?"*

I am a unicorn, it would seem. A (prickly, pissed-off) four-leaf clover. My reaction to their test product, their million-dollar moonshine, unique enough to compel the tech to call in the supervisor, and then the senior researcher. There was talk of a journal article about me, little old me (literally little, at least to my drug-fucked eyes and miswired brain).

I vaguely recall overhearing snippets of muttered conversation: *We screened her for mmmph, didn't we? Of course we did . . . but these things happen . . . we should blargle grph . . .* I wonder briefly what it is that I have in my blood that Charlotte does not that made me react this way, but I'm too groggy and battered to really care.

Lilliputian effect: I am small and you are tall. A problem of perception not grounded in reality. Does it sound funny? Imagine it happening, imagine seeing everything around you spinning, growing bigger and bigger as you descend toward the floor, toward oblivion. Not so funny.

I'm Alice in Wonderland, nibbling from the wrong side of the mushroom. A temporary visual disturbance, they said. A rare and minor side effect, which should (should!) resolve without medical intervention.

I surely fucking hope so. Why was I there again? What were they testing on me? My memories elbow each other, jostling and scrapping, trickling in out of sorts and out of order, the gaps between them stuffed with dark nothingness. Me, insisting I was fine to walk out on my own; me, running, desperate for fresh air; me, signing forms with Charlotte's name, not bothering to read the small print.

"Oh, it's you. What are you doing out here?" The Professor is slowly shrinking back to normal; he's only the size of a Clydesdale now. He offers me a hand, but I wave him away and stand up on my own.

"Did you steal my money?" I ask him as soon as I'm steady on my feet. I try to sound threatening, but it comes out in a watery-sounding bleat.

"Me?" He looks insulted. "I didn't take anything from you. How could I? I just got here."

"Well, did you see who did?"

He shakes his head and then puts on a pair of reading glasses to inspect me more closely. "That's a nasty bump on your head. Maybe we should get that looked at?"

I take a step away from him, blinking away a waterfall of neon eye floaters. "No, I'm fine. I mean, I'm not, but I will be. I just want to go home."

"Care for company, then? I'm going in the same direction." He extends his arm, and it looks as long as a python. *He's a snake.* The thought bubbles out of the center of the pain over my eye, but I take his arm anyway. I don't trust myself not to black out again.

I don't want to go anywhere with him, but it's not like I have many choices. What I want, what I *need,* is Dylan, but he's in class right now, and I know he can't answer his phone.

So I just nod. I start to ask the Professor how he knows where I live, but then I think about the money, what I went through to get it, what it *meant,* and I know that if I open my mouth I'll start to cry. So I don't say anything, not even when he starts in with his questions. *Opportunistic little prick.* I just focus on putting one foot in front of another, tuning out everything else.

He finally takes the hint and shuts up, walking me all the way to my door in silence.

CHAPTER 16

I'm perched on the bathroom counter, the edge of the sink pressing into the back of my thighs. I feel drained, like whoever stole my money also emptied me of blood. Stranger things have happened around the labs, if you believe the rumors, which I don't.

I do look like I lost a fight with a brick wall, though.

Fortunately, Charlotte is an artist. Charlotte is a magician. She's back to her old self again, and I have to keep reminding myself that it's her fault in the first place.

She switches to a lighter shade, switches to a different brush, and I watch in the mirror as my black eye disappears. She's good at this. Very good.

"If there's one thing I've learned from my shitty taste in guys, it's how to cover up a bruise," she says as she dabs more concealer under my eye and all the way up to my hairline. "See? Good as new."

Personally, I don't see the point. In my own experience,

facial bruises function like an invisibility cloak. Nothing like a fresh-baked shiner to make people dance that little *I don't want to get involved* jig and leave you alone to do your thing, but I don't say this out loud. Charlotte's too busy feeling useful.

"Voilà!" She takes a deep bow as I applaud her work.

"You're a master of disguise," I tell her. Dylan's coming over any minute now, dropping everything to come take care of me, so I don't have time to confront Charlotte about tricking me into taking her place in the study. I don't have the energy, either, since my head feels like a semi drove over it.

Besides, my anger is fading. It's like a fizzy drink gone flat from sitting out, and I'm starting to see that it was ridiculous to think Charlotte intentionally set me up, that she could have known what would happen. At this rate, I'm about two blows to the head from turning into one of those crackpot conspiracy theorists, ranting about black-market organ harvests and the evils of fluoride.

Charlotte makes a face. "Yeah, awesome. Why is it that no matter what I do, no matter where I go, I always end up painting over bruises?" She zips up her makeup bag and leans against the wall, chewing on the inside of her cheek a little, the way she does when she's nervous about something, and I wait for what I'm assuming is going to be an apology. I mean, even if she didn't set me up, it was still *her* appointment that did this to me.

But I'm wrong about Charlotte yet again, since what actually comes out of her mouth is about the furthest thing from an apology possible. "Don't you think it's time you took a little break from this thing with Dylan? I mean, come on, Audie, just look at yourself." She squints at me, then reaches over to gently blend an errant smudge of concealer with her thumb. "Look what's happening to you. You're young, you're hot, and you could do a hell of a lot better if you just moved on—"

I bat her hand away from my face and cut her off. "Wait, are you kidding me? You think Dylan did this to me? Charlotte, I told you. I passed out after I left *your* freaking appointment, where I took *your* freaking test meds—thanks a lot for that, by the way—and I hit my head on the curb or something."

She doesn't answer—she just stands there, chewing on her lip now, and I can see that she doesn't believe me. She really *does* think Dylan did this to me.

Whatever anger I had left in me melts away. I mean, how sad is that? I feel awful for Charlotte all of a sudden. All the time she's spent around him, around us, all the times she's seen the way he treats me, how good he is to me, and she still can't get over the assumption that if I come home with a black eye, it must be from my boyfriend.

I sort of get it. When you grow up surrounded by rabbit turds, you don't look at what the Easter Bunny left behind and first think *mmmm, chocolate.*

"Oh, Charlotte. Not every guy is a jerk. You'll meet a nice one one of these days—someone who deserves you." I hop down off the counter and give her a hug. She goes stiff, doesn't return my embrace, but I don't let it bother me. I get it. We're all just products of our environment. Not everyone has the strength to break free from their past.

She finally relaxes a little, and when I step back, she raises an eyebrow, looks like she's about to say something, but then stops herself. "Eh," she says after a few seconds. "Fine. You're right. It's none of my business anyway. Just take care of yourself, okay? You're one of the good ones." She steps around me, gently, and walks into her room.

I can tell she's upset, so I follow her. I finally understand why she's so weird about Dylan, and I feel like a total asshole for not getting it sooner. It's so obvious now—someone like Charlotte, with her background and her baggage, can't possibly see the goodness in someone like Dylan. Because of the life she's had, she just has no concept of genuine, un-fucked-up love. As far as she's concerned, what I have with Dylan might as well be a bullshit fairy tale.

I sit down on Charlotte's bed and watch her for a few minutes. I promise myself that I'm going to be nicer to her, to stop rubbing her face in my relationship. It's not fair to go around flaunting my good luck.

She seems to have moved on, though. She peels off her shirt, sniffing it before she tosses it into a pile on the floor. "Yuck. I need to do laundry. Where'd the damn maid wander off to?"

I laugh with her, glad that we can change the subject, and then watch as she rummages through her closet for something to change into. She looks bonier than I remember. The weight-loss drugs must be working double time. Wasn't she rounder, softer, just a week or two ago? Is it even possible to lose that much weight in so little time?

I'm about to ask her about it when I get distracted by the tattoos on her back. Small circles, a whole series of them, running down the length of her spine. I would've taken her for more of a dolphin-on-the-ass-cheek kind of gal. Maybe a butterfly on the hip, or the Chinese symbol for something or other. Instead, these tats are sloppy and unevenly spaced, almost haphazard, and the one right in the center of her back must be brand-new because the skin around it is a puffy, angry red.

"Hey, what's up with the new ink?" I ask her. Looking closer, I can see that they're not actually circles—they're snakes, chasing their own tails.

She frowns, then grabs a shirt out of the dirty pile and yanks it over her head. "Are you going to the party this weekend?"

She's changing the subject, which is kind of weird, but whatever. If she doesn't want to talk about something, it usually has to do with a guy—Charlotte's the reigning champ of bad break-ups. All the more reason I should quit rubbing Dylan in her face.

Besides, who doesn't have certain things they don't want to talk about?

"Wouldn't miss it," I say.

CHAPTER 17

This is how well Dylan knows me: he shows up with a stack of books instead of a bouquet of flowers.

Flowers are just so *biological,* the way they fade and wilt and die. It's the last thing a guinea pig like me needs more of— further evidence of the mortality all around us. Books, on the other hand, are the perfect gift: tidy little packets of fantasy and escape. From pulp to Poe, I love them all.

I love that Dylan gets that about me.

He takes one look at my bruises, or at least the inch-thick concealer that's covering my bruises, and insists that I get in bed to recuperate. He brings me tea, keeping a wary eye out for Charlotte as he sneaks in and out of the kitchen, then drapes his arm over my shoulder and watches as I flip giddily through the pile of books.

"Here's where I have to make a confession," he says. "I'm actually being a self-serving bastard right now. I'm a little be-hind in English—okay, a lot behind—and I not only have to get through one of these beasts within the next twenty-four hours, I also have to write a five-hundred-word essay brilliant enough to persuade Mrs. Krolnik not to give me an incomplete."

I open my mouth, about to say something about the kind of teacher who would penalize a student dealing with cancer, but I remember just in time that he hasn't actually told me yet that he's out of remission. "So, which one shall we read, then?" I say instead.

"Patient's choice."

"Okay, then. How about this?" I hold up a copy of *1984*. "We were reading it in school when I . . . had to leave, so I never got to finish it." I immediately wish I'd kept my mouth shut.

"Mr. Orwell it is," says Dylan, and for a minute I think I'm safe. But *au contraire*.

"Why didn't you finish school, anyway?" Dylan asks. Of course he does. There are certain topics I do everything in my power to avoid, and now it's my own damn fault, since I'm the one who brought it up. "You like reading more than anyone else I know. I bet you got straight As."

Idiot, I curse myself silently. I scrunch up my face and try to look pathetic enough that he just drops it. "I've told you about it before. Let's talk about something more interesting. Or better yet, let's start the book."

But he won't let it go. "No, you haven't." He lifts my hair and nips playfully at my ear. "Come on, Audie. I'm just trying to know you better. You're such a woman of mystery."

Actually, I have told him, but I always make it a point to downplay things about my past when we talk. *No big deal, noth-*

ing to see here, that sort of thing. Gliding, sliding answers—in one ear and out the other. "It's too nice an afternoon to talk about depressing things. Let's read about totalitarian states and thought police instead."

"Tell me," he says, pulling me in a little closer.

Big Brother is watching, I think, which I know isn't fair. I sigh, and try to decide which version to tell him.

There are several to choose from, and each version is technically true. It all depends on who you pick as your narrator—the social worker, who'd tell you a different version than the principal, who'd tell you a *completely* different version than I would, or one of the bit players, secondary characters with minimal insight and maximal opinions. Even my own version has changed over the years—I see it all differently now than I did back then, when it all happened.

Plus, you have to consider the audience when you tell certain kinds of stories.

I settle on a melted-down explanation—a softened combination of several different versions. "A whole bunch of things happened right around the same time. Bad luck, mostly. It just kept piling on until I couldn't really take it anymore," I say.

He waits.

"My mom died," I tell him, and his eyes go wide and he makes the appropriate little sounds of sympathy.

I don't tell him she'd been walking around half-dead for years, addicted to everything except life.

"And after that I didn't really have anywhere to live."

I don't mention that I wasn't living with her at the time she died—that's kind of beside the point, isn't it? Plus, we'd been talking about giving it another try. I'd run out of options and she was trying to stay clean; for once she actually seemed like she was making an effort. Operative word: *seemed.*

But mothers in Dylan's world don't take anything stronger than extra-strength Tylenol. Maybe Xanax, or an extra glass of Merlot at night if they're hard-core. So I skip ahead a few steps.

"I guess I just kind of lost it," I say. "Grief and all that."

I don't want to lie to him, so I just leave off the messier parts. The things that tend to scare off a nice guy like Dylan. Besides, you really had to be there to understand. Context is everything.

"I had some anger issues to deal with," I say, hoping we can leave it at that.

"Totally understandable," Dylan murmurs.

"But I'm okay now," I reassure him. "I've worked through it."

They didn't press charges. A few legal technicalities, a couple of teachers who spoke on my behalf, and a mutually agreed-upon decision that it was probably best if I just sort of moved on.

There's more, but to be honest, it's all kind of a blur. I don't think I could tell him all the details even if I wanted to. Which I don't. Nobody needs to hear that kind of stuff over and over again—least of all me. And definitely not a good, decent guy like Dylan.

I just want us to have a chance. Just because we come from different worlds doesn't mean we can't start over together.

I push away the thought of the missing money. *Later.*

Fortunately, Dylan doesn't need to hear any more. He wraps his arms around me and pulls me into his chest. "God, I feel so bad for you. You've had it so rough." He sounds genuinely sad, maybe even a little weepy, which throws me a bit. I definitely don't think of him as a weepy kind of guy.

Seriously—is the entire world on mood-altering drugs today? It's gotta be a full moon, or something.

"I told you," I say. "I'm okay now. Besides, it could be worse. I could have cancer." I grin, try to show him that at least I'm at the point where it's okay to have a sense of humor about it.

And, fine—let's be honest. Maybe it's a little jab. A tiny one—just a little reminder that nobody's perfect, that even *he* has things in his background he'd rather erase. It's kind of a shitty thing to do, maybe, but I just want a level playing field.

I want him to want to start over, too. With me.

Dylan doesn't take it as a jab, though. Nor as a prompt to share his own little secret. Can he really have no clue that I know he's sick again? I mean, what kind of person would I have to be, not to notice all the signs? Instead, he sits back and shakes his head, looking so damn sincere I could shake him. "No, don't do that. Don't minimize your suffering."

Shit. I can see exactly where this is going. We're doing the opposite of moving on. And what teenage boy talks like that? I shift my weight and turn away from him while I try to conceal my irritation. I can practically feel the conversation, the whole afternoon, sliding down into this depressing-as-hell emotional vortex, and it's the last thing on earth I want to do on a gorgeous spring day with my gorgeous (though annoyingly weepy) boyfriend.

So I take a clue from George Orwell and play my own

version of thought police. I turn back to Dylan and lean over to whisper in his ear, sliding the stack of books to the floor in the process. He may not want to change the subject, but I pick the one topic that no teenage boy can resist.

A little brainwashing never hurt anyone.

Dylan is shocked, of course, but he gets over it as I whisper more details, and after a minute or two he's no longer an annoying softy on the verge of tears. I mean, it's a *total* transformation, and he doesn't object at all as I take him by the hand and pull him closer.

CHAPTER 18

Promising treatment—
results are anonymous.
May result in death

I'm playing Consent Form Haiku with Dougie, who for reasons unknown (and unasked) is also in urgent need of a quick cash infusion, and who therefore is also participating in this study, which we both know is going to suck big-time.

But: more pain, more gain.

The loss of a week's worth of cash was a serious setback, and the only way I can possibly claw my way back toward my Castillo Finisterre finish line is to relax my standards. No more picking and choosing—I need to enroll in every test that will have me.

"What do you think?" Dougie asks as he rearranges the lines he's torn out of his forms onto one of the logo-plastered clipboards some pharmaceutical company has scattered around the waiting room. As he pushes the clipboard over, I notice one of his tattoos—five dots between his thumb and index finger. Jailbird's Scout badge. He seems awfully young for that. Like, my-age young. Somehow I'm not surprised, though. Something about Dougie has always put me on edge. Plus, he has the rattiest white-guy dreadlocks you've ever seen, which Charlotte claims are a sure sign of questionable judgment.

"Yours is better than what I came up with," I admit, but I show him mine anyway:

An adverse event.
Maximum amount of blood,
when the study ends

"Not bad, Audie. Not bad." He's humoring me. We give each other space, Dougie and me. I think this might be the first time it's ever been just the two of us alone in a room. Which is funny, really, since you'd think two system kids like us might have more in common. I'd bet a hundred bucks we know some of the same people in the outside world. Which is all the more reason to avoid the topic, obviously, since it's always a shame to fuck up a fresh start.

I mean, what're we going to do—plan a reunion? Ha! It's a laughable *and* a redundant idea, since for people like us the system usually sucks you back in and hosts the reunion for you, compliments of the state, no RSVP required.

I go back to flipping through the stack of paper on my clipboard in search of better lines. I'm feeling a little competitive,

I'll admit. I tear out a few phrases here and there, but nothing poetic really jumps out at me. Why do these forms have to be so fucking long? It's not like anyone actually reads them. Blah blah blah, I hereby acknowledge. Mumble, mumble, mumble, I agree not to hold responsible. Hardly lyrical or quoteworthy.

Just tell me where to sign. Again and again and again.

I check my phone. I empty my mind. I wait.

Sometimes there are good days here. Easy, bloodless, paper-work days. No stitches, no probes, no pricks. Days that seem bizarrely normal, like the brown paper bag you're clutching in your hand might actually contain a sandwich and an apple instead of a leaking, stinking stool sample. *Just another day at the office!*

Sometimes there are bad days. Scalpel and retractor days. Large-bore-needle days. Hazy, blurry, time-gone-lost days.

But you know what? Fuck it.

It's a waste of time, stressing about irreversible this and incurable that, thirty-one flavors of gut-scrambling side effects. That's for people whose unpuckered, scarless skin has places to go, for people with reasonable expectations of beach vacations and pool parties in the not-too-distant future, people who have a reason for not wanting to look like a walking autopsy in their swimsuits. It's for people who daydream about strapless wedding dresses, for people who can worry enough about the days ahead to bother with things like flossing and exfoliating.

It's for people who have a very different future than mine.

I know—maudlin much? It's just that Dylan isn't answering

my texts, and his silence is making everything else harder to deal with.

How'd your teacher like my, oops, I mean, YOUR essay?

Then: *Where r u? Everything ok?*

That sounds normal, right? I'm aware that I sometimes fail to consider how my words and actions might seem to someone on the outside. Because of this, I don't mind that Dylan has never introduced me to his family. I get it. I really do.

I'm just on edge right now because of the money. Everything feels more urgent, even something as stupid as an unanswered text.

I look at my watch and instruct myself not to send any more messages for at least three hours. I remind myself not to push him. I know he loves me, and that's enough.

He probably lost his cell phone again. Poor guy is always forgetting where he left it. It's the chemo. That shit seriously messes with your brain cells—I'd probably forget my own name if I'd been through half of what Dylan has.

Focus on the money, I tell myself, and the rest will work itself out. Concentrate on the achievable goal. I just need to dig a little deeper, work a little faster. Tighten the old belt, as they say.

I have plenty of experience eschewing material possessions. Lifestyle-induced asceticism, you could say. As far back as I can remember, things of any resale value used to come and go while I slept, as if carted off in the night by marauding herds of Craigslist goblins:

My first bike—secondhand, probably stolen, then stolen in turn from me. Karma's a bitch, learns six-year-old Audie.

The widescreen TV from the living room—an over-ambitious Christmas gift gone by New Year's. Santa's a flake, learns eight-year-old Audie.

Dad's tool set—bail money trumps home improvement, learns nine-year-old Audie.

A watch, a stack of DVDs, my winter coat, Granddad's coin collection—when the dealer comes a-knockin', your possessions start a-walkin', learns Audie on too many occasions to count.

You learn not to care. You learn not to get attached. Okay, so you also learn to hide and sneak and steal—I'm not pretending to be Gandhi with tits here—but my point is that when you're used to having things taken from you, you learn to get over it and get on with it.

The problem is, it takes more energy every time.

And right now it's harder than usual to shrug off the loss and start over because this time it isn't just about me. This time it's about Dylan and the trip. It's about us, and our chance to do something amazing together.

Money, I can do without. Dylan's happiness, I cannot.

I check my phone again. Two hours and forty-two minutes to go before texting him again. I'll make it casual. *Hey! Coming over tonight?* Something like that. Two hours, forty-one minutes.

It's a relief when they finally call my name, even though I know this is going to hurt.

"Good luck," Dougie says as I stand up. He yawns as I walk by, and as he stretches, his shirt rides up and I catch a glimpse of more of his tattoos. I definitely don't like the tale they tell.

The nurse doesn't look at me. Not as I follow her down the

hallway and into the procedure room, and not as she hands me a paper gown and tells me to put it on so it opens in the front.

The doctor who comes in doesn't look at me, either. Not as he pushes aside the paper gown, not as he swabs my thigh with brown antiseptic, and not as he injects a local anesthetic. Definitely not as he uses small, sharp scissors to cut out a tiny chunk of muscle. "You'll need to come back to have the stitches removed," he says to my tissue sample as he walks out of the room. I've seen more of his bald spot than I have of his face.

"You're welcome," I call out before the door closes, a little loud, a little snarky.

He freezes, then turns and edges, wide-eyed, back into the room, like he's surprised to learn that I can speak. "Oh," he says. "Yes. Yes, of course. Thank you." Obligation fulfilled, he skitters out again.

The nurse shoves a manila envelope at me and then walks out behind the doctor.

I shuffle through the packet quickly. Wound-care instructions, extra bandages, a list of possible signs of infection.

Nothing about getting paid.

"Wait a minute!" I push through the door and chase after the nurse. "Where's the money?"

"Money?" She looks blank.

I want to shake her. *Like I let you butcher me for free, you stupid cow?* "Cash. Compensation. Cashier's check. Whatever. You know, the *money*?"

"Oh. We had to change our terms recently, and now we don't pay until you've completed all the steps. Too many subjects were dropping out before the last phase, and then we couldn't use them in the data set. So now we don't pay until after the final follow-up visit."

I shove my hair back with both hands, tell myself to take a deep breath. "Final visit?" I ask through gritted teeth. "And when is that?"

She sighs and keeps walking, so that I have to trot after her to keep up. "It's all in the paperwork we gave you."

Fuck. The paperwork that lies in jagged strips of five- and seven-syllable phrases. "I, um, I think I might have lost that page. Can you check your records or something, let me know when I can come back?"

The nurse looks at me like I don't deserve to be using up the air on her planet. "I don't have that information," she says in a bitchy, clipped voice. "You'll have to call the study coordinator's office next week. She's on vacation until Monday."

I shred my fingernails against the flesh of my palms and look away so she can't see how she's getting to me. "Can I please have her phone number?" I say as I blink hard. And then before she can even say it: "I know it was in the paperwork you gave me. But can you give me another copy? Please?"

I keep looking away so I don't have to watch her roll her eyes at me as she huffs her disgust and slaps a new consent-form packet onto the counter. "You're welcome," she says in a snarky echo of my own voice.

I spin around and storm off, which is not the smartest idea in the world since it makes my stitches feel like they're tearing through my skin. I'm still numb from the anesthetic, so it doesn't really hurt, but I know it will soon enough. I just want to get the hell out of there.

But when I push through the doors to the reception area, Dougie's there waiting for me. He's limping slightly, same side as me. "Well, that sucked."

I ignore him. I can't deal with him right now.

He doesn't take the hint. He wraps his hand around my upper arm and squeezes, not so tight that it hurts, but firm enough to send a message I can't miss. "What do you say we go somewhere, Audie? Maybe take off our pants and take care of each other's wounds the old-fashioned way." He licks the corner of his lips and tosses back his pathetic faux dreads in a way I think is supposed to be sexy.

"Get off me, Skeevy McFuckerson." I shove him away and practically run out of the room, not even caring when I look down and see a small bloom of blood soaking its way through my pants.

I'm not surprised. I've never liked Dougie—he set off my creepdar from the first time I met him. But he's the least of my worries, and I can't get distracted. My biggest enemy right now is time—a fact I confirm by checking the contents of the envelope in my hand. The final study follow-up isn't for five weeks. Which means no cash until after Dylan's birthday, so it might as well be forever. Just thinking about it makes me almost vibrate with anger. They already have my flesh, but I'm not getting a dime for five fucking weeks. Can they really do that—change the terms like that?

I pull out my cell phone—it's a crappy, prepaid, junkie's phone—and call Dylan. I don't care that it's not time yet. I need to hear his voice. I need to hear that we're worth this.

CHAPTER 19

The first time I got high, it was the moon, full and round.

It was the warmth of the sun.

It was the tide, pulling and lulling in my veins.

It's no exaggeration to say that feeling, that pale, electric, shimmering sensation inside of me, was the light at the end of a tunnel. It was my first breath. It was my introduction to the world. It gave me my voice, that bliss-ed, bless-ed, drug-fueled moment—my first cry a chemical *hallelujah,* a filled-to-the-brim *amen.*

Screw you. Screw all of you who try to tell me it's not possible for me to remember it.

I remember it. I do.

I came out of the womb high as a kite. Every day since has been stained by the absence of that particular feeling, that singular, scene-setting cocktail of opioids and bulking agents (likely suspects, as per police reports thoughtfully included in my hospital discharge file: brick dust, crushed aspirin, sugar. Also, traces of rat feces).

Happy birthday to me, happy birthday to me. Happy birthday, dear Audie. Haaaaaah-peeeee birthday to me.

But nothing will ever touch that feeling again. No drug in the world can give me *life* the way it did that first time, the day I was born, a yowling, yellow, smoosh-faced, too-early, too-small little tweaker baby, crying and shaking in my incubator with nurses tsk-tsking all around.

I remember it all, because every day since then has been an act of withdrawal.

The upside of being born an addict: nothing tempts me. That is to say, nothing satisfies. A twist in my junkie genetics has left me with all the cravings, the bone-deep needs, but none of the fix. I've already experienced the perfect high, and nothing else will ever come close. Not that I haven't tried—just that I've tried and failed. I have apathetic veins. Constipated opiate receptors. It's a shitty way to break a shitty cycle: I am stubbornly and hopelessly unaddicted.

It would be fair to say that my chemical indifference is rare among my fellow professional guinea pigs, however, and tonight a rousing game of Musical Pill Bottles is going on in the living room. *Par-tay!*

A skinny blonde squints at the writing on the small container that ends up in her hands when the music stops. "What the fuck is this stuff going to do to me? I don't even *have* testicles!" She shrieks this loud enough for the whole room to hear, dry-swallows two of the pills, and then starts to laugh so hard she pisses herself, the stain spreading down both thighs, which only makes her laugh harder.

Things like this happen at a guinea pig party, which goes a long way toward explaining why you don't see many outsiders in attendance.

Because, incontinence. Also because, lesions.

See also: Vomiting. Flatulence. Drainage. Not exactly crowd-pleasers.

From my seat in the corner I spot at least four revelers carrying large bottles that look to be filled with apple juice, only it's not apple juice, of course. There's a big trial going on that requires participants to collect forty-eight hours of urine, and a party's no reason to slack on the job, so they rest their bottles full of piss-colored beer next to their bottles of beer-colored piss.

It ain't a pretty scene, but it sure is entertaining—something crazy *always* happens at guinea pig parties. There's just something liberating about handing your body over to science, jumping blindly into the pharmaceutical abyss. Plus, you've never seen anyone dance like a crowd of people all testing a government-sponsored substance designed to counteract the effects of hallucinogens.

I watch a tall, bald man on his hands and knees chasing his imaginary tail in the center of the room. Either he was in the control group, or someone might want to tell the researchers their taxpayer-sponsored psychedelic chastity belt isn't very effective at its current dosage. It's impressive, however, that the man is mere centimeters from actually achieving his goal and nipping himself on his own ass. All around him, the other guinea pigs cheer his efforts, and down the hall, Jameson is dominating a round of pharmaceutical logo bingo. "Pfizer," the caller shouts out, and the other players groan as Jameson raises his hands in victory and scoops up his winnings.

Everyone is having a good time.

Everyone except me. Mostly, this is because my head feels like it's being pounded with a molten-hot sledgehammer—a burning, aching acheburn. Behind my eyes the pain claws to get out, releasing its venom into my blood.

Charlotte lurches by, also looking rough, and I wonder what she's on. The right half of her face is flushed and her pupils are the size of nickels, and whatever it is she's been taking, I'm pretty sure she shouldn't take any more of it. "Still waiting for your 'boyfriend' to show up, Audie?" She makes little air quotes when she says it, then keeps walking. Staggering, more like it.

I'm quiet for a beat, but then something inside of me flares even brighter than the pain in my temple. I've been trying to be understanding, but everyone has a breaking point. "What's your problem, Charlotte?" I stand up and follow her down the hall. "Why do you have to be such a bitch when it comes to Dylan? I know you have issues, but you need to fuck off and let me be happy."

She keeps walking like she doesn't hear me, which is completely impossible, since I might have sort of screamed it and I can feel everyone else in the room staring at me, but Charlotte just keeps going until she's out the door.

I stand there like an idiot. I have no idea what happened, why she's being so nasty. I thought we'd gotten past the Dylan argument during our little bathroom-counter chat, or at least agreed to disagree. But Charlotte obviously walked away from that conversation with a very different conclusion.

I try to shrug it off and go back to enjoying the party, but the fact is that I hadn't been enjoying the party in the first place, since Dylan has once again pulled a disappearing act.

I check my phone. Nothing. He promised he'd come tonight, but here I am, waiting, without receiving so much as a courtesy call to let me know he's running late.

Jameson comes up behind me and puts a drink in my hand. "What is this?" I ask, sniffing it.

"Drink up. It's exactly what you need right now, from the looks of things," he says, leading me away from the door and out onto the cigarette-butt cemetery of a patio. "What's going on, Audie?" he asks.

All of a sudden—seriously, out of nowhere—I realize that I hate him. I know that sounds like a strong word, and I probably made it seem like I thought Jameson was such a great guy and all before, but I only really figure it out just now, standing on this shitty, butt-filled patio outside this shitty freakfest of a party, that I can't fucking stand him and the way he's always mooning around our apartment, like you can barely have your own space or a private conversation, because he's always inserting himself into whatever you're talking about, acting like he knows so much more about *everything* than everyone else.

I mean, a girl can change her mind, right?

"Just stay out of my life, Jameson!" I say, and stalk off to a lone, weather-beaten rattan chair on the opposite side of the patio—the perfect place for a good, solitary sulk. But before I do, I toss back the drink, whatever it is, and wince as the liquid burns its way down my throat. I may not be a druggie, but I'm also not opposed to a little high or a little low here and there.

Damn it, Dylan. Why aren't you here?

But deep down, I already know. He said he'd come, sure, but only after I practically begged him. It was obvious that he didn't want to, and I really can't blame him. The way Charlotte treats him is only part of it. He's too nice to say so, but I know the whole guinea pig life freaks him out, and our little talk about Why Audie Is a High School Dropout Loser probably didn't help, even if I didn't exactly tell him the whole story.

I feel the tingle of Jameson's mystery drink starting to kick in, and my suspicions begin to crystallize into a recognizable form. Suddenly it's obvious that I've been lying to myself all along. Dylan hasn't been pulling away from me, disappearing for hours or days at a time, taking longer and longer to return my calls because he's getting *sicker*. He's pulling away because he's getting *better*.

He's not rejecting me because his cancer is back. He's just rejecting me.

Full stop.

How shitty a person am I that I'd prefer to think my boyfriend has a terminal illness rather than confront the fact he's just not that into me?

I hear a crash, and then loud hooting noises coming from the party, and my face flushes. The healthier Dylan gets, the weirder we all must seem. *Of course* he can't wait to be done with his treatments, to be in full-fledged remission, and never set foot on hospital grounds again. *Of course* he can't wait to leave all this behind. (Translation: leave *me* behind.)

Since my brain is now filling in the gaps I've been willfully ignoring, it occurs to me that Dylan almost never talks about his illness anymore. You can sit and talk to him for hours, and he'll never say the word *cancer*. Not once. He's done with it. Beat it. Over it. And next up on the discard list? Me. *I'm* part of his sick world. Why would he want to be around a constant reminder of the worst years of his life, once he's better?

I feel kind of woozy and off balance—that must've been one hell of a strong drink. (Or was it two? The details are going hazy.) But even through the shifting prism of intoxication, I know with a singular clarity that only one thing can fix this downward spiral.

Patagonia. The castle at the end of the world.

Dylan and I need to get away from here for a while, away from both of our pasts, so we can build something healthy. We need to start over in a different context. In a better place.

All of a sudden I can't get out of here fast enough.

I shove past Jameson and back into the apartment, then keep shoving, all the way through the crowd, until I'm out the front door. *Whose apartment is this, anyway?* I feel like I knew the answer to that at one point during the evening, but the answer eludes me now. Doesn't matter. Guinea pig apartments are all the same. Revolving roommates, minimal decor. Clean. We're compulsively clean people, which makes sense. The labs put the fear of contamination in you. We've all seen what happens when things aren't kept sterile: Fungal Jungle, maybe a visit from Mademoiselle MRSA or that most unwelcome houseguest, necrotizing fasciitis. Only us guinea pigs realize that the true zombie apocalypse is microscopic, that the zombies aren't outside the gates. *They're inside the house, people!* Or, more accurately, in your veins. The early signs of infection have been drilled into us so much that at one point Charlotte turned them into a nightmare of a nursery rhyme:

> *Hickory, dickory, dead.*
> *Your wound is swollen and red.*
> *Your glands are sore,*
> *There's pus galore,*
> *Hickory, dickory, dead!*

We're a hand-scrubbing, Lysol-spraying band of freaks, we are.

Once I'm outside, I scroll through the texts on my phone, hoping to find answers. Hoping to find proof of . . . what, exactly? Even I don't know.

Him: *Dinner with folks, then b right there.*

Me: *c u soon!*

Me: *Where r u?*

Me: *Still coming?*

Me: *I love u.*

Me: *?*

Him: *On my way.*

The texts offer no proof of anything, except perhaps indifference. Two hours have come and gone since his last message, which I think officially makes him a liar. I pace outside the door and shove away the stinging realization, but I feel it coming on, like an infection.

Don't do it, Audie, I tell myself. *Don't turn on him. I'm sure he has a good reason for not being here yet.*

But anger, that most invasive of infections, has already found a way in and now it's slowly eating through my thoughts. If he didn't want to come, he should've just said so.

I'm talking to myself, stamping my feet, when the Professor walks up. He's about the last person on earth I want to see at the moment, but I do have to admire his nerve, the way he keeps showing up where he's not wanted. He must know people lie to him all the time, when they agree to talk to him. He has to know Charlotte's full of shit when she tells her wild stories. But he keeps showing up, keeps filling his notebooks full of lies.

You have to admire that sort of dedication, even if it is pointless.

"Are you okay, Audie?"

I don't say anything. But since people usually aren't shy about telling him to fuck off, get lost, he seems to take my silence as an invitation.

"You look a bit troubled. Can I buy you a cup of coffee? Maybe go somewhere and chat?"

Fucking weirdo little gnome. Professor LikesToWatch. Guinea Pig Groupie.

But I do want to get out of here. I'm sick of the party. Sick of checking my phone for texts that never come. Why not? If nothing else, it's a chance to practice the fine art of telling a good lie.

"Fine," I say. "Lead the fucking way."

CHAPTER 20

There's a diner close by, the kind of place that smells like a few decades' worth of grease and plumbing problems. Stepping inside, I feel a brief sputter of panic, since I have no recollection of walking (driving?) here. It's one more small black hole in my memory, which doesn't speak highly of either my sobriety or my short-term memory.

But here we are.

The hostess leads us over to a dingy booth, where she flicks a brown-edged piece of lettuce off the table with her fingernail and then slams a half-full carafe of coffee between us without even asking if we want it.

I wipe two different colors of lipstick off the rim of my coffee cup before I fill it myself. "This place is a shithole."

The Professor scratches at a fist-sized patch of dried ketchup obscuring the words on his laminated menu and then gives up. "I'll just stick with the coffee," he says when the waitress comes by. "But decaf, please."

This is the type of restaurant where Charlotte would eat if she wanted to get into an *E. coli* study.

This morning she told me she never washes her hands after using the toilet anymore, and she's been eating eggs sunny-side up every day for weeks. "You wouldn't believe what they'll pay you to test new salmonella treatments," she said. "The poultry industry is loaded." She's never tried eating raw chicken before, but she will if she has to.

She may be a bitch sometimes, but you have to respect her work ethic.

"Here's your decaf." The waitress sloshes coffee all over the table when she fills the Professor's cup, then walks away.

"Miss, can you bring me a towel?" he calls after her, but she ignores him.

He sighs and then asks me to hold his briefcase so it doesn't get wet while he sops up the mess with a fistful of paper napkins.

I take the case, then unzip it and start flipping through the contents. He raises an eyebrow while he watches me do this, but he doesn't tell me to stop.

"See anything interesting?"

I shrug. "I'll let you know."

I'm being a brat, but it's only because I know exactly why I'm here. The Professor is famous for these little "interviews." Almost everyone I know, except Jameson, who goes out of his way to avoid him, has sat down and answered the Professor's questions at least once.

Most people like talking about themselves.

Most people like to believe they're interesting.

It's sad, really—some asshole spends fifteen minutes asking you nosy, leading questions and you feel like a rock star for a day.

I start to feel pissed off at myself for even being here. "What exactly are you researching, anyway?"

His face twists as he takes his first sip of coffee. I could've told him it was lousy, but then that would be one more thing he learned vicariously through someone else's experiences. Better he figure it out on his own.

"Interesting question," he says, even though it's not. See what I mean about how phony these conversations are?

"I study human behavior," he says after another minute. He had to think about it first, like no one's ever cared enough to ask. Which probably doesn't bode well for his research. "Specifically, human behavior in extreme or unusual circumstances."

I snort. "Which category do my circumstances fall into? Extreme or unusual?" Before he can answer, though, I pull something out of his briefcase and hold it up. "Jesus. I'm guessing this is what you mean by extreme?"

It's a magazine: the *Journal of Artistic Body Modification*. On the front is a picture of a man who barely looks human. Which, apparently, is the point; the cover model has painstakingly transformed himself into a human cat, complete with surgically clefted upper lip, sharpened teeth, and pointed ears. Tattooed whiskers traverse his acne-scarred cheeks.

I open the magazine to the middle and pick a random sentence to read out loud: "The decision to declare scleral tattooing illegal in the state of Oklahoma is a clear example of government overstepping." I stop and look up at the Professor, who smiles grimly and points to his eyes.

"Whoa. Scleral, as in eyeball?" I say. "People tattoo their freaking eyeballs? Seriously?" I should put the magazine down, but it's too gruesome, too fascinating, to stop looking. I flip through the pages.

Holy fucking freak show.

Holey, wholly, holy fucking freak show.

The pictures in the magazine make my rashy, sutured, piss-toting brethren look like farm-fresh Mormon missionaries. From children's books. Heavily bleached children's books. These are the stumpy-est, bumpy-est, inky-est, holey-est people I've ever seen.

Flesh zippers. I did not know there was such a thing.

Branding: it's not just for cattle.

A four-page spread covers a recent performance by a troupe of dancers who perform while hanging from hooks piercing the flesh over their shoulder blades. The pictures look like crime-scene photos, except for the fact that the victims are smiling and posing with pointed toes and gracefully extended arms. It's all surprisingly bloodless, and one of the performers is quoted as saying that he finds the act of suspension "therapeutic." His dance partner is his wife; one of the pictures shows them gently skewering one another.

They look like ballerina kebabs.

"This is real?" I ask the Professor. "*This* is what you study?"

He reaches over and takes the magazine out of my hands. "Not exactly. May I have my briefcase back?"

I wait a beat before I hand it to him.

"I'm studying a variety of populations. The unifying theme, at least as I would argue it, is a desire for control. Over oneself, first. And by extension, a feeling of control over one's circumstances. Sometimes people cause themselves harm just to prove to themselves, and perhaps to the rest of the world, that they can."

"Or before someone else can hurt them first," I say, without thinking.

"Or that," he says.

I sit back and think about this. Then I grip the table and lean forward again. "Wait, you're comparing *us* to those freaks in the magazine? That's ridiculous. Totally fucking idiotic."

"Is it really?" He's pulling on his beard, enjoying my reaction. He has his notebook out and his pen in hand. Sneaky, baiting bastard. "Why does the comparison upset you so much?"

It *does* upset me. But I'm having a hard time expressing myself. Some of the pills I've been taking lately slow down my thoughts and stretch out my words, especially at night, and I had to double up today because I'd forgotten to take them yesterday. They're combining forces with the pain meds, plus the one or two or three drinks I may have had this evening, and now the chemicals are all mixing and churning and burrowing like hungry maggots in my thoughts.

I hate it when I get like this. I'm not normally an angry person, I don't think, but certain combinations just set me off. The wrong people plus the wrong pills, and *bam,* it's like someone lit a fuse in me. I take slow breaths and remind myself that bad things happen when I let my temper take over.

"We're nothing like them. We're just making a living," I finally say. "We get paid to do what we do. *Those* freaks pay other people to mutilate them. If that's not a good indicator of insanity, I don't know what is."

The Professor is scribbling notes so fast he bumps his cup with his elbow. "Damn!" he says as coffee spills across the table for the second time. But his eyes are glittering and he keeps writing, ignoring the growing puddle. "So the difference lies in the exchange of money? Is that what you're arguing? That the decision to willingly allow another person to inflict pain upon you is a rational one, as long as you're being compensated?"

"No. And don't write that, either, because that's not what I said." I can tell that he's trying to provoke me. Unfortunately, it's working. "*We*—guinea pigs, professional volunteers, whatever you want to call us—serve a purpose. We're part of a scientific process. What we do has a point. It isn't just . . . self-butchery."

"Ah. Yes, I see. It's for science. So what you do is altruistic as well as lucrative. Which makes it all . . ." He mimics my own pause with a mocking smile. "Which makes it all perfectly sane."

The smile fades from his face as he notices the fork gripped in my fist. *Stab him!* the maggots cheer me on.

His eyes go wide and he raises his hands in surrender. "Whoa, settle down. I apologize, Audie; I didn't mean to insult you. I just thought it would be a fun debate. Two intelligent minds turning over a juicy, complex topic. No disrespect intended. I may have taken our chat too far too fast."

I relax my grip on the fork, but I run my thumb over the tines, checking for sharpness. Just in case.

I may enjoy the look of panic on his face slightly more than is healthy.

"How about this, Audie," he says. His eyes have lost their glitter, and the taunting edge is gone from his voice. "Instead of me always asking questions, how about we talk about anything you'd like to. Anything at all."

It actually makes me feel sorry for the guy, the way he says it. I mean, it's pretty pathetic—here's this grown man who doesn't even exist except as a shadow following other people's lives.

Whatever. He wants to chat? It's not like I have anything better to do right now.

It's not like Dylan has called or texted.

"So let's talk about books," I say, only because it's the first remotely polite thing that comes to mind. Small talk, you know?

The Professor beams at me. "What have you read lately?"

"*1984.* You know, Big Brother, all that good stuff. George Orwell." I fidget in my seat. The only reason I agreed to talk was to avoid thinking about Dylan. And yet, here we are. All topics lead to Dylan, it seems.

But the Professor lights up even more. "I actually reread that fairly recently; it's one of my favorites. The main character, Winston, says a number of things that echo my own work. For example, he says in the beginning of the book that 'freedom is the freedom to say that two plus two make four. If that is granted, all else follows.' It's a powerful statement about the need to maintain control over one's own thoughts and beliefs and truths."

I fidget around in my seat, making sure I look bored. Dylan

never even bothered to tell me how he did on the paper I basically wrote for him.

The Professor doesn't notice; he's still rambling on. "It articulates a sentiment that I see in the various groups I study—a fundamental desire for autonomy, even if that self-control has to be gained or expressed via extreme behavior."

He pauses, waiting for me to say something, but I take my time stirring more of the greasy artificial creamer into my cold coffee. In a booth on the other side of the restaurant, a quartet of overmuscled teenage boys loudly order french fries all around, and their normal boyish drunkenness, of course, makes me think even more about Dylan.

Which makes me upset again. It's like I can't escape him—he's everywhere. His *rejection* of me is everywhere.

Which makes the maggoty dark spots in my thoughts start to buzz and fidget.

Which makes me lash out against the Professor again, even though, up until this very moment, I had no strong feelings about either his research theories or his literary analysis, one way or the other.

"What a crock of shit," I say. At this point I'd say that to anything that came out of his mouth. I've been called a contrarian little bitch on more than one occasion. Watch me earn the title.

"The right to say 'two plus two equals four' isn't freedom. It's just spouting off a fucking formula somebody more convincing drilled into your head."

The Professor is staring at me with a strange little smile

on his face. He isn't taking notes. *Pick up your fucking pen!* the maggots chorus. My voice gets louder.

"Screw four," I say, and the teenage jocks turn to stare at me. "Maybe that's somebody else's pathetic idea of freedom, but what if I want more than that? Maybe I want five. I want more than numbers, more than science. I want the magic beans, you know? And, hell yes, I want control. So, when everyone else says four is the answer—the "truth"—well, maybe I still want five. I want the power to make five happen. *That's* freedom."

I don't even know where this is all coming from, or why I even care. But like I said, certain combinations just seem to set me off, and I guess this is one of them. Maybe I should stop taking those birth control pills. At the very least I'm going to report the mood swings.

But even though I'm annoyed with the Professor—and I'd never admit this to him in a million years—it actually feels kind of nice to sit here and talk about a book. About ideas. About something other than my family's medical history or my allergies and current prescription medications. About something other than Dylan.

It's kind of nice to remember there's still a brain lurking around inside of this price-tagged body of mine. I may be a slab of meat, but I'm a slab of meat with a head still attached.

But the shit-eating smile is back on the Professor's face and his pen is resting on the table, like nothing I have to say matters half as much as Charlotte's bullshit sexcapade stories. He's always in a hurry to capture every motherfucking word of those.

She's probably right about him. He probably is a little pervert. Maybe that's why he does what he does—it gives him a chance to hang out with other deviants without admitting his own sick and twisted tendencies. *I have a friend . . . I know this guy . . . I'm studying someone who . . .*

While I'm thinking this, little bits and pieces of *1984* are running through my head. A word from the book flashes like neon in my mind: *doublethink.* Two contradictory beliefs, simultaneously accepted. Welcome to my life.

Big Brother is watching. Don't I know it.

The maggots wriggle and squirm in my brain, and I flash-glance at the grinning faces of the jock posse in the booth. They're elbowing each other, pointing and laughing. I turn my head and see the pinched straight line that is the waitress's mouth as she walks over, probably to ask me to shut up or leave. Then I turn back and look at the pen sitting abandoned next to the Professor's blank page.

Book club for freaks is over.

"You know what? I don't have time for this bullshit." I push away from the table, spin toward the door as more phrases from the book flare up in the corners of my thoughts.

"Shove it up your memory hole!" I yell as I walk out the door, covering my ears so that I can't hear anyone else's voice saying anything at all.

OmniOnce

"*I feel great. Really, I'm doing so much better.*"

I smile as I lie to the doctor. I imagine his skin peeling off his face. I imagine machine guns loaded with hypodermic needles.

rat-a-tat-tat, how d'ya like that?

He smiles as he lies back to me. Bullshit is the new black.

"*Audie, the terms of your stay here have changed,*" *he's saying.* "*There's a question of consent, and the legal department is concerned. Without a signature from a legal guardian . . .*" *He trails off, waits for me to fill in the blank.*

I'm too busy trying to keep the smile floating on my face. It's not easy, keeping this skin mask on. It takes all of my concentration not to let it slide right off.

He sighs. Tries another approach. "*There is one other option. My department is starting a new clinical study. It combines a new medication with a . . . procedure that I think could really help you. It is experimental, but you'd be under my care, so I would be your medical guardian for the purposes of the study. That would eliminate the consent problem.*"

Consent problem. *That's one way to describe it. It's also one way to describe* me.

I could reach him. My thoughts are turbocharged calculations of force and distance and trajectory. I could reach that sharp, sharp pen in his pocket. Stupid, careless man, sitting there so foolishly close to me with his Proud Doctor Pen winking in the light. It's silver, topped with two tiny snakes coiling around a tiny winged staff. The caduceus—a symbol of poisoners and torturers and thieves.

How do I know that? Where did that word come from? Words like that don't float around in defective junkie heads like mine.

Then I understand.

They whispered *it to me. The snakes. They're moving, teeny, tiny little metal snakes the width of a string, and I can hear them hissing words at me. I can feel their scales as they circle around my ankles and squeeze.*

As I watch, one snake stretches its jaws wide and then devours the other. It slowly, smoothly eats its twin, and then it loops back and begins to feast again, this time beginning with its own tail. The snake's hunger is greater than its will to live, and it slowly begins to turn against its own flesh.

The snake hisses my name in greeting. The pain of being consumed and the burden of flesh in its mouth make it difficult for it to speak, but I understand. Even covered as it is with blood and gristle, the snake is beautiful in its wholeness. Life and death, hunger and pain, beginning and end. It is infinite perfection.

It is truly everything.

"Audie?" The doctor's voice breaks my concentration. "Audrea?"

I hate that fucking name, and I wish the snake would eat the man speaking it.

"Do you understand what I'm saying here? I think it's our best option."

I stare at his face for too long—I keep forgetting to blink. The snake in his pocket doesn't blink, either. I nod.

CHAPTER 21

PANCAKE MOMENTS™: A FAMILY AFFAIR!
Directed by: Yours truly

Fade in. Soft-focus, wide shot of brown-eyed,
shaggy-haired father figure (handsome, not too)
making a delightful (!) mess in sun-kissed kitchen
with small, brown-eyed progeny (three or fewer
to avoid negative socioeconomic overtone).
[Props: bowl, spoon, spatula]

Cue montage: 1) Slow-motion spill followed by
wide-eyed pantomimes of guilt (child) and forgiveness
(father). 2) Touching moment involving dab of flour
either brushed off or dabbed onto (better) adorable (!)
button nose. 3) Playful mishap involving syrup.

Pan camera to bathrobe-clad mother figure
entering kitchen, shaking her head (tousled, but not

suggestively so) in mock consternation. Cut to flour-nosed child proudly serving plate of pancakes. Smiles and hugs all around, music swells, that's a wrap!

**Postproduction note: Rough edits of discordant images/sounds already completed, per client request. Pls confirm deletion throughout of: Mommy's scrunchy hangover face. Daddy's sleep-gruff voice calling out for his *goddamn cigarettes*. The sound of foster brothers rattling lockless bathroom doorknobs. Sponsor confirms lack of brand compatibility: these are not Pancake Moments™.

I wake from a night of vivid dreams feeling so much better.

I finally feel like myself again.

My anger has evaporated. It was obviously only a temporary side effect, and I have my head on straight now. I do.

I'm apologizing with pancakes. I found a package of powdered mix in the back of a cupboard, which makes me laugh a little, because it's just one of those things that would never even occur to me to buy.

Things got a bit weird for a little while, but not too long, right? It will all be fine. Because, pancakes! The Disneyland of breakfast entrees. The Hallmark of griddle fare.

I've never made pancakes before, but they're turning out perfect. Pancakes: the fresh start of breakfasts. I crank up the stereo and dance while I flip.

I think about calling Dylan to invite him over, but then decide against it. I have this very strong feeling that he'll come on his own. He always shows up when I need him the most. We joke about it sometimes, about how it's like we're on some private mental Wi-Fi network.

I'm sure he has a good explanation for not showing up last night.

I'm sure there's no reason to worry.

When the clock hits 11:00, the larvae in my head start to wake up, but I rinse them away with orange juice and make extra noise as I wash dishes and rattle the utensil drawer. At 11:20 I turn the music up to a semi-obnoxious volume. At 11:25 I pound on Charlotte's door, then Jameson's. No answer at either.

I have enough pancakes for an army, but I'm the only one home.

At 11:31 the key rattles in the front door and Jameson drags himself in, bleary-eyed and stubble-cheeked. His clothes are usually starched and pressed to the point of squareness—he's the rare kind of guy who might actually look natural in a bow tie—but now he's wearing a stained hoodie that makes him look like one of his druggie customers. He looks like shit.

"Where the hell have you been?" he asks as he punches off the stereo, not even acknowledging the leaning tower of pancakes resting in front of him on the counter. "I've been calling you for hours."

Crap. I picture the last place I remember seeing my cell phone: on the table in the diner last night. "Why? What's wrong?" I can't even think of a single time that Jameson has called me—I mean, we *live* together, so it's not like I'm hard to track down—so I can't figure out why he'd care now. I step closer to the pancakes, waiting for him to notice my peace offering.

He rubs his hands over his face, hard, like he's trying to squeegee away a bad dream. "It's Charlotte. She— I don't even know how to describe what happened. She completely lost it last night not long after you took off. I've never seen anything like it. We were trying to get her under control, but then she just . . . collapsed, I guess. I didn't want you to hear about it from someone else."

Sad but true: this statement alone triggers no warning bells. Among the guinea pig crowd, people collapse/black out/pass out/faint/fall fairly often. Side effects and substance abuse both tend to leave you with a wonky equilibrium and bruises on your ass. I make a *so what?* face at Jameson.

"Audie, she—" He stops talking, and just sort of deflates in front of me. Everything about him wilts, and his voice sounds airless when he finally continues. "We didn't think it was a big deal at first, either. I mean, you know how it is around here."

I nod, not breathing, starting to understand what's coming next.

"So by the time we called for help, she was too far gone. I didn't— I mean, *none of us* realized how serious it was. We all thought, hey, this is Charlotte we're dealing with here. She'll snap out of it, she always does. . . ." Jameson rakes his fingers through his hair, making it stick up in greasy spikes. "Except this time she didn't. Jesus, I can't even wrap my head around it. She's fucking gone, Audie." He doesn't look at me when he says this. He says it to the floor. To his feet.

We become statues.

I'm just standing there, the goddamn spatula still in my hand. Even my brain has frozen midthought. All I can think about, for a long, stupid minute, is my pancakes. Like, if Charlotte's dead, who's going to eat all these pancakes?

But then I unfreeze, and what he said punches me in the stomach.

Hard.

"Fuck" is what I finally say.

You always think you'll be eloquent, or at least admirably stoic at times like this, but that's not how it goes. Not for me, anyway. "Fuck," I say again, slow and drawn out. It's the only word I have that captures the moment. *Sorry, Charlotte. No disrespect intended.*

"I don't understand. What happened?"

Jameson shakes his head. "Nobody knows. She was on a lot of stuff, Audie. Way too much stuff. But I don't know exactly what did it—the docs wouldn't tell me jack since I'm not family." His face is blotchy, like he's been crying.

My throat closes. Something wet and vicious is strangling me from the inside. I grab the edge of the counter, because there's nothing else to hold on to. "Are they going to stop the studies she was doing? Do an autopsy? Anything?"

Jameson looks at me hard when I ask this, and I feel my face go red, since it must be pretty obvious that I'm not just asking out of curiosity. I admit that it's pretty shitty to be worrying about myself at a time like this, but in the back of my mind I'm thinking that Charlotte and I were in quite a few of the same studies recently.

Asshole, I call myself, and force my thoughts back to Charlotte. "Does she have . . . do they know who to call? Her next of kin, or something? What will they do with her . . . ?" I leave the question unfinished. I can't bring myself to say *her body.*

Jameson shrugs, then scratches at the shadow growing across his cheeks, so hard his nails leave red lines. He's still staring at the ground. "I don't know. All this time I've known her, and I never once heard her talking about her family. I don't even know where she's from."

"Detroit. She grew up in Detroit. That's all I know." I don't say it, but it's pretty obvious that when someone never talks about her family, ever, they're probably either dead or scumbags. That's kind of the deal for people like us, isn't it? We're not the kind of people who have anyone to call.

We're the people with empty chairs at our funerals.

Jameson and I just stand there, on opposite sides of the kitchen counter, and the silence between us turns awkward. Like we're supposed to be saying more, but we both forgot our lines. "We should do something for her," I finally say, mostly because one of us has to say *something.*

"Yeah. We should do something." Jameson answers like he's in a trance. Finally, after a few more seconds of silent weirdness, he looks up at me, but it's more like he's looking through me. "I need to take a shower. Maybe grab a few hours of sleep."

I just nod. I wait until I hear his door close and then I dump the pancakes in the trash. I'm not crying, exactly, but my chest hurts and my eyes burn and the vicious wetness is starting to win. I can't seem to move or even think very fast, either. I try to

136

wash the pancake plate no one ate from, but I have this weird, clumsy sensation like my hands just don't belong to me anymore, and it occurs to me that the dishes are, *were*, all Charlotte's, so it seems especially important not to break anything. I set the plate down in the sink as gently as I can and slide down onto the floor. I sit there for a very long time not *not* crying.

At first I'm thinking how much it sucks that the last time I saw her we were fighting. I've only known her for what, about a year? But I haven't lived many places for a whole year at a time, so it's almost like I've known her forever. And the thing is, I *liked* Charlotte. I really did. It may not be saying much, but she was the closest friend I've had in a long time. Maybe ever.

So then, sitting there in that suspended tears, not-crying way that actually feels way worse than crying, I start trying to figure out why, exactly, we were fighting anyway, and I realize that the fighting bits in my memory are sort of blurry. And it's not just one of those *don't speak ill of the dead* things, either. It's more like all of a sudden I'm not so sure she *actually* said or did the things that made me upset. Maybe I just thought she was thinking those things. Like, did she really take a dig at Dylan when we were at the party last night, calling him my "boyfriend" with those little air-quote fingers, or did I edit those in myself?

I do that sometimes. I project bad stuff where it doesn't necessarily exist. I put words in people's mouths, fill in gaps with my own worst thoughts. And I was definitely feeling insecure about Dylan last night.

The more I think about it, the more I'm sure: Charlotte and

I weren't fighting at all. Okay, so I did call her a bitch at the party. But it was loud, and she didn't even turn around—I'm totally positive about that part—so that means she probably didn't even hear me say it. Which means that my last words to her, at least the last words she heard, weren't nasty after all. And it's not like I was ever actually mad at her. Not Charlotte. She was a good egg.

She was my friend.

I feel a little better when I realize this. My hands start to feel like they belong to me again, like they've been reconnected to the rest of my body, and I push myself up off the floor because now I'm motivated. Charlotte was my best friend, and now I need to do something for her.

I feel good about this. And the better I feel, the more angry I feel; the more angry I feel, the better I feel. Does that sound weird? There's such a thing as good angry. Good and angry. Good. And angry.

Yes.

CHAPTER 22

Charlotte's still dead when there's a knock on the door. I'd been willing the news away, eyes closed, when the sound broke my concentration, and so she's still dead.

I ignore it at first, but then it crosses my mind that it could be Dylan. He must have done it again, picked up on my need for company from our pretend psychic network.

"Works every time," I say as I swing the door open.

But no one's there.

On the ground is my cell phone and a brand-new hardcover copy of *1984* with a business card—the Professor's—marking a page with a single line underlined in red:

We shall meet in the place where there is no darkness.

I understand immediately that it's the Professor's weird way of offering his condolences for Charlotte, and I appreciate it. Quite a lot, actually. Maybe the little garden gnome isn't such a bad guy after all. I see now that he means well.

There's a single message on my phone, from a number I don't recognize. I access my voice mail with shaking fingers. I don't know how, but somehow I just know it's going to be bad. It's just the way things have been going lately. Downhill, no brakes.

I hear a male voice I don't recognize. At first I think it's a wrong number or maybe a butt dial, because there's all kinds of noise in the background, and the voice is so muffled I have to listen twice to understand what the caller is saying. The second time around, though, I realize that the stranger's voice is actually Dylan's, and that there's a very good reason he doesn't sound like himself.

He's back in the hospital.

From beneath my squeezed-tight eyelids, real tears finally start to escape.

CHAPTER 23

Of course Dylan had a good reason for not showing up.

I never doubted him. Not for a second.

I stop in the little store just off the lobby and spend money I should be saving on an arrangement of the ugliest helium balloons they have in the place, which says a lot, since have you seen the tacky shit they sell in hospital gift shops? The worst of the bunch has a picture of Eeyore with a thought bubble floating over his mopey, sad-fuck donkey face: "After all, one can't complain. I have my friends."

It's so morose and awful I know it'll make Dylan smile.

I remind myself to keep my own smile in check. I wouldn't want him to think I'm glad he's sick, or anything. I was just so relieved to hear from him, period, that it's hard not to feel a little bit happy. Appropriately happy, I mean.

"Just coming to visit my sick boyfriend," I tell the old-lady candy striper I ride up with in the elevator.

"I hope he gets better soon, dear," she says back, and pats

me on the shoulder. "I'm sure he'll be thrilled to see you. Visitors do our patients *so* much good."

This visit is going to help me just as much as it helps Dylan. I need something to take my mind off of Charlotte before the grief paralyzes me. I need good news.

The news *is* good: he's not in the cancer ward. This time it's a secondary infection—the unfortunate result of a good treatment gone bad. It's one of those *the cure is worse than the disease* kinds of things, and they're pumping enough antibiotics into him to sterilize the Northern Hemisphere twice over. I recognize the name of the drug—I'm pretty sure I tested it once. It chewed my stomach to bits and made everything taste like copper for a month after I stopped taking it, if I remember correctly.

I'm sure that's why he only pokes at his odorless lunch while I sit on his hospital bed trying to entertain him. "Seriously, why doesn't it smell like anything at all? I mean, it's a grilled turkey and cheese sandwich. Shouldn't it smell like meat? Or cheese? I'd even settle for a faint whiff of toast. But there's nothing."

There are so many topics of conversation that must be avoided. Like Charlotte, obviously. Dylan doesn't need to hear about that. They may not have been friends, but he would care because *I* care. It's better to stick to positive subjects. My current strategy: avoid anything from the past. Only the future is safe.

And food. Talking about food is safe.

Dylan grins, and you can hardly tell he's sick. Okay, so he's paler than usual, and maybe he's a little more subdued than normal, but nothing dramatic. His doctors are always overreacting—I can tell that he's going to be fine. "You can't have smelly food in a hospital," he says. "It's insensitive. I mean, can you imagine if your death, your final swoon, your great swan dive into the sky, was accompanied by a bacon smell track? Or, like, Tater Tots? Those things smell for freaking miles. It would take away from the dignity of the moment."

I shift as a nurse glides into the room to glance at Dylan's monitor. "Wait. Did you just say *smell* track?"

His eyes are twinkly. It could be the meds, but I don't think so. "Hell, yeah. If there can be such a thing as a sound track, why not a smell track?"

I steal a bite of his sandwich, since he's obviously not going to eat it. It tastes exactly like it smells. Like nothing. "Personally, I want my death to be accompanied by the smell of marshmallows toasting over a campfire," I say.

He raises an eyebrow. "Interesting choice. A little more Girl Scout-y than I would've thought from someone like you."

I take another bite and think it over while I chew. "You're right. Cancel that. I'd rather have something spicy. Something exotic. Something that smells like you're in the middle of an adventure. Paella, maybe? Nothing boring can possibly happen in a room that smells like paella."

Dylan goes rigid for a second, and his face loses about two more shades of color. He breathes through whatever it is for a few seconds before saying anything. "I've never had paella" is all he gets out before closing his eyes and sinking back into his pillows. Apparently, his pain meds have kicked in. Lying like that, he looks slight, almost frail. He's definitely neither, but seeing someone you love semiconscious in a hospital bed can mess with you a bit—it can make even someone as tall and broad-shouldered as Dylan seem small and vulnerable.

It makes you want to do whatever it takes to protect that person, to crawl in bed and fight his battles right alongside him.

I shake him softly. "Wait, don't fall asleep yet! I want to tell you something." It's a spur-of-the-moment decision. All of a sudden I feel an overwhelming need to tell him about my plan, about how close I am to making our trip to Castillo Finisterre happen, before he gives in to the twilight. I happen to know that when you're suffering the worst, just having something to look forward to can make all the difference.

Plus, now that his secret is out—he doesn't have to hide the fact that he's sick from me anymore—I want to tell him my secret, too. I don't want secrets between us anymore.

But he's too far gone. He mumbles something barely comprehensible about the party last night, probably an apology for not coming, and then he closes his eyes, smiles, and says "nice to meet you," in the voice of a happily oblivious drunk. I'm about to tease him for sounding so loopy, but he's out cold, the traces of the smile lingering just enough to make it look like wherever he is right now, it's a decent place to be.

I curl up next to him while he sleeps, kissing him and whispering travel plans in his ear. At first it feels nice, and I can almost tune out the hospital noises and pretend it's just the two of us in a cozy little honeymoon suite. But after a few minutes his words come floating back, like they always do, and they start twisting around as they play on repeat in my head.

never had paella never had paella never had paella

I'm trying so hard not to dwell on anything negative, but the more I think about it, the more it starts to seem like the saddest fucking thing in the whole world, and it doesn't take long before I'm totally depressed.

I sit there, in a funk once again, looking at this amazing guy who could die without ever eating paella, and think about how even if I were to go out and find someone to cook him some god-damn paella, it would be one of those depressing-as-hell make-a-wish type things where it wouldn't even taste good, because you'd be sitting there picking at it, knowing this is, like, Death Takeout. And then the quicksand that is my brain sucks my thoughts over to death-row inmates and their last meals, and all of a sudden I'm wondering how many of them actually eat what-ever their last meal is. I start picturing empty jail cells filled with uneaten food, murderers' pork chops and kidnappers' mashed potatoes, and then I'm just staring and staring at all the food left on Dylan's lunch plate and thinking about all those pancakes I made for Charlotte, who I still can't think of as being dead.

So not even five minutes after he goes to sleep, I'm sitting there next to my sick, sleeping boyfriend, ugly-crying with snot smearing my upper lip, all because of the goddamn smell of paella and a stack of uneaten pancakes.

Hold your shit together, I tell myself. *Quit spiraling.* The solu-tion is obvious.

The solution, as it has always been, is Castillo Finisterre.

I don't even know if they eat paella in Patagonia, but I don't fucking care. I'll have it flown in from Spain if I have to. It's all gotten wrapped together in my head and I don't care what I have to do, I'm going to put everything on fast-forward and make this trip happen. Soon.

CHAPTER 24

We all raise a glass to Charlotte, cold and stiff.

Besides Scratch, no one cries, and even with him it's hard to tell whether he's actually crying or if it's just his usual allergy-induced dampness.

This is not a weeping crowd.

It *is* an angry, wall-punching crowd. There's something in the water. Outrage in the air.

"The people running this fucking place destroyed her. They're a bunch of fucking criminals." I don't think the guy who says this even knew Charlotte. I've never seen him before in my life. A few other people in the room rumble their agreement that yeah, *someone* should pay, but it doesn't go anywhere. We're all guinea pigs here. We know that the hand that jabs us is the same hand that feeds us.

So the anger remains hazy and unfocused. It's a missile in search of a target.

To diffuse the tension Jameson shows us a video he took on his phone ages ago: Charlotte goofing around on a ukulele. She played badly, sang worse, but damn could she liven up a room. In the video she's tipsy, sitting crooked in her seat (has anyone, ever, played a ukulele sober?), and she's making up goofy lyrics to the tunes of kids' songs. She did that all the time—some of her lyrics got pretty raunchy. She had an X-rated version of "Old MacDonald" that nearly made me piss myself every time I heard it, it was that funny. This one, the one in Jameson's video, is relatively tame, set to the tune of "The Chicken or the Egg," but she's singing it in this weird, really intense voice, instead of her usual jokey sort of way.

> Oh, which came first, the crazy or the pill?
> Which came first, the crazy or the pill?
> How could something so cruel and spiny
> Come from something so smooth and tiny?
> Which came first, the crazy or the pill?

She starts rocking back and forth a little while she sings, and she's staring at—no, staring *down*—whoever is recording. She looks seriously pissed, like she *hates* the person behind the camera, like she's about to leap out of her chair and rip his head off. It's all pretty weird, honestly, since I assume that Jameson is the one who shot the video, but as far as I know they were pretty tight. I never knew Charlotte to act so hatefully toward him.

It starts feeling really awkward, and you can tell that other people are noticing, too, so no one protests when Jameson puts his phone away before the clip ends.

Dougie's holding ice on his knuckles, glowering through a matted curtain of his stupid wannabe dreadlocks, and I start feeling like I should go say something to him, no hard feelings, that sort of thing, to let him know that I'm not holding a grudge or anything. I mean, we're in my apartment after all, so I should probably at least try to act like a good host, even if Dougie is a fucking idiot.

My phone keeps ringing, but I don't answer it because I know it's not Dylan, and I've been getting a bunch of wrong-number calls lately. A few of them have been pretty nasty, and I'm starting to think that maybe somebody played a joke on me and wrote my name in a bathroom stall. *For a good time, call Audie,* that kind of thing.

Now that I think about it, it seems like something Dougie might do. In fact, I start feeling kind of annoyed that it took me this long to figure it out. Of course Dougie did it. I watch him sulking on the other side of the room, how he makes a big point of ignoring me even though it's my freaking apartment, and I'm sure of it.

I'm not going to confront him, though. Not tonight, anyway. Tonight's about Charlotte.

Besides, I don't feel so hot at the moment. Somebody raises yet another toast, and everyone in the room gets a little drunker and a little madder.

I pull out my phone and text the number on the Professor's business card. *Want to observe a guinea pig funeral ceremony? Come over.* I don't even know why I do it, why I invite him. For some reason I just want him to be here, doing the little note-taking thing he does. I want Charlotte's name written down somewhere. I want someone to have a record that she existed, and that she died doing this. I like the idea of having her name in a textbook somewhere. She'd get a huge kick out of that—generations of college students highlighting her name. Or even better—how cool would it be to have a multiple-choice question about you on a test?

Was Charlotte's death:

A) A tragic accident
B) Medical malpractice
C) Murder
D) Suicide
E) All of the above

I know—I'm quite the life of the party, aren't I? But just thinking about Charlotte's death like that, like a question, makes me realize that not a single person in the room, myself included, has a fucking clue what happened to our friend. Okay, fine, like Jameson said, it's a reasonable assumption that she OD'd. We all know she was dumping a whole lot of a whole lot into her body, but was it a drop or a flood that killed her? I want to know exactly *which* pill, *which* vial, or *which* combination took my friend.

Am I the only person who wonders?

Maybe I shouldn't. It isn't that big a mystery; she's just one more test bunny who died a foreseeable, and therefore unremarkable, death. She's the warning label everyone ignores: MAY RESULT IN DEATH. *It doesn't apply to me*, people tell themselves. *Those things only happen to other people.*

Except we, the scary, scarry people gathered in this room, *are* the other people.

I finish my beer and stand up to get another, even though I know it's a bad idea.

"Hey. Quiet. Can everyone shut up for a second? I want to have a moment of silence for Charlotte." Even Jameson is sloppy tonight, and everyone ignores him. "She's in a better place. She really is . . . ," he trails off.

You can tell he doesn't believe it by the way he says it, though, like he's reading from a cheesy sympathy card. He's just saying it because that's the thing that people say when someone dies.

The Professor texts back to say he's on his way, and pretty soon Charlotte's wake begins to resemble every other guinea pig party. People are yelling, there's a guy running around in drooping tighty-whities, and the smoke detector goes off. I have another drink, because tonight's for Charlotte, and after a while the Professor shows up. I see him talking to people and taking notes, and I have another drink, and none of it fucking matters anyway.

As individuals, we're all statistically insignificant.

There's a swirling energy in all of the buffoonery that starts to lift me up a bit, though. It's obvious that all these ridiculous pillheads really do care, and that's no small thing. Eventually, all I can do is stand there and grin, because I feel like Charlotte would be laughing at all these lunatics right along with me, and even though she's dead, and even though her absence feels like a goddamn hole in my chest, I feel sort of happy right now, standing here thinking about my friend laughing, thinking about Dylan, and thinking about how I'm going to come up with the money for Patagonia even if it kills me.

Scratch wanders over and stands next to me. "Hey, Audie," he sniffs.

Poor Scratch. I can't look at him. He's been trying to grow a mustache—it's a patchy, sad little thing crawling across his lip—and he has all these ingrown hairs that look like they're probably infected nestled in between the few pube-y tufts he's managed to grow. He's a nice enough guy, I guess, but he's just so exhaustingly revolting.

I do my best not to shudder as he scoots closer, then closer still, until he's almost leaning against me.

Oh shit. He wants a hug.

I go stiff and try to give him one of those touch-minimizing, back-patting things, like the hug equivalent of an air kiss, but he's not having any of that. Once he has his opening, he dives right into full body contact, pulling me against him. He's a couple inches shorter than me, so he ends up kind of snuffling wetly into my neck. A little moan escapes me as I think of the mucus trail he's probably leaving on my shirt, and Scratch mistakes the sound for crying, which he takes as a cue to open up the floodgates. Soon he's weeping and snotting all over my shoulder.

"I can't believe she's gone," he sobs.

I pull back as much as his damp embrace allows, but he's obviously taking Charlotte's death pretty hard, so I don't pull all the way away. To be honest, I'm getting a little weepy myself, just watching Scratch break down.

"I know, I miss her, too," I say. Poor Scratch. Now I feel really bad. I mean, I know Charlotte threw the occasional pity fuck at him, but I didn't realize he had real feelings for her. I'm pretty sure the feelings weren't reciprocal, but obviously he doesn't know that. I give up on my shirt and on holding back the tears, and for a minute we sort of cling to each other and just have a good old cry. It feels good to mourn Charlotte together. Comforting. And phlegmy as he is, Scratch actually smells kind of nice. Clean. Like he made an effort.

"I know you guys were close," I say when I finally extract myself from our wet embrace.

He shrugs, then starts fingering a nest of blackheads inside his ear. "Sort of. I mean, we hooked up a few times. But we weren't, like, *close* close."

"No? I just assumed from the way you were . . . I mean, you seem to be taking it pretty hard. I thought maybe . . . ?"

He lifts the bottom of his shirt up to towel off his face, giving me a flash of the silvery-pink eczema blooming out of his belly button. Volcanic pimples and puckered biopsy scars dot his chest like dozens of extra nipples.

Good Lord, Charlotte. How could you?

I bite the inside of my cheek and focus on a smudge on the wall behind him until he tucks his shirt back in. "Nah, it's not like that. It's just the timing, man. It sucks. I mean, I was *this* close to closing the deal on a little, uh, investment opportunity, and Charlotte was gonna help me out. Make the dream happen, you know?"

I tilt my head at him, work my jaw a little.

He misunderstands my confusion. "I was going to pay her back. With interest, obviously."

"*That's* why you're wailing like a fucking banshee? Because you asked her for a fucking *loan*?"

He shrugs again, goes back to digging into those blackheads in his ear, really going for it this time. "What? I was counting on it, you know? I have *commitments*. And she supposedly had some sweet thing going on, tons of cash coming in."

He finally looks at the expression on my face. Picks up on my rage. "Hey, don't get me wrong—it's not just the money. Do you think I'd be crying like a baby if I didn't care? I'm totally going to miss her. Totally. It's some sad shit, man. It's sad shit *and* bad timing, that's all I mean."

I think back to one of my last conversations with Charlotte. Our Marry, Fuck, Sack Tap game.

I pick option C and leave Scratch mewling and sputtering on the floor in fetal position as I walk away. "Get bent, you nasty fucking pustule," I say over my shoulder. "Shove your stupid investment opportunity up your crusty, leprous ass!"

I hate it when I'm so wrong about people. It makes me question my own judgment—like, who else am I misinterpreting?

I see the Professor trying to get my attention as I push my way out of the apartment, but I ignore him. I'm done wasting time with this crowd.

It's cold tonight, and raining pretty hard, but I don't care. I tuck my head down and head over to the hospital. It's way after visiting hours, but I know how to sneak past the nurses. Dylan's pretty much the only person I can count on these days, and since he can't come to me, I'll go to him.

CHAPTER 25

GUINEA PIG CAREER PROGRESSION: A TWELVE-STEP GUIDE TO CLIMBING (DOWN) THE CORPORATE LADDER

Step One

You will start by selling plasma. Everyone does. It's easy money and the standards are low.

Step Two

Because that was easy, you will rationalize the giving away of small samples of potential yous. If you are male, this means sperm. (Why not get paid for what you're already tossing off, er, away?) If you're young and female, this means egg donation, but only if you can get through the screening process. (Are you pretty-pretty-pretty enough? Perhaps a gymnast or a cellist? And, by the way, what are your SAT scores?)

Step Three

Because the slope is slippery and the pay is good, you will next allow something other than your skin to be pierced and probed. It will feel uncomfortable and you will not like it.

Step Four

Because you did not like it, you will decide to take pills for profit instead. Especially when the odds are good that you'll be given a harmless placebo anyway.

Step Five

You will get a sugar pill and therefore feel nothing at all except a distinct sense of superiority over the poor working stiff you used to be before you discovered the world of drug trials.

Step Six

You will take more pills. Some of them will work as expected. Some of them will not. Some will do nothing at all. Some will do far too much.

Step Seven

Because some of the pills work as expected, and also because some work as not expected, you will no longer be so uncomfortable when strangers in lab coats stick things down your throat or up your ass. The money is good, and you feel good. Most of the time, anyway.

Step Eight

Because you are now letting strangers stick things down your throat and up your ass on a routine basis, you take more pills, and then more, and then more. You begin to hope that you do not get a placebo, because those do fuck-all, and that is now a problem.

Step Nine

Because you are taking many, many pills, most of which do *something*, holding down a regular job has become impossible. This does not bother you, as even the idea of a regular job has now become intolerable. Side effects from pills are usually temporary. Side effects from real life are usually not. Also, you like to be in control. You're your own boss now, you tell yourself.

Step Ten

Because you make a full-time living from the steady sublet of your veins/skin/bones/bowels, things that once seemed unbearable are now routine. You hardly even notice the pain anymore, and you've begun to feel pleasantly indestructible. You are definitely in control.

Step Eleven

Because you are indestructible and in control, and also because the money is very good, you will start to see every day as another chance to play chicken with the universe. It's a powerful feeling, and you will usually win.

Step Twelve

Until you do not.

Rest In Pieces, Charlotte.

CHAPTER 26

It's a sign of just how broken up we are about Charlotte that Jameson and I wait another full day before we go through her stuff.

Jameson brought her ratty purse home from the hospital, so he gets first dibs on the wallet. He cradles it in his hands for a minute, then unsnaps it and opens it slowly, all reverent like it's a ceremony.

We are solemn and respectful thieves.

He extracts a thick stack of money, and I let out a low whistle. "That's a lot of cash."

Jameson reaches into the purse and pulls out an envelope filled with even more; I see fifties and hundreds as he fans through the bills. This isn't quick-trip-to-the-ATM kind of cash. This isn't a handful of crumpled ones and fives. This is serious money—one hell of a payday or ten. I can't believe Charlotte would even think about loaning any of it to Scratch, but neither can I think of any other reason she'd be walking around with so much cash. It'd be just one more in a string of poor choices;

she'd be the first to tell you she had a long history of bad judgment when it came to guys.

Jameson turns pink and shifts around, looking a lot less reverent than he did a minute ago. He splits off a stack of bills—a very small stack—and hands it to me. He tries to stuff the rest into his own pockets, but there's too much. He finally gives up, his face dark red by now, and puts the money back into the envelope, which he slips into his jacket.

I count what he gave me. Two hundred bucks. I'm guessing he kept at least ten times that for himself. I start to object, but he cuts me off. "We were working on something together. She owed me this much and more."

Well, isn't that interesting. Now that Charlotte's not around to set the record straight, she suddenly seems to have owed money to all sorts of people.

Jameson's almost certainly lying, but what can I do about it? This is technically his apartment, after all, and I haven't paid him my portion of this month's rent. He hasn't said anything about it yet, but we both know a conversation is overdue.

Now that I think about it, I don't remember paying him the rent last month, either. That doesn't necessarily mean I *didn't* pay him. I forget a lot of things. Still, it's my turn to flush red, heat creeping up my cheeks as it occurs to me that Jameson may be lying about Charlotte owing him money only because he's too nice to point out that *I'm* actually the one who owes him a shitload of cash.

Either way, it stings a little that he's lying to me. That he can't just come right out and say what's on his mind, especially on a day like this. That we can't just put it all out there and acknowledge that one of us is screwing over the other. I shouldn't be surprised, though. Guinea pigs aren't exactly play-by-the-rules sorts of people.

We do whatever it takes to survive, up to—and including—stealing from our friends.

The thought comes full circle, then slams into me like a fist. A large sum of cash disappears from my backpack one week. A large sum of cash appears in Charlotte's purse the next. Coincidence?

I think back to the way she begged me to take her place in the study that day. *Please, Audie? My head is seriously killing me. . . .* She knew my schedule, knew exactly where I'd be. She could have been watching me, waiting for her chance to pounce, to steal the money I'd been working so hard to save. . . .

No. It's a stupid idea. I mean, we freaking lived together. She could've just taken the money while I slept, or while I was in the shower. There'd be no reason to stalk me around the lab on the off chance that I might pass out in the alley.

It was a ridiculous thought, and I feel like an asshole for even considering the possibility that Charlotte would rob me. Charlotte was my friend. She'd never do that to me.

I wouldn't put it past Jameson, on the other hand. Between his little pharmaceutical resale business and the way he just pocketed most of Charlotte's cash, he doesn't even try to disguise his . . . entrepreneurial interests. I know for a fact that just last week he resold a bottle of my leftover pills to some poor bastard for eighty bucks. He paid me five.

Did I pay him rent? I must have. . . .

Jameson pokes around the remaining contents of the purse

briefly, then pushes it over to me without taking anything else. He looks away while I pick through the tampons and ChapStick and crumpled fast-food receipts. The only thing even remotely worth keeping is a leather appointment book. It's nice. Refillable. It's something for a person with a real life, someone with things worth keeping organized. I keep the book and the wallet, and shove the purse away. I'm not a purse-carrying kind of girl, and besides, it would make me too goddamn sad to look at it and think of Charlotte every day.

He must realize that he's being a greedy shit, because Jameson tells me to go ahead and keep whatever I want from her room. "I'll go in there and clean out whatever you don't want some other time," he says. "I can't deal with it right now."

And then that's it. It's done.

This is how it works for people like us. No reading of the will. No last testament, except what you have crumpled in your pockets. Leave enough behind and you can at least rest in peace knowing the scavengers are singing your praises. *Peace be with you and your up-for-grabs stash.* Otherwise, it's like you never even existed.

Jameson's skewed division aside, there's no shame in taking what we need from Charlotte. It's the universal code of the slightly less unlucky, like a Civil War soldier taking the boots off a gutshot comrade. An unbegrudged matter of practicality. I fully expect the vultures to descend when I die. Let 'em pick my bones clean—less of me to rot in the ground.

Jameson stands up and wipes his hands on his pants, like the whole process has made him feel dirty. He's avoiding eye contact. "I'm gonna go get some beer and pizza. Dinner's on me tonight."

I nod, still not sure whether I have a right to be pissed or whether I should feel grateful, and he takes off fast, his pockets heavy with thousands of dollars of our dead friend's money.

Once he's gone, I go into Charlotte's room, glad for the chance to be alone there. It's a lot like mine, meaning there's nothing in there but dirty clothes, more tampons, and a wheezing hair dryer that probably won't survive the month. A handful of change. A lighter and a cheap alarm clock, mismatched earrings all missing the backings. A crusty tube of mascara and four black eyeliner pencils. This is all that's left of her. A bunch of useless crap that could belong to anybody. It's depressing as hell, really.

But even with so small a presence in the room, this is still all I have left of Charlotte, so I take my time. I touch all the surfaces. I breathe in the air. This was my friend. This is my goodbye.

There are no pictures on the walls. No mementos. There's fuck-all for tchotchkes or knickknacks. Something about the guinea pig life, all that gambling with your mortality, makes a person unsentimental, I think. Like it's hard to appreciate the value of any object, any *thing,* if you've already started selling off your own flesh to the highest bidder. Because what's more valuable than that?

We are not yearbook people. We have no trophies or stuffed animals held on to from childhood. We don't display our pasts in frames.

I crawl under the covers of her bed and then open up her wallet. No pictures there, either—not so much as a single credit, debit, or gift card. *Damn.* Just her driver's license and a punch card from the falafel place down the street. One more stamp and the next combo meal's free. A real golden fucking ticket.

"Thanks a lot," I say out loud. But I have a smile on my face. The girl did love a good falafel. How's that for an epitaph?

It's when I crack open the appointment book that the cash starts to make more sense. I let out a whistle, and the sense of relief I feel takes me by surprise.

Charlotte didn't need to rob me. She was a busy, busy girl. A genuine test-tube entrepreneur. She'd been double-booked, triple-booked in studies every single day for months. How did I not know she was testing so much? And why did she wait so long to bring me in on her plan?

I'm going through the last week—the week before she died—line by line when I notice the extra appointments. In addition to the studies we did together, there are several entries I don't recognize. I assume they were follow-ups for long-term studies she started before we partnered up, but I can't be positive, because she tended to use a bizarre kind of shorthand, with scrawled words paired with doodles and codes, only some of which I can figure out. The only thing I can be sure of is that she was far busier than I realized.

Why so much? Testing like this is just asking to die. Anyone could see it, even someone like Charlotte, who was convinced she'd live forever.

"What were you doing, Charlotte?" I ask her room.

I understand need. I understand hunger. I totally get the desire to make enough money to go a little wild, and then enough on top of that to feel safe, and maybe even a little more on top of that just because. But the pace Charlotte had been keeping for what I now realize was *months* was completely insane. Dumping all those chemicals into your body takes a toll. And then there's the blood—so many vials drained from her in the name of somebody else's science.

Why would she let herself get sucked dry like this?

I shiver a little under her quilt. Chemicals in, blood out. Poison in, life force out. Day after day. Over and over. I feel like I'm looking at a scheduled suicide. Death by testing.

"Why?" I ask her room again, but I don't expect any answers. We're an unsentimental bunch, remember? When we pack up and leave a place, we're gone for good. What little she left behind won't tell any tales.

I know there's nothing worth keeping, but I crawl out of Charlotte's bed and poke through her dresser just to be sure. Sweaters and jeans in the bottom drawer. A few shirts in the middle. One top drawer full of socks and underwear, and the other full of drugs. It's a pill graveyard, filled to the brim with dozens and dozens of different medications—Jameson must not have known about them, or else he wouldn't have been so quick to leave me the contents of the room. Half the bottles are uncapped, and tablets and capsules rattle around loose as I yank hard, then harder, to get the stiff drawer to open further. I yank too hard and the entire drawer comes flying out in my hand, spilling pills all over the carpet.

Damn it. I get down on my hands and knees to clean up the mess.

It's doing this, picking up what I spilled, that gives me the idea. Crouched down on the floor like that, my hands full of the half-empty bottles and random, mismatched pills, any one of which could have been the thing that killed her, *I feel like Charlotte is sending me a message. Giving me a gift.*

I know I'm being morbid and ridiculous as hell, but it's just the way I feel. Charlotte was my friend, and this idea, this *plan,* is coming from her. It sounds like woo-woo, poltergeist-y bullshit, but I know what I know. This is Charlotte giving me rent. This is Charlotte giving me a chance at the castle at the end of the world. This is Charlotte finally approving of Dylan.

Jameson may have snagged Charlotte's cash, but I can earn that and a whole lot more if I'm smart about it. Smart enough not to die, I mean.

I walk over to her bed and pick up her driver's license. It worked once before, and it'll work again. I open the appointment book to today's date. It's too late now, but starting tomorrow I will be a very busy girl. A test-tube entrepreneur.

I'm doubling down on my doubling down. I'll go to my appointments *and hers*. Not for months and months, like Charlotte did, obviously. This is a short-term solution—I'll do it just until I have enough for Patagonia. All the income, none of the dying. And if they catch me and kick me out, so be it. This is my grand finale here, anyway. My exit plan. My golden parachute.

Charlotte was right about one thing—it's time to move on. She just took things too far. I'll do it the right way. Just far enough.

I feel good about this. Happy and hope-y. It'll be a cinch stepping into Charlotte's place. Tomorrow, after I'm done being me, I will be her.

Except, not dead.

InterThen

They keep bringing it. More medicine, in impossible quantities. They pour and inject; they load it into me by spoonful and pitchfork and truck.

I am diluted.

Audie in a bottle, one part per million.

Shake well to avoid separation. Shake well before serving. I can feel the good bits, the me bits, dissolving in the bad blood.

shakemeup shakemeup shakemeup

Keep it together. Keep me together.

They add even more medicine. I had no idea I was so empty, that I had so much space that needed filling. They crack me open and pour it in, day after day after day. I'm being reconstituted. Regenerated. New and improved.

A whole new, homeopathic me.

CHAPTER 27

Being Charlotte gets easier with practice.

I panicked the first couple times I had to sign her name. Was she right-handed or left-handed? I felt guilty for not knowing this, so I signed using large, gratuitous swoops, the opposite of my compact scrawl, just to give Charlotte's name more space on the paper. No one questioned a thing.

In her name I give samples. On her behalf I swallow pills. As Charlotte I spread myself wide open and say aah. Nothing to it. It's just like being me, except busier.

It's also more fun. *I'm* more fun. It's hard to explain, but when I walk into an office and tell them I'm Charlotte, it's like I become her. Like I'm channeling her. It feels good to be someone else for a little while.

Charlotte had energy. Charlotte had stories. Charlotte was sarcastic and funny and bouncy and flaky, and she had this way of ice-skating over the shitty parts of life. Charlotte made liberal use of her middle finger. Charlotte put hot sauce, the hotter the better, on everything she ate. Charlotte lit up a room.

And now I do, too.

It's not as creepy as it sounds—this isn't some beyond-the-grave Single White Female thing. I'm not actually trying to be her. I'm just taking her best parts and . . . borrowing them.

So Charlotte pisses cheerfully, a happy, tinkling stream of gold. Charlotte holds out her arm with enthusiasm, never wincing as the needle plunges in. Charlotte lies on tables in peaceful repose. Her sacrum is sacred. Her ventricles are venerable. Her medulla oblongata is an open book.

I am out of body, out of mind. My follicles and my spleen and my metatarsal bones and my bronchial tubes all pay tribute to my friend, and the money comes rolling in, and in, and in.

I'm Charlotte Incorporated, businesswoman extraordinaire. My complexion is glowing, my bikini line is hair-free. I have a newfound appreciation for laser technology.

I even need less sleep than I used to. Charlotte was always complaining about insomnia—maybe it's contagious on some subconscious level? Or maybe I'm just highly suggestible.

In any event, I am she and she is me. Together, Charlotte and I are profitable. We are in the black. We shampoo and chew and scrape with great efficiency, and the castle at the end of the world shimmers brightly in the back of my mind.

Dylan's birthday gift is a bright and shiny *maybe*. A quickly growing *nearly*.

But between appointments, between procedures, between the pages of my well-thumbed Castillo Finisterre brochure, something festers when I let it. A dark and rotten clump of questions I do my best to ignore.

why did she die what happened what will they do with her body

But mostly, as Charlotte, I feel fine. I feel good. There are uppers and downers and wires and isotopes, but everything seems remarkably survivable.

so why did she die

It's a question I ask a lot, actually. I know I can't just reap the rewards, collect all this good fortune, without repaying Charlotte in some form. And so the more money I make, the closer and closer I get to the cost of round-trip airfare for two and six—no, seven!—nights of eco-luxe heaven, the harder I look at faces and procedures and ingredients. *Which one of you killed her?* I silently inquire.

So far, I've found no clues.

"You're in a good mood," Dylan says when I visit him between appointments. I come as often as I can, although we both prefer visits when no one else is around. Not that we've ever discussed it explicitly, but we don't have to. It's obvious that neither one of us likes to share our time together with anyone else. If I show up and someone else is in his room, I tiptoe away and come back later.

"Of course I am. You're getting out tomorrow." As my plan solidifies, the secret is becoming even harder to keep. I'm going to tell him soon. The time is almost right.

"Right. Tomorrow." Dylan is grinning—he has his own secret plan. "That's what my mom thinks, anyway. Hmmmm . . .

my bad. It's actually today." He checks his watch. "Within a matter of hours, as a matter of fact."

"You sneaky, fantastic bastard," I say, and flop down next to him in his bed.

"*Oof,* easy there, sparky. All is not yet operating at one-hundred-percent capacity."

"Sorry," I say. "Does this mean you're coming over? For the whole night?"

He nods. "My mom always comes by after work. They'll discharge me as soon as she leaves and then I'm all yours."

Butterflies and experimental double-action antacids flutter in my stomach as I lean over to kiss him. "Do I even want to know how you pulled this off?"

"Sexual favors for the nurses." He kisses me back, but he's moving stiffly and protecting his abdomen. "I feel cheap and used. And chafed. You wouldn't believe what a bunch of deviants they are."

We lose it as one of the nurses, who looks about eighty-five years old and has a face like a deflated balloon, walks by his room and gives us a disapproving look.

"Seriously, Audie." He takes my hand. "This has been amazing. *You've* been amazing. Your visits have been the only things keeping me going in here."

I mock-punch his shoulder, light as a feather since I know he's still in pain, to try to lighten the mood. "You've done the same for me," I say.

He shakes his head. "No, I haven't. Not even close."

I kiss him to shut him up. The big dope doesn't even realize how much he does for me, how just being around him makes all the other crap in the universe disappear into the background.

I try not to worry that he's favoring one arm. It can't be a good sign that the pain seems to be spreading to new parts of his body every week.

His kissing, on the other hand, gets better and better every day. It doesn't matter what crappy thing happened that morning, or how lousy I might be feeling. As soon as his lips touch mine, the slate is wiped clean.

Just yesterday, for example, I actually managed to have a polite conversation with Scratch. It was only a *hi, how are you* kind of thing as we passed in the hall, but still. Without Dylan I'd still be holding a grudge, carrying around all sorts of unnecessary anger.

I have one more study today, but this time when I leave I know it's only for a few hours, so I don't have those itching, crawling worries I usually have when I walk away from Dylan. "See you tonight," I tell him. I like saying that. I like not having a question mark at the end of our goodbye.

"Promise me you'll be gentle," he yells at me down the hallway, loud enough for the nurse to hear and glare anew. "Remember, the chafing!"

Charlotte's appointment book says "Memories, 2:30, Rm. 1321," with a little smiley face with stars for eyes drawn next to it. She does that—*did* that—a lot. Used weird little doodles as shorthand. I haven't seen this particular version of a smiley face before, but it can only mean good things.

Room 1321 is on the psych floor. That's Jameson's territory.

Candy Land. Overthinkers Anonymous. Shrinkydink Central. The Nut House. Wonderland. There are a lot of nicknames for this particular corridor—it's a love-it-or-hate-it kind of place. Jameson won't do any other kind of study; he gets off on twisted mental stuff, likes to feel smarter than the tests. I was under the impression that Charlotte avoided psych studies—she always called them mind fuckers—but that's just one more example of how little I actually knew about her.

I've been here a few times. The experiences were okay, I guess. I'm pretty sure I got a placebo the last time because the meds didn't do anything at all, but then I had to spend hours answering inane questions about my freaking "emotional experience" and the pay was only meh, so I haven't been back since. It just isn't worth the grief.

But now's not the time to be choosy, so I walk into the reception area, rattle off Charlotte's study ID number, and hand over her driver's license. The receptionist photocopies it without even glancing at the picture, then hands me the consent forms.

I laugh when I read the study description: the effects of psilocybin on long-term memory recall. Leave it to Charlotte to find a way to get paid for taking a ride on the Magic Mushroom Express. The starry-eyed smiley face makes perfect sense now. *You crazy little stoner bitch,* I whisper affectionately.

Two other people are already sitting in the waiting room. One of them, a leathery older guy missing a bottom tooth, looks up at me and winks like we're sharing a joke. Which, I guess, we kind of are.

"You done this before?" he asks.

I shake my head and he cackles. "Hoo boy. You're in for a treat. Just relax and enjoy it, girlie. Let go o' the reins on your brains, know what I mean?" He cackles again, a wet, lecherous sound, and I'm glad when a nurse pokes her head in the room to call him back.

I pick up a magazine to help me avoid eye contact with the other person in the room, but after a minute it's obvious I don't need to bother. She's middle-aged, frizzy and unfocused, smiling at a spot on the wall. There's something strangely chilling about her stillness, about the complete lack of recognition that I'm sitting just a few feet from her, almost like *one* of us doesn't exist.

By the time the nurse comes back into the room and calls Charlotte's name, I'm almost spooked enough to bolt. Something just feels wrong here. *Take the drugs, then take the money,* I tell myself. *Calm the fuck down.*

I stand up and follow the lady.

CHAPTER 28

I know exactly where I am—nothing about the room has changed since the nurse led me in and made me open wide to prove I hadn't cheeked my pill. (Silly me, expecting an actual mushroom.) But somehow things have shifted, and I'm both *here* and *not here* at the same time. No, it's worse than that. It's more like a feeling of being simultaneously dead and alive, like a furless version of Schrödinger's cat.

I obviously didn't draw the placebo card this time.

In the distance of the not-here I see when I close my eyes, a carnival tent splits open. It's the lone splash of color against an otherwise never-ending stretch of murky grayness.

From inside the tent a low-pitched, slurring voice starts to gather tempo and volume. It sounds like the Professor's voice, with the curious addition of a carny twang. He's like a drunken ringmaster, and as he speaks, the fog begins to lift and when I open my eyes, images from not-here superimpose themselves on the previously white walls of the room. Slowly the familiar pages of a magazine come to life around me, and somewhere, a curtain lifts.

Ahem.

Welcome.

Welcome, and don't be shy! Step right up, ladies and gentlemen, mesdames et messieurs. See before you a motley crew—fine and fearless individuals transformed, transfigured, and bound by neither flesh nor physics. Feast your eyes on tongues split in two . . . wait, make that three! Watch the clever pink tentacles flitting nimbly from pierced, bedazzled lips—the tongue is surprisingly dexterous when freed from its dreary, unforked form, don't you think? And look at those teeth, neatly filed to points. Someone's dentist had better be on his best behavior. Hahaha!

Step to your left to enjoy the next display. A dazzling array of decorative scarification and newly unsplinted elvish ears. So pointy and droll! (Let's not get into the mechanics just now, sir—there are children present.) And don't be concerned by the startling number of missing digits and other appendages, kind audience. All amputations are performed on a strictly voluntary basis.

Now look, look over there. See those horns? No, no, save your gasps. The fine gentleman sporting them is neither devil nor billy goat. He's merely modeling the finest in decorative titanium implants. Because why should your epidermis have all the fun?

Let's move on—there's not a moment to waste. The grand spectacular is about to begin!

Shhhh. Hush now. The surgeon needs to concentrate. Oh, no, madam—he's not an actual surgeon, at least not in the conventional sense. But observe the confidence with which he plunges the hooks through his victim's flesh—I guarantee you've never felt sturdier hands upon your bones. If you won't take my word for it, you need only look at the bliss upon said gentlewoman's face as she's hoisted by—let's count together, are there six?—metal hooks through tender flesh. Watch as she dangles, suspended in midair like a chrysalis in wait. Watch her breathe deeply, and begin to sway as she grows comfortable with her newly stretched flesh wings. She's dancing now, do you see? Flying, really. Behold, and envy her freedom! Envy her beauty! She's conquering her mortal coil, transcending the limits of her very flesh! So graceful, so brave . . .

Something is wrong.

This isn't my memory.

The instructions were clear: focus on an early memory. Happiness. Yes. My earliest happy memory.

I need to think about this. I need to focus while they take snapshots inside my brain. *Click click click click.* I need to ignore the wet darkness that is filling the room around me and think about pony rides or sitting on Santa's lap or Grandma's special just-for-me cookies. These are the examples they gave, and somehow I didn't get the chance to tell them before they strapped me here that I only have a hole where those memories should be.

I am a drain. I am a whirlpool. I am suction and vacuum.

Now something is wrong and my mind has sprung a leak.

Liquefied thoughts pour from my ears, puddling around me on the metal table, then overflowing into a drain on the floor.

Somewhere, out of sight, Charlotte begins to sing:

Ashes to splashes, we all fall down.

I scream to block out the sound.

A tinny voice comes from a speaker. "Charlotte, try to stay calm. Remember, we need you to hold still while we complete the scan. Try to focus on the topic."

I am strapped to a table, stuffed into a machine that clicks and thunks as it eats my memories.

I start to scream again, but everything I need to say melts into a pale gray puddle and oozes from my pores before any sound comes out. The vibrations from the machine splatter and scatter the liquid.

The topic. Focus on the topic.

What is the topic?

Memories. Yes. They must exist in here, somewhere.

The mechanical noises fade away, and I go limp. A cool breeze sweeps through the room, and I release. *Let go o' the reins on your brains.*

But the liquid soon returns, first in speckles and in drops, and then in great, arcing arterial sprays. I vaguely register that it's now red.

Through the mist, the electronic voice chirps out. "Hang in there, Charlotte. Not much longer; we're getting some great prefrontal-cortex images."

I go stiff because I know that something terrible is coming, and before I can cry out for help, the swirling redness fills my mouth and my ears and my eyes, and the pictures I see, all those memories that don't even belong to me, are tinted with the angry color of spilled blood.

The machine roars back to life, this time in reverse direction, and now I can hear the sound of its mechanical claws kneading past and present into a sticky ball of muddled time, then rolling it out flat. The machine twists and braids the dreamdough, and I can't tell where all the red is coming from or why my skin feels like it's on fire even while I'm drowning. . . .

I'm relieved when the darkness finally returns; I breathe it in with great, grateful gulps.

"Charlotte? Charlotte, are you okay? Can you hear me?" The tinny voice breaks through my thoughts. "We're finishing up now. I'll get you out of there in just a minute."

"I'm okay." My voice is a croak.

I am okay. Somehow I know the worst is over—that I've come through it intact. But part of me is still anxious. Did they get the direction right at the end? Is time moving forward again? I have this terrible feeling that something has gone wrong, and time is moving forward and backward at the same time, weaving and looping around itself in a never-ending figure eight.

I want to ask, make them check their machines, but the speaker stays silent, and before anyone comes into the room, I slide gently back into the grayness and the empty place where memories should be and then it's too late anyway. What's done is done.

CHAPTER 29

All the way home the lights play tricks on my mind.

I'm well enough to walk, but my balance is off and I keep veering to the right even when I mean to go straight. I swat away the buzzing gnats of the hallway fluorescents overhead, and then I spit at the stabbing, jabbing floodlights that line the sidewalk outside. I weave through the parking lot and slam my fist down on the trunk of a car whose turn signal is mocking me with its pointless on-off, on-off sounds (*FUCKyouFUCKyou FUCKyou*). The white-haired driver looks at me with startled round eyes and slaps quickly at the door lock as I walk by.

One-block, two-blocks, one-block. The distance contracts and expands as I walk home, and the streetlights follow me, stretching their necks to hand me off, relay-style, to the next glowing guard. There'll be no shadows for me to hide in, no sirree. The spotlight shines on my back, making the skin on my neck tingle and crawl as I stop and lean against the wall to vomit.

It's fortunate for me now, as it has been before, that guinea pigs don't drive to work. Too many blurry, side-effected nights like this one to survive the commute.

Halfway home my brain unwinds itself enough that at least I can tell the difference between fact and symptom—I can recognize, I can articulate to myself, that *this* thing or feeling or apparition is just the drug gripping my mind, and, most likely, so is *that*. These things, these creeping, whispering bugaboos peering out at me, are not real—they are figments of my test-addled mind. Knowing this does not stop me from seeing them, but it does stop me from *believing* in them. Someone who has never had this experience, this breakthrough, might not recognize the significance, but it is profound.

Fuck me. Chalk up yet another recreational drug my junkie genetics won't let me enjoy. My mind feels tinkered with, toyed with, in a most unpleasant way.

Apparently, I prefer a good close rein on my brain.

When I finally squint and stumble my way into my apartment building, it takes me several panicked minutes—two? five? time is too stretched out to tell—to find my keys, since the act of sticking my hands into my pockets assaults my overwrought nerve endings with unpleasant sensations. Glass-sharp lint and razor-blade crumbs wedge themselves under my fingernails when I reach into my jacket, and even the fabric feels like woven barbed wire against my skin.

I guess that I find the key somewhere in the middle of a stretch of time that my brain absorbed and discarded, because then all of a sudden I'm in the apartment, where a different sense assaults me. The living room is messy, messier than it's ever been, and beneath the clutter, wafting in swamp-colored tendrils through the air, is the unmistakable stink of decaying flesh. Part of my brain notes the overflowing wastebasket in the kitchen, deduces it's the smell of chicken tossed two days ago and begging to be taken out, but that doesn't stop the other sector of my brain that's still dancing in circles from whispering terrible things in my ear. *It's Charlotte. She's here. This is how she smells now. Dead and rotten, just like you.*

I slap the thought away from my ear and walk into the stench.

Jameson is sitting at the table, staring into space. "Hey, Audie," he mumbles, but barely. He's wearing the same clothes from yesterday, and I can smell the vinegary stink of his sock-clad feet even over the smell of decay.

I open my mouth to ask him if he's okay, maybe make a joke about the messy apartment, but someone knocks on the door behind me before I can say anything.

I open the door and the fog in my head lifts a little as soon as I see Dylan standing there. I press against him and kiss him, I mean, *really* kiss him, and Jameson makes a disgusted snort behind me.

"Come on." I grab Dylan's hand and pull him past Jameson, who just sits there and shakes his head at me like he's a fucking school principal debating whether to send me to detention.

I almost lead Dylan into Charlotte's bedroom by mistake, since I've been sleeping in there for the last couple of nights, but I catch myself just in time and we go into mine, where I shut the door against the smells of the apartment.

"That dude hates me," Dylan says as I'm pulling his shirt over his head.

"He's having a rough week."

I pretend not to notice how much weight Dylan has lost—how he seems to be shrinking before my eyes. His jutting ribs look like gills, and the new peaks of his face catch the light in ways they never did before. *He's fine,* I remind myself. *Nobody eats the hospital food.*

I turn off the light so that I can fill him. Rebuild him. Fortunately, he's familiar in the dark. Wrapped together, skin pressed to skin, his changed appearance no longer matters.

Afterward, he falls asleep. Once he's been out for what feels like long enough, I sneak from the bed and pull his wallet from the pocket of the jeans crumpled on the floor.

I have enough money saved up now to buy our plane tickets, and I've finally decided how I'm going to surprise Dylan with the news that we're going to Patagonia. I want the big reveal to be fun—I'm going to fill out a passport application with all of his information, then hand it to him to sign. See how long it takes him to figure it out. I already have most of the blanks filled in, but I need to fill in the rest soon if there's any chance of getting the passport back in time for the trip. Even with expedited service, we're cutting it close.

I freeze as he stirs, then rolls over in the bed. I wait until he settles back into his slow sleep-breathing before I pry his ID out of the wallet in order to fill in one of the gaps remaining on the form—his middle name.

Alexander. How did I not know that? It makes me feel bad,

like the world's shittiest girlfriend, for not even knowing my own boyfriend's middle name.

But at least now I know: Alexander.

It suits him. I imagine his parents quarreling about names, wanting, needing to come up with just the right one. A family name, I bet. A gift from an earlier generation. The kind of name you get from parents who care, from a family with roots that grip the earth and don't let go. A name shared and bestowed.

Not like my name, which looks like a drunk person's typo. Audrea is bad enough. Pair it with my middle name, Makayna—Hawaiian, a random thought from parents who've never come closer to any tropical location than a Malibu Rum hangover. I have a dollar-store, grab-bag name. They might as well have called me Final Discount. Little Miss Odds and Ends.

Whatever.

I'm smiling, feeling victorious as I slide the ID back in the wallet, when the numbers on the card start to fidget and scatter. Dylan's birth date rearranges itself before my eyes, and as I watch, next month becomes three months past.

No. No.

It's not right. It's the drugs. They're still in my system.

I remind myself of this over and over until my heart slows down and my gut unclenches. It's not real. Of course I didn't miss his birthday. It's an optical illusion. My eyes still playing tricks on me.

I toss the wallet onto the floor—no sense letting the ID pull its nasty stunt on me again—and curl up against Dylan, my forehead pressed to his back and my eyes squeezed shut.

When I wake up, the room is flooded with sunlight, and everything is clear again—the numbers and letters and facts and shadows have all returned to their correct places. *Keep the reins on your brains, Audie,* I tell myself. *You'll get through this.*

JustUntil

He waits until the end of the hour to tell me he wants to increase my dose and also start me on yet another new medication. "I'm very pleased with your progress, Audie. You're becoming one of my success stories."

"Progress according to what?" the girl using my mouth asks. She sits on my fingers to keep me from scratching.

The doctor's eyes pinch a little at the challenge. "Well, we've certainly made significant progress as far as your cognitive functioning and the delusions go. But I will admit that, on some fronts, it does feel like we're slipping a bit. I haven't seen you smile in weeks, for example, and several of the nurses have commented on your flat affect. You seem to have lost some of your fight, which I suppose is both good and bad. Anyway, I'd like to start you on an antidepressant, see if we can hold off another slide into major depression."

I wrestle control of my mouth back long enough to say something, even though I know it will cost me. "I've never been depressed in my life."

He raises a doubting eyebrow, then looks down to flip through the pages in my chart. It takes him a long time to scan through the alphabet soup of my diagnoses.

Finally, he frowns his confirmation that I'm right. "Well, Audie, nonetheless I'm seeing some unmistakable signs of depression. Insomnia. Lethargy. Decreased appetite. Do you really disagree?"

"I'm not depressed. I'm unhappy. It's different." The itching is almost unbearable. It's her fault—she wants me to stop talking.

The doctor leans back in his chair and steeples his fingers, the way he always does when we only have a short time left. He thinks the pose disguises his wandering attention. "How so?" His eyes are welded to the clock on the wall behind me.

It takes the last of my energy, but I say it anyway. "Depression is irrational. I'm unhappy because my life sucks. That's rational."

I can tell that the clock has finally reached the hour, because the little tension lines around his eyes relax. "You know, Audie, sometimes I forget that you're still a teenager." He smiles. Gives the shallow little rumble that is meant to be his laugh. He is the only person I've ever met who actually chortles. "Okay. We can hold off for now if you feel strongly about it, but I'd like to revisit this next week."

I do feel strongly about it, but I can't say so because I've lost control of my mouth again. As payment, the girl who isn't me lets me snake my hand out for one quick scratch, deep along my thigh. I dig in my nails, make it count. "No, it's fine," she says in my voice. "If you think changing my meds will help." She tilts my head one way and then the other. Blinks away the fading edges. "You're the doctor."

CHAPTER 30

After a long day in the pill mines, I go to a movie with Dylan. It's something action-y and futuristic, but I can't concentrate on the plot because I'm too focused on the actor's hairpiece and how it slips around from scene to scene. Our aging but still-muscular hero has found love on a distant planet, but all I can think about is the fact that his hairline was noticeably higher back on Earth. Has NASA ever studied gravitational effects on follicles?

It's the drugs, of course. Charlotte must have self-reported a severe case when she filled out the enrollment paperwork for the ADHD study, so I'm on the maximum dose possible. For three days I've been hyperfocused on one thing at a time.

One.

Thing.

At.

A.

Time.

So you know how you usually have at least a few things

floating around in your brain at once? Like, yeah, this movie is awesome, and oh shit I forgot to charge my cell phone, and damn my boyfriend's hot? Not me. Not anymore, anyway—the usual matrix of competing thoughts has shrunk into a single laser-beam point of concentration. I process the world in staccato, single-task bursts.

It turns out that this completely ruins the act of making out, which is fundamentally supposed to be a holistic experience. Dylan tried kissing me as soon as the lights went out in the theater, but it was kind of pathetic since I couldn't help getting fixated on stupid details. Like, I'd never noticed the way he makes this weird clicking sound with his tongue right before our lips meet, or the way he traces little circles into my thigh with his thumb while we're kissing. Suddenly it was all I could think about and it absolutely annoyed the crap out of me. Which kind of defeated the whole purpose of making out.

I miss my free-form brain ballet. There's something to be said for random. There's something healthy about distraction.

Nobody's perfect if you stare long enough.

Now please excuse me while I focus.

The actor stands on the planet's windswept surface, marveling at his newfound ability to breathe alien air, but his hair barely flutters in the Martian breeze. And: his part is a quarter inch closer to his left ear than when he first emerged from the transport pod. He moves off camera and I hold my breath until he reappears. Hey-ho, cut scene, and his phony cowlick has shifted portside again!

I turn to examine Dylan's hairline. Now that he's given up

on getting any dark-theater action—apparently, I didn't disguise my lack of responsiveness very well—he's enjoying the movie and doesn't notice me staring. Wait. Has his hairline changed, too? I could have sworn he wore his hair parted on the other side. I replay various scenes in my mind, zeroing in on his hair. *Click click click,* I shuffle through memories, frowning at hairline discrepancies. Finally, a pattern emerges.

Oh.

Scrutiny is the enemy of perfection.

I stretch my arm over his shoulder, pretend-casual, and ruffle my fingers through his hair to confirm what I already know. He turns his head and gives me a brief distracted kiss, then returns his eyes to the screen. I pull my hands back into my lap, ashamed of myself for only now realizing how much his treatments have thinned his hair, which used to be thick and full.

At least he's put back some of the weight he lost.

My excessively attentive brain gloms on to any good news at all lately, since life as Charlotte has not gone as smoothly this week. Two studies busted me, shooing me out the door in disgrace. One, upon noticing discrepancies in my blood type. Charlotte: A-positive. Me: O-negative.

Make that *O* for oops. Definitely a big fat negative, as far as the lab was concerned.

The other study did the unthinkable: they actually looked closely at the ID I handed over. "This isn't you," the study coordinator said after frowning at the driver's license for a long minute.

I wasn't going to argue with her. I reached for the card, prepared to walk out without a scene, but she snatched it away, holding it just out of my reach. "This isn't a game, you know," she snapped. "You people think this is just an easy way to make a buck. Do you not understand that we're trying to do something important here? Do you even care that pulling stunts like this, lying on your forms and swapping participants, can completely invalidate our results? You're messing with real lives here."

Like my life isn't real. Like Charlotte's wasn't real.

We stared each other down until I finally lunged across the desk to grab Charlotte's driver's license and then walked out of the office.

"I'm going to warn the other offices about you," she called after me. "I'm sending an email to the whole department. Good luck pulling off your little switcheroo in the future."

She's full of shit. The studies are staffed by a rotating cast of graduate students, visiting faculty, interns, and technicians who have their noses buried so far into the data that they can't be bothered with details about individual test subjects.

But still. It's a concern. Good thing I can't worry about it for long. I have hairlines to inspect.

The movie climaxes. At last, the hero's hair comes under control; it maintains its Astroturf-y stasis and the integrity of its side part through two galactic battles, several sexy alien romps, and an interplanetary award ceremony. Two-thirds of the way through the film and someone on the production set finally started paying attention to details. Perhaps the good makers of AttentiQuil DX (patent pending!) should commence their marketing efforts in Hollywood.

Dylan wants to get something to eat, but the meds have killed my appetite. "I'll split something with you," I say, and he makes a face.

I recalibrate. "How about Mexican?" I say, trying to look hungry and enthusiastic.

I really hate disappointing him.

CHAPTER 31

TODAY'S RANT: REFLECTIONS ON THE (MOTHERFUCKING) NOBILITY OF SCIENCE

Dearest gentle readers,

It has come to our attention that certain among us stand accused of taking advantage of what was once a process above reproach. Our crime: eking profit from science.

Foul exploiters! our critics cry. *Perverters of knowledge! Defilers of wisdom!*

And what say you, wise guinea pig brethren?

What's that? What is that faint rumbling noise I hear percolating deep within your collective bowels? A pang of conscience? A clang of doubt? A viscous *kersplash* of guilt, perhaps?

Could it be that you actually agree with those who seek to banish your generous and practiced bodies from these hopeful hallways of untried cures?

Ah. It appears I was mistaken, and quite so. Those were not gurgling noises of agreement. Please—the restroom is just down the hall, if you need it.

But what of the Scientific Method? our wide-eyed critics lament. *What of the dissertations? The research? The government grants?*

"Data integrity," they chant in wholesome, educated unison.

Do their protests concern you? Worry not, my cottontailed test-rabbit friends. Furrow not your furry brows. For the scientists shall not suffer. Not as long as we loyal volunteers continue to draw breath, and not as long as science beds faithfully with commerce.

Lo, we need only envision the intrepid researcher, woken in the darkest of night by a thunderbolt of inspiration surely equal to Archimedes's own. *Eureka!* this wise one cries. *There must be a better way to shrink a pimple,* thinks this eager and selfless soul. *I shall not rest, I will not stop, until the dreams of my nine years of doctoral studies, not including two years of unpaid fellowships, are fully realized. I will find a better way! I will shrink the pimples of the world faster than anyone has before! I shall not rest until I have achieved my mission, my very goal in life.*

It is you and only you, darling human subjects, who can make such dreams come true. You offer your pimples to the great gods of science. You dedicate your spotty complexions to the betterment of humanity. And all you ask in return is fair and just compensation for your vital (in the most literal sense) contribution.

For *ours* is the truly noble calling. Or at the very least, ours is the truly necessary one. Because theories, as you know, are cheap and plentiful.

Proof, on the other hand, is precious.

And that proof, dear guinea pigs, is what lies deep within *our* veins and tissues. So carry on, darling lab rats, confident in your role, and assured of your value.

Carry on.

CHAPTER 32

On the fifth and last day of my participation in the AttentiQuil DX trial, my fixation du jour becomes (drumroll, please): Charlotte's tattoos. I quickly become obsessed with the circular snakes I saw inked on her back the day she died.

The only reason I think of them in the first place is because of all of the funny little doodles in her calendar. For certain things—appointments, anniversaries, reminders, who the hell knows?—she didn't even use any words. Just a doodle next to a date and time—like that starry-eyed smiley face. I've figured a few of them out; it's kind of like a twisted little puzzle game.

Want to play? Then guess the meaning of these little red circles.

tick tock tick tock tick tock

Stumped? Here's a clue: they tend to show up roughly every twenty-eight days, usually for five days in a row.

Yes, boys and girls, you guessed it. Red dot = red period

= Charlotte was having her period. She was many things, but Charlotte was definitely *not* subtle.

I'm a little embarrassed, then, by how long it took me to figure out the meaning of one particular symbol that appears every Thursday evening for the last three months: a half circle, flat side up, with smaller circles poking out of it.

A pot of gold, I thought. Some kind of payday. This, naturally, piqued my interest. I won't tell you how long I scavenged around her room, emptying her drawers, and even pawing through the pockets of the dirty clothes in her laundry basket, until I finally figured out that the pot of gold was Charlotte's rendition of a falafel sandwich. Her way of reminding herself of the Thursday-night two-for-one special at the deli down the street.

She was many things, but Charlotte was definitely *not* artistically inclined.

I figured out almost all the other symbols fairly quickly. You just have to take a minute and get into a Charlotte-y frame of mind—she had kind of a tipsy, literal way of thinking, with a healthy splash of good-tempered anarchy and a firm commitment to toilet humor. Once you manage to squeeze into her thought patterns, it's easy to figure out what her doodles mean.

Except for the snakes.

They look exactly the same in her calendar as they did on her back—snakes curled into circles. The drawings appear three times over the last six months, and there's one more next week. Wednesday afternoon at 2:00. There's no other information—no names, no locations, no text at all.

Normally, I'd shrug it off, but the AttentiQuil won't let me.

It shackles my brain to the symbol, and won't let my thoughts wander no matter how much they want to.

It's annoying as hell, to be honest.

I get back at the AttentiQuil people by scrupulously listing side effects when I fill out my paperwork. I check off almost all the possible boxes: anxiety, insomnia, irritability, twitching, abdominal cramps. You name it, I report it. I have a little fun with the open-ended section at the end. "List any side effects not previously mentioned," it says, so I do.

I write: blue urine, nighttime teeth grinding, preoccupation with other people's follicles, compulsive ChapStick use, degenerate thoughts, pyromania, incurable laziness, and general insufferability.

And then in all caps, I write and then underline:

MASSIVE WEIGHT GAIN. 40+ POUNDS PER WEEK.

Someone once told me that's the worst feedback a pharmaceutical company can get. People will tolerate all kinds of nasty side effects from their prescription medications— they'll put up with heart palpitations and liver damage and blinding headaches every day of the week, but weight gain is the kiss of death for a new drug. That and erectile dysfunction, but I'd probably destroy my credibility if I tried to tack that one on.

The study coordinator flips through my paperwork to make sure I completed everything, and I see her wince as she looks at what I wrote. She looks pissed, but she doesn't have a choice, so she hands me the envelope with my money. She sort of hurls it at me, actually, but I'm still Charlotte in here, so I just don't care.

I go straight from the study to the area of the labs where the Professor tends to linger, hoping to find him. I know it's the medication, but that snake doodle is really starting to bug me. I'm starting to feel a little obsessed, actually.

Fortunately, he's there. He's lurking around with his notebook in hand, as usual. Also as usual, everyone is ignoring him.

He gets this ridiculously overjoyed look on his face when he realizes I actually *want* to talk to him. It almost makes you feel sorry for the guy.

"Audie!" he says. "To what do I owe the pleasure?"

I grab his notebook and pen from him, which makes him stutter and panic a bit, but I make a big point of flipping to a blank page, not reading anything he's written, and he calms down a little.

"What is this?" I ask him, and I hand him back the notebook so he can see what I've drawn. "What does it mean?"

If anyone would know, it's the Professor. It's exactly the kind of trivia that fills the minds of people like him.

He does know. "Your sketch is a bit rough, but if I'm not

mistaken, that's the Ouroboros. A serpent devouring its own tail."

His answer makes me even more impatient. "Okay, Ouroboros. Got it. But what does it *mean*?"

He sinks into a cushiony chair and strokes his beard in contentment a few times before motioning for me to grab a seat nearby. "I'd want to double-check my sources, of course, but I seem to recall that the symbol is Egyptian in origin. Or is it Greek?"

He talks himself through it slowly. So slowly I suspect he's stringing out our conversation on purpose. Not that it's much of a conversation—just him talking and talking and talking. I have to force myself to shut up and listen. It's important that I know.

The Ouroboros symbol appears throughout history, the Professor says. *Curiously universal* are the words he uses. Quetzalcóatl, the Aztec serpent god, sometimes took on its looping shape. It shows up in Norse mythology. Alchemists wrote about it. Jung did, too.

It represents infinity. Continuous renewal. The joining of opposites, creation from destruction. Blah blah blah. On this topic, at least, the Professor knows his stuff.

Maybe he knows a little too much, I start to think.

"It also makes for a helluva tattoo, don't you think?" I ask, just to see how he responds.

But from the way he blinks and tilts his head like he's confused about why I'd interrupt his little soliloquy with this not particularly deep observation, I realize he doesn't know what I'm talking about. He doesn't know about Charlotte's tattoos.

I let him ramble on a little more, but I already know enough. The Ouroboros obsession box has been checked off my mental list of side effects, and I finally feel released from its grip.

"Thanks for the info," I call over my shoulder.

The Professor, looking a little dejected about my rapid departure, frowns and waves goodbye.

CHAPTER 33

I go home between appointments to stash my cash under my mattress.

Yes, my mattress. Shut up.

It's an embarrassingly obvious hiding spot, but my options are limited. All the real furniture in the apartment belongs to someone else. Everything was already here when I moved in, and I don't even know who actually owns what. The couches, for example. Who bought those—Jameson? Charlotte? Or some other, long-gone roommate?

And do I have any claim to whatever was Charlotte's? Not that I even care whose crappy coffeemaker it is now, or who should be called the rightful owner of the hand towels. But it might be nice to have a sense of ownership, of permanence, for once, instead of living like a goddamn nomad for the rest of my life.

Everything I own can and has fit in the back of a cab with room to spare. A futon mattress, a set of stackable plastic organizers in lieu of a dresser, and a duffel bag full of miscellaneous crap I haven't had the energy to toss. There are depressingly few nooks and crannies among my meager possessions, so under the mattress it is. Better than in the hands of a thief. Again.

Sadly, my hidden treasure is not growing as fast as I hoped. I'm so very, very close to the magic number that can make Dylan's birthday trip happen, but two more studies turned me-as-Charlotte away this week, and everywhere I go I can feel people looking at me in all the wrong ways. The halls are lined with tilted, turning heads and smirking, narrowed eyes.

What's that famous quote? Sometimes paranoia's just having all the facts? Well, I'm still sorting through the facts, but it's starting to become obvious.

I've been blacklisted.

Not that there's an actual list. My face is not displayed on WANTED (or, more accurately, UNWANTED) posters in back-hallway administrative offices. *Blackfogged* might be a more accurate description of my current status. As in, there's a noxious, slow-moving cloud spreading misgivings about me, damply telling unflattering tales.

The money has slowed to a trickle.

Sometimes paranoia's just having eyes and ears.

Jameson is home in the middle of the day, smelling riper than ever. He used to be so clean.

"Aren't you working today?" I ask him.

"What do you mean? Of course I am." He's jumpy, which I'd normally assume was a side effect, but I haven't seen him leave the apartment all week. Whatever's making him anxious isn't chemical in nature.

"So help me out, then." And when he makes a face, "C'mon, Jameson. You always have some kind of hustle going on. Can't you hook me up with anything? I need to make some quick cash."

"No." He gives me a weird look, takes a deep breath. "But, hey, can we talk?" He waits until I get closer, until he can be sure I'm paying attention. I've stopped taking the AttentiQuil, so, admittedly, there's room for doubt.

"Audie," he finally says, "I like you."

Shitballs. Where is this coming from? I've never gotten that vibe from him, like, *ever*, and it's pretty much the last thing I need to deal with right now. I'm about to give him that whole stupid *I like you too but* speech when he shakes his head.

"No. Jesus, no. Not like that. You're a freaking kid. Plus—" He stops, then shakes his head again like he's trying to get rid of a disturbing image. "I just mean that I like you as a person, and I worry about you. Maybe you shouldn't be doing this stuff to yourself anymore. You're too smart for this place, for this shit. You need to get out of here, get a real life." He looks away, his face turning pink. "Get out of here before you end up like Charlotte."

He keeps talking, but I'm fixated on his fingernails—long on the left hand, chewed to the quick on the right—and I'm too focused on his jagged cuticles to listen to whatever he's saying. I may have stopped taking the ADHD meds two days ago, but I'm still getting little burst effects.

Little solar flares of temper, too. Like now.

"Okay, got it," I say, sarcastic as hell. "You feel guilty. Guess what? So do I. It turns out that none of us had Charlotte's back when she needed us. But last I checked nobody takes guilt in lieu of cash, so thanks a lot for all your help. Forgive the fuck out of me for even asking, since you obviously don't want to lift a finger. Just don't blame me if next month's rent is late." I'm about to walk away when he raises both hands into the air in defeat.

"Okay, okay," he says. Shakes his head like I'm a lost cause. "Forget I said anything." He sighs, and I can smell his stale breath from three feet away. "Give me a day or two. I may be able to help. But in exchange, all I ask is that you think about something." He pauses until I give him a sharp, angry nod. "I just want you to think about the fact that I knew Charlotte for five years. I watched her survive *five years* of this shit. It's not really surprising, what happened to her, when you think about it like that. You can hardly expect to just waltz out of here, no harm done, after putting in that kind of time."

Five years ago I was twelve years old, spending my days angling for sleepovers at friends' houses and making up excuses for erratic school attendance. Five years *does* feel like forever. And I had no idea Charlotte had been working the labs for that long. She must have started doing the pediatric stuff. You see that occasionally, scared parents dragging scared kids in for tests, hoping for a shot at getting a miracle cure.

"*You've* been here longer than five years," I say. "And you're still breathing."

He kind of half smiles. "What can I say? I'm a lifer. If I can somehow manage to hang on for twenty more years, I'll get a gold watch and a pension."

I snort, and my anger dissolves a little. "Yeah, right. Wouldn't that be nice. A guinea pig retirement plan."

He looks at his feet. Doesn't laugh.

Now I feel bad. It's no joke. He really is a lifer, and here I am rubbing his nose in it. What's he going to do after all these years of farming out his brain cells? Fold shirts at the Gap for just above minimum wage? Clock in and out, ask his twenty-year-old boss for permission every time he needs to take a piss break? He wouldn't last a week. None of us would. Once you get the chance to control your own fate, set your own schedule, it's too hard to give it back.

I look at him sitting there, morose and greasy-haired, and I soften up. Jameson isn't the enemy here. I know that. "I know you mean well, and I appreciate it. I don't plan to do this forever, I promise. Okay? But I really do need to make some fast cash. Can't you *please* help me out?"

He nods vaguely, mutters something about making a few calls, but he won't look at me. Instead, he slumps even further in his chair and stares down at his hands, and I can already tell the fingernails on the left are going to be chewed to the quick by nightfall.

"Thanks, Jameson," I say. And, "I miss her, too." I hold my breath as I give him a small peck on the top of his head and then get out before his funky smell and funkier mood wear off on me.

CHAPTER 34

I head back to the labs and check the boards. I need cash. I can't afford to be picky.

While I'm standing there, Dougie walks up. "Looking for some action?" He waggles his eyebrows to let me know I can take that question any of several ways.

"Jesus, lighten up, Audie," he says when I don't answer.

I can't deal with his oily energy, so I start to walk off.

"Too bad," he calls after me in a taunting voice. "I was gonna let you in on a little secret, tell you how you can make a fast five bills."

I grit my teeth and turn around slowly. Try not to look as hateful as I feel. I can't afford to be picky, I remind myself.

"Attagirl," he says with a smirk on his face. "Why do you hate me so much, anyway? I've never been anything but nice to you."

"I have good instincts," I say. Then, "I'm pretty sure you screwed me over in a past life."

He laughs. "Well, you won't hate me so much after this."

It's not posted on the bulletin board, he says. Word of mouth only. "I'll walk you over myself," he says, holding out his arm, which I don't take.

"Suit yourself." He shrugs. "Follow me." But he insists on walking too close, our shoulders brushing, as we head over to a different building. His route cuts through the alley where I woke up with the black eye, and I can't help looking around for bodies. None today.

It's all about family history, Dougie tells me as we walk. He takes hold of my elbow, steers me through a set of double doors. Cancer stuff, blood stuff, all the usual crap. Check yes for this, no for that. He rattles off symptoms and conditions. They'll catch me eventually, once the blood test results come in, but somebody screwed up when they wrote the forms and they have to pay you five hundred bucks even if you get kicked out.

He's proud of himself for knowing this.

"We're all signing up before they figure it out and shut things down. Today might be your last chance."

He leaves me at the lab door with a slow, blatant scan of my body and a sharp squeeze of my upper arm.

"Thanks," I say automatically, then bite my tongue hard as punishment. I don't want to encourage him.

I sign in at the front desk and sit down to fill out the forms, eager fucking beaver, already feeling the weight of that cash in my hand. I start to get excited. With five hundred dollars, I'll have enough to cover the whole trip. I'll tell Dylan. Finally.

I space out for a few minutes like that, thinking about how

he's going to react, and I'm sure I have a giant stupid grin on my face. But after a few minutes I snap out of it and look around and I realize that certain things seem . . . off. Different from other studies.

It's the other people. *They're* different.

All around me, sitting in those ugly waiting-room chairs, everyone looks gray and boneless, like it's too much work to sit upright, so instead they're drooping and puddling over the edges of their seats.

They move differently, too. They shuffle like old people. They lean on things. They hunch when they stand. Guinea pigs almost always look hungry—it has as much to do with personality as it does with malnourishment. These people, though, they look *starved.*

It takes me a minute to figure it out. This is what is different about the people in this waiting room: these people are Sick.

There are a lot of different ways to be sick. I know this now.

There's sick as in mildly ill. *Oh man. That cafeteria meat loaf made me sick to my stomach.*

There's sick as in disgusting or disturbed. *Did you see Dougie kick that dog? He's one sick bastard.*

There's even sick as a compliment. *Gavin is so hot—he has sick abs.* Actual sick people, I suspect, do not use the word this way.

Here is what I realize now, sitting here surrounded by these melting, shuffling people: guinea pigs are, indeed, sick.

sick in the head sick as fuck sick puppies sick of waiting sick humor sick and tired sick at heart sick of this shit make me sick

What we are not, however, is Sick. As in, deserving of treatment. As in, in need of care. As in, desperately, hopelessly ill, the way the people in the chairs around me clearly are.

I put my paperwork down and just look at the other people in the room. I force myself to look at Sick, *really* look, for the first time, and compare it to what else I know. What else I've seen.

Dylan, in his hospital bed. Watching even the nurses avoid eye contact with him.

Charlotte's empty room.

Here is what I realize: *Real* Sick doesn't flaunt its presence.

Real Sick whimpers and turns its back to the door. Real Sick is quieter than the noises in the room. Real Sick whispers underneath the sound of the monitors and the pumps and the optimistic voices of well-intentioned visitors.

Real Sick sits patiently in the waiting room for as long as it takes. Real Sick does not ask the receptionist for the second time how late the doctor is running. Real Sick knows the value of time.

Real Sick savors the taste, the *essence* of minutes.

I sit in the waiting room, my lie-spattered paperwork resting in my lap, and I understand what's going on. I'm competing with these slow-moving people, these *Sick* people, for a golden ticket—a slot in an experimental treatment for people with a family history of dying in a really terrible way. I'm bullshitting my way through the forms so that I can take a chance away from someone who really needs it.

You probably want me to tell you that I stand up immediately and storm out, don't you? Take A Stand. Do The Right Thing.

Sorry to fuck up your after-school special. This is not what I do.

It's five hundred dollars.

i'm sick too

I don't walk out.

I finish filling out the paperwork, drafting page after page of fiction. I answer the questions exactly the way Dougie told me to.

sick in the head sick at heart

How do you like me now?

But there's this one lady sitting in the corner. Same as everybody else in the room—middle-aged and ancient all at the same time. A used-up sponge. Unlike everyone else, though, this lady has a kid with her. A boy. About nine years old, maybe? That age when most kids are kind of ugly, with teeth too big for their heads and awkward haircuts. He's ugly like that. And this homely, big-toothed kid keeps glancing over at his mom with this look on his face that just about punches me in the gut. It's hard to describe, but it's like this cesspool of hope and fear and resignation and horror, all spun together in a fucking nine-year-old's eyes. It's like he can't even look at his mom without imagining her dying, right there in front of him. He just looks so goddamn helpless and hopeful and so fucking sad.

I stand there with the finished paperwork in my hand, watching this kid watching his mom. And all I can think about is, *What if I get into the study and that kid's mom doesn't?* For all

I know, it's a first-come, first-served system, and the lady's hand is shaking so much it's taking her forever to fill out the paperwork. I'm standing there in the middle of the room like an idiot, willing her to just hurry the fuck up, get her paperwork turned in before I do. I even start getting mad at her for taking so long. *Lady, you gotta want this more,* I want to yell at her. *You need to act less starved and more hungry.*

No kid should have that kind of look on his face. No kid should have to feel like that.

So, finally, I leave.

Reluctantly.

Slowly.

Subtracting money from my pocket with every step until I reach the door with nothing at all.

How d'you like me now?

PerpetuNever

The doctor frowns at the piece of paper while I hold my breath. He sits back and steeples his fingers in silence, making me wait for what I can already tell is going to be a no.

"I'm only asking for a day pass," I say. I keep my voice soft. Nonconfrontational, with no jagged edges. "Just to get out and walk around a bit. Visit some friends."

control my mind control my feet control my voice

"But what do you hope to accomplish with that, Audie? Especially considering what happened last time. We've seen several times now that outside influences too early in your recovery process tend to set you back. I'm inclined to advise against it for now, but we can revisit the issue during your next appointment if you really feel like you're ready."

"Okay."

He pauses. Waits for anger and argument and fists and shouts. When none appear he smiles, makes a small note in his file. "Don't feel discouraged, Audie. I think we're close. Very close."

I nod and tether my stare to the edge of his desk.

"The new medication seems to be working well. How about the blackouts? Have you had any recently?"

"No."

I feel his disappointment with my one-word answer. He wants cartwheels and gratitude for his work. He wants me to worship at the same altar of pills he does. I try to generate a more enthusiastic response, but my voice is slow to cooperate and nothing comes out.

"No blackouts at all since our last appointment?" He sounds skeptical.

"No, none," I say. Technically it's true. True-ish. I no longer have grave-sized hunks cored out of my weeks. Hours and days no longer wander off, never to be seen or heard from again.

But.

Of course there's a but.

But the order of things is . . . off. Things that can't possibly have happened appear in my mind as memories. Ancient history recurs on a random Tuesday.

The sequence of my life is all wrong lately. Dead people show up at birthday parties. I wake up in houses that burned down years ago. I find myself in the middle of tasks I never would have agreed to.

It's no longer so much a matter of blacking out as it is a problem of blocking out, though. As in, I'm no longer able to block out those parts of life I'd rather not experience.

I don't even try to explain this to the doctor. It must be the pills he's giving me—his oh-so-carefully-crafted treatment plan—but I don't want him to know this. I hate to disappoint people.

Starting today I'll cut back. Maybe spit out every other dose when the nurse isn't looking. No reason for anyone else to know.

See? I feel better already, just thinking about it.

CHAPTER 35

I've lost my keys, and Jameson's not home to let me in.

This is what I get for trying to do the right thing: empty pockets.

I close my eyes, do that trick where you try to visualize the last place you saw something, but all I get is a headache. I paw through my pockets, but for the life of me I can't remember where the keys *should* be, much less where they are. I can't even conjure up the muscle memory for the way they should feel if I had them, for the heft of the key ring in my hand, can't even remember how many keys there should be. *Were they on a key ring? They must have been, so why can't I picture it?*

When I was eight, the spare house key was in a rusty Altoids tin, behind a cobwebby planter full of long-dead ferns. I always held my breath as I reached into the dark, spidery space to fish it out.

When I was thirteen, my foster father du jour made a big deal of giving me a key on a ring with a little silver teddy bear on it. "Giving you this key to my house proves I trust you, Audie.

Do *you* trust *me*?" I can still feel his humid whisper in my ear, extra quiet so no one else would hear.

I can remember a half-dozen other key-ring configurations, other secret hiding places—magnetic boxes, fake rocks with clever, key-sized hollows in the center. So why can't I picture the keys I need to open my apartment now?

The black holes in my mind are growing again. The headaches are getting worse.

I'm too freaked out to try any more of the studies Charlotte has in her appointment book today, so I sit on the ground and pull out my phone. My hands are shaking, so it takes me a minute to shuffle through my list of contacts to find Dylan's latest phone number. How many times can one guy lose a cell phone, anyway? I have each version saved: Dylan(a), Dylan(b), Dylan(c). I dial Dylan(d), hoping it's the right one. The latest one.

When he answers, it makes the blackness recede a bit. "Hey!" he says. He sounds good—better than he has in a long time. I can feel his health, his energy, coursing through the phone line. I feel better immediately.

"Hey back. What're you doing right now?"

"Not much. Thinking about you, of course." He says it in that teasing, suggestive way that always makes me laugh. It's amazing what just hearing his voice does for me. It's infinitely better than any fucking pill.

"I'm at my place right now, but I'm locked out. Are you anywhere near the hospital? I can be there in five minutes, meet you for coffee or something."

"A date in the hospital cafeteria, huh? I always knew you were an incurable romantic. I'm on my way—can't wait."

I flinch a little when he says *incurable*. I can't help it. I hate that so many words are off-limits, tainted by association. It makes me wish I could order up the mental equivalent of a colon cleanse to purge the bad thoughts—let them spill out my ears in filthy torrents, like the messy aftermath of an old-fashioned enema. An emotional laxative. Prozaxative.

There'd be a huge market for a drug like that. I'm surprised no one else has thought of it.

I push myself up off the ground and balance against the door for a minute until the wavy lines clear from my vision. One of the pills I'm taking is doing a number on my equilibrium lately.

I totter the short walk to the hospital wishing I had sunglasses, since the bright sunlight is laser-beaming even more pain into my skull. I'm sure I'm quite a sight, with my drunken-sailor walk and my face scrunched up against the daylight. Not to mention my jeans, which are hanging off my body like they belong to someone twice my size. When did I start shrinking again?

I'm so focused on cursing the midday sunlight that I don't think about the fact that, *duh, Audie,* it's so fucking bright because it's the middle of the day, and the middle of the day is when Dylan is supposed to be in school.

I forget normal things like that a lot. I don't have a lot of normal in my life, so it feels strange when I know someone who does. Like the other day, Dylan was talking about going to the mall with his mom to buy new shoes, and the whole idea of that just blew me away. I mean, he might as well have said they were about to board a rocket ship for a family vacation to Mars, that's just how crazy his normal life stuff feels to me.

So I'm thinking about how weirdly normal Dylan is, realizing too late that he shouldn't be meeting me here in the middle of the day, when I push my way through the glass doors of the cafeteria. He's nowhere to be seen.

Of course he isn't. It's the middle of the day.

I just stand there, and the black holes in my memory start joining forces with the headache that's tearing up my vision, and I start feeling more and more confused. *Wait, was it just now that I called Dylan?* I start wondering. *Or am I remembering a call from a different day?*

I'm standing there, half freaking out and half laughing at myself for being such a space cadet, when Dougie comes up to me from behind and grabs my elbow, spinning me around so that I face him.

I hate that.

"Hey," he says in a greasy tone, with a greasy smile to match. "I'm glad you called. I *have* been thinking about you."

He sounds just like Dylan when Dylan is joking around, using his pretend-skeezebag voice, except Dougie is totally serious when he talks this way. Like, he *actually* talks like that.

I pull away from him so I can keep looking for Dylan. I stand on my toes, stretch my neck up as I scan the room, corner to corner. Everything is getting jumbled in my mind, and my headache is pounding so goddamn bad that I can hardly think straight.

"Audie." Dougie grabs me by the elbow again. Always the same place. Always that possessive, hard-enough-I-can-feel-all-five-fingers-digging-in kind of grip. I *really* fucking hate when people do that.

I whirl around, tear my arm out of his greasy hold, and mostly without meaning to, I sort of backhand him across the jaw in the process. Pretty hard, actually.

I guess I've been feeling pretty tense.

His hand goes up to his mouth and comes away bloody. Only a little bloody, no reason to freak out, but he still looks pissed. And ugly. And mean.

I've never liked Dougie. Everything else is sort of blurry and confusing right now, but not that. I'm not at all confused about Dougie being bad news, or about not wanting to hear anything that could come out of his ugly, twisted mouth.

"You fucking psychotic bitch." He growls it, so low that no one looks up from their table, no one even glances at us.

Almost like it's not happening.

"This is how you repay me? I didn't need to hook you up with that study, you crazy whore. There're way easier ways to get into your pants."

I wish he would stop talking. I wish he would disappear.

Wishes are like assholes, Charlotte used to say. *Everyone has them.* Or, when she was in one of her moods: *Wishes are like assholes. They both leave you sitting in the same old shit.*

"What's the matter, Audie? I'm too healthy for you? You here to choose another dying guy to fuck? Look around. Plenty to choose from." Dougie steps closer, baring his teeth right next to my ear, an animal that needs putting down. "There's a guy in a wheelchair over there. A double amputee—just your type. Someone who can't run away once he realizes what a complete psycho you are."

I won't let him talk about Dylan that way. My hands make claws and I go for his face, but Dougie just laughs and bats me away. "You're famous around here, do you know that? Everyone knows how to get you into bed. Everyone knows the secret."

I look around, and I see that he's telling the truth. People are staring at us now. At me. They all have that look on their faces, like they know something about me. Something ugly and dark.

My vision is clouding over with steam, the whole room is pulsing and glowing, and I lunge at him again, trying to hurt him any way I can, but Dougie is already walking away. Laughing at me. "What's the name you like again? Dylan? Baby, you can call me anything you want if you treat me nice, the way you did last time. Oooooh yeah." He grabs at his crotch, does a few obnoxious pelvic thrusts, and more people are turning to look.

Which means that he's real.

Which means that what he's saying is real.

The pain behind my eye explodes in a red mist and then everything goes black.

Forlfver

"One of the burdens of being exceptionally intelligent, Audie, is that your delusions are both tightly fabricated and highly effective." For once the doctor isn't watching the clock. Even as he's scribbling notes with that manic enthusiasm that had all but disappeared recently, he peeks up at me between words, between lines, like he's afraid to miss something. He wants to see every frame of the train wreck playing out across my face.

It's a breakthrough, he says.

breakthrough, breakdown. potato, potahto.

His breakthrough is my apocalypse.

He is fascinated, enthralled, as he documents my total destruction. He is proud of his role in the annihilation of Me.

"It's a clever construct, really. Your delusions serve a very real purpose for you. They're all designed to maximize your feeling of control, which is something that has always been in short supply in your life."

I turn my head away, focus on the framed diplomas hanging

on the wall. So many letters. MD, PhD, Fellowship of this, Doctorate of that. Professor of Dust and Air and Shit, those gold-embossed certificates might as well say. So much time studying. So little time living.

What could he possibly know?

"It felt real." My voice comes out as a whimper. The sound of my weakness makes me want to curl up and finish dying. "He felt real."

He finally stops taking notes and puts down his pen. He strokes his ridiculous beard for a minute—it's overgroomed, pointy and so white that it looks fake. He looks like a goddamn garden gnome.

Did I tell you that already? I've been repeating myself a lot lately. It's like hearing echoes everywhere I go.

He sighs, and looks genuinely pained. "You're talking about Dylan. Or rather, the construct of Dylan." He flinches a little when he says the name, tenses up like he's afraid of my reaction. He looks ready to duck.

Past predicts future.

But I'm too weak to defend myself, much less attack. My hands stay in my lap, curled into limp approximations of fists.

"I know this is difficult for you. But it's a good starting point. It's necessary for us to address your promiscuity, for the sake of both your physical and your emotional well-being."

"My promiscuity? I'm not a fucking whore."

The doctor shakes his head. "Of course not. It's never been about sex, Audie. Like I said, your delusions are highly functional. For example, in the case of Dylan, or more accurately, the concept of Dylan, you were able to experience a perfect relationship.

You created an idealized notion of what a boyfriend should be, and each person you spent a night with had some element of that ideal. In essence, you sought out the best qualities in every young man you brought into your life."

"Into my bed," I correct him. No need to soft-pedal things now that it's all out in the open, now that we're sitting here talking so openly about *Just How Crazy Audie Really Is.*

Perfect.

Dylan.

I know there are other words coming out of the doctor's mouth besides these two. I know he's surrounding Perfect Dylan with words that negate everything I know and love, but I try not to hear them.

"He was hardly perfect," I say. "He had cancer."

The doctor raises a triumphant finger in the air, then catches himself, tries to cover the gesture with another stroke of his beard. "In a less complex framework, the idea of a terminal illness would indeed be considered a flaw. But once again, Audie, both your intelligence and the intricacy of your fantasy world come into play. In this case, by seeking out potential partners with serious medical issues, you were actually bolstering your psychological construct."

I am suddenly, inexplicably, exhausted. I can barely keep my head up, and the doctor's words sound like they're coming at me from the other end of a tunnel a hundred miles long. I'm too tired to hear more, but I'm also too tired to escape his words.

But the doctor won't stop. "Think about it this way, Audie." He doesn't even seem to notice that he's torturing me, killing me. It's like verbal vivisection, sitting here listening to him. *"It's* considered bad form to speak ill of the dead, correct? When people die, we put them on pedestals. We, myself included, forgive, and sometimes quite literally forget the negatives. It's a coping mechanism. There's something about loss that makes us reset our hard drives, so to speak. So we purge the bad memories, which allows us to remember the dead with artificial fondness. It's an act of self-preservation we all engage in when we lose someone close to us—we get to keep all of the good, comforting memories, and rid ourselves of the bad ones."

He finally pauses for a second and tilts his head at me. He wants me to chime in. To agree with him.

I'm too busy trying to curl into myself and disappear.

"In other words, Audie, you chose boys who, even if they disappointed you, or hurt you, would be the easiest to forgive. By extension, this allowed you to preserve your idealized notion of Dylan as the perfect boyfriend."

Dylan. Perfect boyfriend. I try my old tricks—to at least block out what I can't black out—but they're not working.

He sits back in his chair and smiles. "As I said, Audie, it's ironic that part of the problem here is your intelligence. Your delusions are so complex that they're sometimes difficult, even for me, to untangle."

His eyes shine with pride. He is impressed by my crazy. To him, I am fascinating in my brokenness. Clever in my delusions. I am the prized possession of this Professor of Dust and Air and Shit. A paper waiting to be written. A case study served juicy and medium-rare.

"The good news is that we're making progress," he says. "The *fact that we're even having this conversation is proof. I just want you to be prepared for the hard work ahead, and to understand that I need you to do your part. You're going to continue to have good days and bad days."* He stops here and chuckles. *"Or, good* hours *and bad* hours, *as the case may be, and I know that can feel confusing."*

I don't laugh with him. And I'm not the least bit confused. I know that his cure is my destruction, and that somehow, somehow, I have to find the strength to fight back. To fight for what's mine.

Fortunately, I've already taken the first step: no more pills. I've been chemically celibate for two days already; I'm snipping the strings that bind me, one skipped dose at a time. Soon enough I'll be born again. I'll be me again, just like before.

Only better.

CHAPTER 36

 EXPERT TESTIMONY

Hey.

You over there.

Yeah, you—junior-college lifer. You too, high school dropout. Gather round, Little Miss D in Chemistry, Mr. Incomplete. And get that drunk guy over there, while you're at it. I'm talking to you, teeming masses. The Great Unwashed, and the early peakers.

Hoi polloi.

Riffraff.

Scumbags.

Losers.

Want to know something interesting? It's a dirty little secret, kept hush-hush by people with fancier degrees and clothes and cars than you'll ever have.

You know those doctors, those know-it-all, white-coat-wearing motherfuckers, supposed guardians of science and chemistry and endless co-pays?

Well, they don't know jack.

You go to them for help, humbly baring your ass and your soul and your wallet. You supplicate in germ-filled waiting rooms, where you're kept forty-five minutes past your appointment time on a good day, just so you can turn your head and cough. *Tell me why it hurts,* you beg. *Save me. Cure me.*

And yet, for all their diagnostic manuals and insurance codes and prescription pads, guess who actually does the real work when it comes down to it?

That's right: you.

Welcome to the world of self-reporting.

Say it with me, loser brethren. All together now: *self-reporting.*

You'd be amazed how many illnesses are diagnosed and drugs dispensed simply because you say so. YOU.

How much does it hurt? Where does it hurt? Is your cough productive? What do the voices in your head tell you to do? Are you experiencing difficulty breathing/sleeping/climaxing/digesting? Are you anxious? Depressed? Filled to the gills with violent sociopathic tendencies? When was your last bowel movement, and are you a threat to yourself or others?

They ask. You answer.

So tell me, fellow Alumni of the Streets, who's really doing the heavy lifting here?

The fact of the matter is this: unless there's a specific blood test for it or unless you have a gushing, gaping hole in obvious need of sutur-

225

ing, there's a metric shit-ton of guesswork involved in this little field of pseudoscience that we call medicine.

And psychiatry? Don't even get me started.

Well, maybe a little. Since you asked.

Actual conditions listed in the DSM-5, the bible of mental health professionals everywhere:

—Internet gaming disorder (step away from the *Candy Crush*!)

—Caffeine withdrawal (when a Starbucks on every corner just isn't enough)

—Tobacco use disorder (because cigarettes cause cancer *and* crazy?)

—Frotteuristic disorder (a laughable medicalization of those nasty dudes who rub up against you on the bus)

Do you suppose there's a blood test for pedophilia? Excuse me. *Pedophilic disorder.* I don't think so.

They only know what you tell them, friends.

Yeah, but some things are obvious. That's what you're thinking, right? You know a pervert when you see one. You can spot crazy from a mile away. Surely those doctors can, too.

But you've had a different sort of education. Your certificates bear very different sorts of distinctions. *Involuntary commitment. Parole violation. Ward of the court.*

How many psychiatrists do you think have actually been energetically and wetly frottaged while crammed in the back of a standing-room-only city bus?

How many doctors knew by age six how to zigzag their way home from school, avoiding *this* house, and *that* guy, and *this* corner, since the direct route would've gotten them killed before puberty?

Not many.

No, they seal themselves off in luxury sedans and take the long way around *our* neighborhoods. They don't know crazy the way *we* know crazy.

They also have very different definitions of sane.

So the question becomes: What label would *you* like to see pasted across your file? Which fancy new medicines would *you* like to give a try?

And even more importantly—what, friends, do *you* believe to be true? What do you want the world to know about you?

Because if you self-report it, then it must be true. Nine out of ten doctors agree.

So name your own symptoms.

Write your own disease.

Prescribe your own cure.

Because the truth is whatever *you* say it is.

CHAPTER 37

I lose a fistful of time trapped in that dark fog, but once it finally lifts, I see that only a few hours have lapsed, and I still have just enough time to make Charlotte's last appointment of the day if I hurry.

I run, hoping that a little money might help me salvage what has so far been a complete ruin of a day. I'm barely two minutes late, but the office manager is waiting for me with a frown on her face. She gives me a form to sign, then picks up the phone, tells someone in a clipped voice, "She's here." She follows me with a pinched-face stare, doesn't let me out of her sight until a man in a lab coat comes to get me.

Lab Coat leads me to the tank room, and once I'm undressed he starts attaching the electrodes to my body. I kind of expect him to check out my tits, since they're pretty much right in his face, but he doesn't. It's like I'm not even human, like I don't even merit the usual degradations. "Just like last time, these are perfectly safe. They're specially designed for this kind of study, and I promise you won't get electrocuted even when you're in the water." He checks something off on a clipboard. "Everybody always worries about that."

He turns on a monitor and then helps me climb into the warm saltwater that fills the metal tank. He's silent as he fidgets with the wire leads, testing the signals and then making adjustments until he's satisfied that everything is working.

"Okay," he finally says. "You know the drill. Signal if you need emergency attention, but try hard to make it until I come get you out. If we interrupt the process, we have to start the whole thing over." He starts to close the tank, to seal me into the darkness, but then changes his mind and swings the round door open again. This time his face is heavy with pity, and when he opens his mouth to speak again, I hear his embarrassment. He's embarrassed *for* me, a realization that coats me with shame even before his words sink in. "I'm supposed to tell you that you can't come back after today. We probably shouldn't even be using you now, but we're almost done with this data-collection phase and we can't afford to lose any more subjects this close to the end. But everyone's been told to watch out for you, not let you into any more studies. So today's the last time here. Okay?"

I close my eyes. Nod. *Everyone knows,* says Dougie. *Everyone's been told,* says Lab Coat. Their voices echo and collide with a hundred others in my head. *Crazy, crazy, crazy,* they all say.

"Okay. Then here we go. Good luck, and I'll come and get you when we're done." The metal door closes, and I hear the compartment seal engage.

Cue ominous music: I am alone with myself. Me, myself, and I. Quite the diverse group, it turns out.

I wait, one minute, two minutes, then blink my eyes. Open, shut, it makes no difference. There's only blackness, so complete it has an almost tactile presence, velvety and thick as pudding, and the only noises are those that come from me—stomach gurgles and hitching breaths that sound almost deafening now. I can literally hear myself blink—my lashes make tiny, wet clicks as they clap together—and my hand wiping away a tear sounds like a limp body being dragged across a floor.

It's my second time here, and apparently my last, since I am officially unwelcome and officially undone. Without Charlotte's identity to hide behind, I have no choice but to face the world's reaction to the real me, and judging from my last few inter-actions, that's not going to be pleasant.

It's good that I'm here now. It's calm in here.

Also, I can't hurt anyone.

I was right to come. I feel better already—maybe what I needed all along was just a little escape.

I unclench my hands, which keep sneaking into fists, and begin my long, blind float. I tell myself to accept the nothing-ness, the darkness, as a gift. The gift of total isolation. I bludgeon my thoughts into silent submission and try to just . . . exist. To extinguish my needs. To dissolve the memories of the day.

I slow my breathing and try to empty my mind.

It's all very Zen for about half a goddamn minute, but who am I kidding? This is me we're talking about, so ninety seconds later I'm making little whirlpools with my hands and trying to come up with as many words as possible that rhyme with *tank*.

dank, stank, rank. spank, tranq, yank.

I'd make a shitty monk.

"Om." I chant it out loud. No one can hear me, so I draw it out, loud and long. *Ohhhhhhhmmmmmm*. It goes downhill from there. I do mental cartwheels to keep away the unwelcome thoughts. Show tunes are involved—a sure sign that I've lost my mind completely. I dictate a letter of complaint to the makers of the dissolvable sutures that still haven't dissolved from my thigh. Sharp ends poke from the skin high on my leg, like alien pubes run amok.

I cry in rough, unsatisfying bursts.

With no point of reference, it's impossible to tell how much time has gone by. Probably more than I think. Or possibly less. The only certainty of being truly alone with your thoughts is that whatever you're thinking is probably wrong.

Drunk on isolation, I sing one of Charlotte's rewritten songs at the top of my lungs:

> *Om, om on the range*
> *Where the beer and the Lexapro play*
> *Where seldom is heard*
> *A non-drug-addled word*
> *And your thoughts remain cloudy all day*

Only when I truly can't avoid them, when I have completely, totally, thoroughly, strenuously emptied my mind of all other content, a process that includes the recitation of every phone number I've ever memorized, only then do I allow myself to think the forbidden thoughts.

They're ugly little gremlins, these thoughts. Sneaky, devilish bastards.

They tiptoe out of the darkness, bearing proof. Mental snapshots, a slide show of intimate moments captured by an unseen lens. At first glance, the images please. They're of me with Dylan—freeze-framed smiles and caresses. Full-color bliss.

Extended sensory deprivation may result in visual hallucinations, warned the consent forms for this study. Hallucination: the perception of something that seems real but does not actually exist.

What might the opposite be called? The perception of something that actually does exist, but seems unreal?

At first, the images are vague.

Click.

Here, Dylan's head tilted back, both our mouths open wide in a moment of shared laughter. A happy scene, yes, but why so fuzzy?

Click.

In this one, a last-minute turn from the camera blurs the face. It's Dylan, of course, but you'd have to *know* that to know it.

Click.

Here a passing shadow obscures his eyes. It's like the best part of him is being hidden by a trick of the light.

Click.

Now the two of us sitting on a bench, legs intertwined, but

an aggressive flash obliterates Dylan's features. In each of the pictures, in each of the moments, my coy lover's face hides in oblique angles and shadowy blurs.

But as I float in my silent darkness the images eventually grow clear, and soon enough the truth becomes impossible to deny.

Deprived of distractions, I can't hide from it any longer. Here, now, I am naked and alone with the truth. I'm dripping in it, bathing in it. Hunted by it.

Cornered.

Here in the darkness, the truth takes on its true form: clawed and slavering. Red-eyed. Fanged. It's a fast and vicious predator, covered in matted, stinking fur.

Oh, Dylan.

At first I try to fight for him. Because why should it matter? I love him in all his forms. In every image. With long hair or short. Dark skin or light. Tall, short, somewhere in between, heavyset or slight, I love him in every configuration. I love each version of him. I love each version of us.

Click.

Here: a tattoo on his left shoulder, a scar on his abdomen.

Click.

There: smooth, perfect, unblemished skin. Those same locations now uninked and unscathed.

Click.

He's always been there exactly when I needed him most. He's always been exactly *who* I needed most.

So what do a few little discrepancies matter?

But truth is a hungry beast, and before long it tires of toying

233

with me and goes for my throat. I scream and thrash about in the water as I am bled dry.

As I weaken, the facts take on sound and form. Dylan's voice goes high, then low. His hands are smooth on Monday, rough on Wednesday. In one memory, his touch is firm and assured. In the next, it's nervous. Hesitant. His eyes are dark. His eyes turn light. Amber, blue, brown, then green. The rainbow effect of my Dylan's loving gaze.

Gradually his kaleidoscope face becomes clear. His *faces* become clear.

None of them are Dylan.

All of them are Dylan.

a prank on the skank in the tank

I scream until I choke, and I cry until my tears and the saltwater I'm immersed in mix together and I feel myself start to dissolve.

CHAPTER 38

When Lab Coat opens the tank, I have to shield my eyes from the light. He eases the hatch open slowly and gives me a few minutes to adjust to the glare of the real world before saying anything. He seems to realize that it's a difficult transition to make.

Or maybe he heard my agonized howls in the tank and now he's afraid of me.

Either way, I appreciate it. When I finally emerge from my dark steel cocoon, I feel shrunken and dehydrated, and my throat is scraped raw from the crying. I know I look like an animal being pulled from a cage, so I'm glad that he doesn't even ask if I'm okay, since it's pretty obvious that I'm not.

It's amazing what you notice when the noise gets stripped away.

Lab Coat guy, for instance. I see things about him I didn't before. Now I see the way he turns his face away respectfully as he hands me a towel, then a robe. When my eyes finally adjust to the light, I notice that he has nice teeth. I can tell that he's probably a decent person by the way he hands me an alcohol wipe to remove the residue from the electrode adhesive before I even have to ask, and then gently wishes me well. When he turns his head just so, his profile reminds me, just slightly, of someone I know and love.

Let's not say his name just now. It's all confusing enough as it is.

Now that everything has been stripped away, I can see that this is how it happens. This is how so many faces and bodies and names become Dylan to me.

Is it really such a bad thing to be able to recognize people's best parts? To find something to love in everyone I meet?

Because I'm aware of myself now, aware of the tricks my mind plays on me, I also notice when things start to go blurry around the edges. I force myself to read the name stitched on Lab Coat's breast pocket in navy thread. *Jacob.* I force myself to say it out loud. "Jacob." *Not* Dylan.

Because this is how it happens. This is how I fall in love.

If you squint hard enough and hold your hand up just so, you can block out anything you don't want to see—the past, the present, the future, or the changing color of your boyfriend's eyes.

Don't judge me. Just because Dylan doesn't exist doesn't make our breakup any easier.

It's worse, really. Because he's perfect. *Was* perfect. Whatever. Do you know how much it hurts to lose perfection? People toss out the phrase *soul mate* so much it's become a cliché. But Dylan was the real deal. Because he came from inside of me.

He *was* my soul.

Just try ripping your soul out of your body. That's how much it hurts.

Or if that's too melodramatic, then at least grant me this more pragmatic explanation: my breakup with Dylan is really a breakup with AidenEricEvanLukeConnorDougieJonathan OrionPaul. It's a dozen breakups, rolled into one. It's one breakup splintered into multiples.

It's pain multiplied by each new face.

The doctor gives you a sugar pill, and your headache is gone by dinner. The pill may be a sham, but the cure still counts, doesn't it? The relief is as real to you as the pain was.

So don't tell me it doesn't hurt. It was real in all the ways that count. Dylan: my perfect placebo boyfriend.

Lab Coat—does his name even matter?—walks me to the door, where Pinch Face hands me my money. They stand shoulder to shoulder like two bouncers holding back a crowd until I walk away. Bruised and mute, I stumble home. I must fade out a bit, my feet on autopilot, because no time at all seems to pass before I arrive at my door.

I remember too late that I've lost my keys, but Jameson appears out of the fog behind me almost immediately, bearing his own key. "Hey, Audie. You look like hell." He unlocks the door, holds it open for me, but does not come inside.

"Aren't you coming in?" I ask him from the doorway, and he gives me a funny look, then starts to walk away.

His clothes are clean again. So starched and pressed it almost looks like he's wearing a uniform.

He stops abruptly, looks left and right like he's making sure no one is watching, then comes back. "Hey," he says in a low voice. "Were you really serious about needing extra cash so bad? There's a study going on tomorrow. I'll be honest—it's a nasty one. Bottom-of-the-barrel stuff. But it pays well."

He's acting squirrelly, talking out of the corner of his mouth and keeping his body angled away from where I stand in the doorway. "But you have to swear you won't dime me out to Dr. O'Brien. He's already breathing down my neck, and I don't want to lose my job over this."

A dagger of pain and confusion twists in my head, and it's all I can do to stay on my feet. "Who *are* you?" is all I can manage to say.

Jameson tilts his head and studies me. "Audie? Are you slipping on me again, girl? Because you know I'm the last one on earth who wants to get O'Brien involved, but I will if I have to. I'm not going to be a part of you going down this road again."

I'm not so confused that I've lost my survival instincts. I force my mouth into the shape of a grin, reminding my eyes to play along. "No, I'm fine. I'm just messing with you."

He frowns at me. Scans me again with narrowed eyes. *Judging, judging.* "Okay, if you say so," he finally says. "I'm off tomorrow, so meet me in the back parking lot at 10:30. Think you can behave long enough not to lose day-pass privileges before then?"

I give him my best annoyed-teenager eye roll, which seems to convince him I'm normal enough to leave unattended.

"Okay. Just don't let anyone see you get in my car. I'll get shit-canned for sure if anyone sees me with a patient on a day I'm not even scheduled to work."

His words are like little electric currents cauterizing parts of my brain, obliterating whatever used to make sense. I just nod, too unsure of what's going on to speak.

CHAPTER 39

May I tell you a story?

It won't take long, I promise. Mostly because the details keep shifting. Little earthquakes keep rattling my thoughts and shaking the words around.

Have a seat. Yes, right here. Right next to me on this twin-sized bed. The one with the institutional linens and rounded edges and complete absence of exposed screws. It's a remarkably *safe* bed, don't you think?

Did you know there are companies that specialize in making furniture specifically for crazy people? I mean, think about it: they can't just build a plain old chair that looks and functions like a chair, and then call it a day. No, they have to consider some very un-chairlike things when they design their furniture.

Things like the effects of bodily fluids and psychotic rages and creative suicidal tendencies. Things that tend to be tough on furniture. Also, potential lethal uses of screws and hinges and knobs. It's amazing just how many things can be dangerous in the wrong person's hands.

Yes, that is very interesting. It's also a good segue into the story. Shall I begin?

Okay.

Once upon a time, there was a young girl who was batshit crazy. She was stupid, too. Very, very stupid.

She might have been pretty, were it not for the scars.

She might have been smart, were it not for the pills.

Anyway, our stupid, ugly girl was very lonely, as stupid and ugly people often are, so one day she set out in search of companionship. Having little to lose, she decided that she would do anything, anything at all, to find her one true love.

She would go to the end of the world, if need be.

She was unsuccessful, of course—that much goes without saying. How many crazy, stupid, ugly people do you know in happy relationships?

But she wanted this one thing so very, very much that the crazy part of her mind took over, and she managed to fool herself into believing that she *had* succeeded in finding happiness and love. She tossed in some friends and lots of money, too, because, why not? If it's all imaginary, you might as well go all out.

Just think of it as a form of mental alchemy: where you or I might see shit, she saw gold.

For quite some time she was a very happy crazy girl, since, in her mind at least, she had everything she had ever wanted. She even started to look prettier, or at least less ugly, on account of that special glow that true love brings.

Perhaps she wasn't so crazy after all.

But, alas. Crazy or not, her happiness was not meant to be.

One day, an evil wizard came along and decided to test the strength of his magic against the strength of the girl's crazy. He spent a long time studying her crazy lies and her stupid mind tricks, and he spent many nights stroking his pointy white beard, pondering. Pondering and stroking. Stroking and pondering. Finally, after all this time studying and stroking and pondering, he developed a potion that he was certain would defeat the demons in her mind, and he used his powers of enchantment to make her drink it.

Wait—where do you think you're going?

I don't care if you don't like fairy tales. Sit your ass down, shut the fuck up, and listen.

Besides, the door is locked from the outside.

Did you happen to notice these subtle little slots on the side of the bedframe? They're designed to accommodate restraints. Isn't that clever? Sometimes a bed isn't just a bed. Now, where was I?

Oh yes.

The potion was very powerful, and the wizard watched proudly as it did its work—as everything in the poor girl that was crazy and happy vanished in a puff of smoke.

In no time at all, our newly lucid girl was once again alone and miserable, once again surrounded by shit instead of gold. Worse still, she was now fully aware that true love did not, in fact, exist. The wizard declared her cured; his experiment, he decided, was a smashing success.

But.

Of course there's a but. What kind of story would this be without one?

But, unbeknownst to the wizard, there was still a tiny little glimmer of crazy deep within our girl. It was on account of her stupidity, actually. She was so stupid that while she was taking the potion, she became distracted and accidentally spilled a few drops. Embarrassed by her clumsiness, she mopped up the spilled liquid with a handkerchief and hid the evidence under her mattress so that no one would be the wiser. And since the wizard had given her only just enough to do the job—he hadn't wanted to kill her by mistake—that last, hidden ember of crazy remained aglow.

And because she now *really* had nothing left to lose, the girl decided to use that last tiny spark to do something *truly* crazy. So in her darkest hour, in the depths of mourning for a life that never was, she began to transform herself into something altogether different. In one final hurrah of insanity, she turned herself into a giant snake.

If she couldn't be happy, then perhaps she could be fearsome.

If she had to be lonely, then at least she could be strong.

The wizard, of course, was terribly disappointed. In a fit of rage he sealed her into her chambers, bricking over the door and windows so that his failure would never be known to the outside world.

Locked away from any source of comfort, the girl who was now a snake quickly began to starve. And because she was crazy, and because she was hungry, our stupid girl who was now a snake decided to nibble on her own tail, just to see if it might satisfy her, even for a moment.

Surprisingly, it did.

So because she was crazy and stupid and hungry, she bit down again and again, barely even noticing that she was destroying herself in the process. That's how great her hunger was. How empty she felt.

Her snake body coiled into a giant, infinite loop, her head consuming her tail, and her tail nourishing her head, until finally, she was happy once again. And perhaps not quite so stupid after all, because she no longer felt alone, though, technically of course, she was.

She had found the solution, don't you see? She had to consume herself in order to survive. It was all within her; it was all within her control: love, power, sustenance, *will*.

Because she was both the source and the outcome.

The cause and the cure.

Don't bother with that button on the wall. It hasn't worked for ages. A vicious cycle? Really? That's how you interpret the ending of the story?

Not me. No, definitely not. I mean, can you even think of a more literal act of self-sufficiency than that? I think she was her own hero. She saved herself, don't you see? She took control of her life and her death.

And every story needs a hero.

CHAPTER 40

All those *I woke up in someone else's body* stories I've read or watched over the years, and not one of them does fuck-all to help me now.

I don't care if it's Kafka or yet another *Freaky Friday* remake—they all use pretty much the same basic formula, amiright? Person wakes up, checks their shit out in the mirror, and is all *ohmygawd, holy shit, wtf* for a while. Then, later on, they get used to their new body and play around and have fun with it for a while, like, *look at me, I'm a big hairy cockroach climbing up the walls, wheee!* Little girls check out their new grown-up boobs, little boys have fun learning to shave their overnight-adult faces, whatever.

You can practically hear the fledgling screenwriters pitching their film agents on their latest version, their spin on a spin on a spin that's been done a hundred times: *Who hasn't occasionally wanted to wake up as someone else?*

I've certainly wanted to wake up as someone else. Of course

I have. But the whole goddamn *point* of that fantasy is to wake up in someone else's body, with someone else's life. Instead, I wake up with the same shitty life, the same scar-blasted, toxic waste dump of a body, and someone else's memories layered on top of mine. I'm me, but not me. I'm doubled down—all of my problems and hang-ups and deficiencies multiplied by Fact and by Fiction. I'm someone's sick-joke version of "cured"; I'm me to the power of fucked.

I'm not seeing the potential for slapstick antics here.

I think the film rights to this one will remain safely mine.

Sunlight filtering in through safety glass and the sound of a lunatic gargling somewhere down the hall jolt me out of the stupor that has replaced sleep, but I don't get up just yet. There are too many cobwebs and fissures still crisscrossing my thoughts to be able to face the day. So I lie in my bed, which isn't really my bed, and untwist the snarled braid I seem to have woven from the details of my life.

Fact: my name. Several people confirmed it last night, including one of the many nurses who fade in and out of my field of vision like pill-pushing ghosts, and Jameson, whose clothing I now realize matches the uniforms worn by several other key-ring-wielding men I've seen wandering around—men who fall below the nurses in the pecking order, but above the cleaning staff. Orderlies, maybe, though do they still use that word? It sounds too old-timey, so I'm sure it's been replaced by something stiff and modern and ridiculous: Psychiatric Sanitation Engineer, or Certified Cranial Technician.

The nurses are familiar, too; I've seen them all before. But back on the flip side of this little breakdown, this total mental meltdown of mine, they were lab administrators and research assistants.

Here on this side they don't ask for my consent. Here, I'm supposed to hand over my veins and swallow their pills for free. Here, they think *they're* in charge.

And yet, here's another fact: there *is* money under my mattress. (Un)grand tally: two hundred and thirty-one dollars. Hardly enough for the trip of a lifetime. Does Castillo Finisterre even exist? Add that one to the mountain of questions already towering over me.

Also under the mattress: hundreds of other pieces of paper, all folded with maniacal precision into rectangles the size of dollar bills. Sad, crazy counterfeits that make my today-face burn with shame. The pathetic currency of my delusional mind. But this discovery is almost comical considering what's *also* under the mattress: a shitload of pills. They're faded and crusty, like they were held in someone's mouth just long enough to start to dissolve.

Someone's mouth. How delightfully passive of me, no? Just thinking about it, I can feel the sensation of a smoothly coated capsule rolling under my tongue. I taste the memory of that first bitter release of what's inside, and I reflexively start to push the taste out of my mouth. *My* mouth.

If there was ever a time not to be passive, it's now. So . . . Fact: those are clearly *my* pills, which I clearly spit out of *my* mouth. I have no conscious memory of doing so, just the muscle memories of ingrained habits. I don't know why I refused this hidden cache of medicines, but there must have been a good reason. Which brings up yet another question, this one with some urgency: Who can I trust? Doctors and nurses proffering questionable cures, or my (less than reliable) self?

Neither option holds much appeal.

I shove my hand under the mattress and pull out a handful of the folded pages, flicking away two crusty capsules that stick to my sleeve like burrs. My Madwoman's Monopoly Money mostly consists of tissues, random flyers, and articles torn from magazines. My fortune is a practical joke, played *on* me, *by* me. Perhaps there's comedic value to my story yet.

Nope. *Not funny, Audie. Not funny at all.*

Fortunately, among the useless trash are dozens of identical brochures bearing glossy and copyedited answers.

Because if it's in writing, it must be true. (And if you believe that, then have I got some great drugs to sell you!)

I unfold one of the pamphlets with shaking hands and read.

Facts, as spelled out in tactfully euphemistic jargon: "The Cedar Hill Center for Transitional Living provides residential psychiatric care for adults and adolescents with persistent mental illness. Various levels of intensity are offered in our apartment-style community, which is conveniently located on the grounds of a top-ranked, university-based hospital system, thereby ensuring that residents have access to state-of-the-art treatments and facilities."

Whoever designed the brochure chose a mint-green tree motif for the cover, which makes zero sense at all, since what the hell do trees have to do with crazy people? Personally, I would've gone for an ice-pick design. "Cedar Hill Psych Ward: Not just for lobotomies anymore."

Fact: I am crazy. Crazy crazy crazy crazy crazy. Insane in the membrane. Out to lunch. Cuckoo for Cocoa Puffs, wack job, nutso, loony tunes. Fucked in the head.

Sick.

Or so they say.

It takes a very long time before I can convince myself to get out of bed.

When I finally do, I'm relieved to find that my home today is much the same as it was yesterday. Yesterday, back when I was still . . . on the reality-is-optional channel, shall we say? Not that I'm not anymore, just, I don't know. Something has cracked. Something I took, something I stopped taking, something Dougie said, something I did, I don't know what, just *something* has changed and now I'm seeing certain things I didn't before. And not seeing certain other things that I used to see.

Eeny, meeny, miney, moe. Audie's mind catches up slow.

The truth has now achieved critical mass in my mind, and it's forcing out all the beautiful, happy stories. My fantasy world is a smoldering wasteland.

Fiction: Dylan, whispering (*lies*) in my ear. Arms around me, holding me, keeping me centered, his (*stranger's*) flesh on my flesh, keeping me (*in*)sane. His whispered (*lies*) promises, *we'll get through this together, baby.*

Liar, liar, brain's on fire.

I can't deal with this particular crack in my brain right now, so I seal it shut. It's a temporary fix at best, but it allows me to get up and stumble around my half-familiar world.

The apartment is almost the same as yesterday—same curtains, same toaster, same couch. It's just smaller than before; a twee miniaturization of a real apartment. Kitchen(ette). (Mini) fridge. A faux home—a dollhouse for the institutionalized set.

I think back to that day I woke up in the alley, the way everything looked huge for a few hours. Lilliputian effect, they called it. Today I'm experiencing the opposite. Today, my world has shrunk.

Reality: a most unwelcome side effect.

Different versions of events continue to unfold like origami. The Professor walked me home that day.

Zzzzzzzap.

No, Dr. O'Brien walked me home that day.

crazy stupid crazy stupid crazy stupid

second verse, same as the first, a little bit louder, a little bit worse

I stare at the door to Charlotte's room. She was real, I'm almost certain. My thoughts about her have more heft, somehow. But . . . is it possible that I imagined her death? Maybe it's just a part of this whole fucked-up, delusional whatever it is that's going on in my head. A fight between friends that my smoke-and-mirror brain morphed into a tragedy? For a second my heart races with hope that one thing, just this one thing, might actually turn out in my favor, and that Charlotte may actually be alive. But then I open the door. It's a vacant room, the mirror image of mine—utterly anonymous with its institutional, bolted-down furniture and paste-colored walls. Anyone could have lived here. No one could have lived here.

I close the door to the empty room and try to find solace in the fact that at least now I know what I don't know.

I fail to find solace in this fact.

It turns out that ignorance is *not,* in fact, bliss. Ignorance is a hole in the head and a knife through the heart. Ignorance is a terrifying void too quickly filled with Styrofoam facts and junk-food hopes.

Outside my apartment, which is not, of course, actually my apartment, the *same but different* trend continues. I explore the alternate universe of my shrunken world, walking through hallways that just yesterday were city-blocks long, down a stairway that used to be an alley, and across a small, grassy quad that used to be the neighborhood park. I keep my head down in order to avoid conversation with any of the quasi-familiar faces that drift by.

I'm not ready for any more reality at the moment. I'm already at a toxic saturation level; I'm *this* close to overdosing on the truth.

But I change my mind when I see Scratch sitting on a bench. He's revolting as ever, but he's also someone I know and remember—for some reason he seems to straddle the gap between my delusions and my reality. Plus, he might be able to help me sort out the whole Charlotte business, which is as confusing as ever.

Scratch. Good old Scratch.

Except it turns out that today's version of Scratch is not quite the same as the version in my recent memories.

How did I not see it before? Was I so fixated on his rashes and boils that I never even noticed his eyes—the way they're focused so intently on something just out of range of everyone else's vision? How did I miss the tics and twitches?

"Hey, Audie," he says as I sit down next to him. "How's Dylan?" His voice is sharp and mocking.

I jump up from the bench and stare at him. The scabby little fucker is grinning at me. A teasing, toying grin. So this is how it is? I'm a joke around here, laughed at even by the likes of this pus-pocked fool? I wonder if I'm at the bottom of some un-written psychiatric pecking order: a crazy person who doesn't know she's crazy.

Zzzzzzap.

Make that: a crazy person who *didn't* know. I walk away from Scratch as fast as I can without calling attention to myself, not feeling the least bit elevated by my newfound knowledge.

CHAPTER 41

Apparently, I fall into one of the more lenient of the "various levels of intensity" described in the Cedar Hill Center's brochure, because no one tries to stop me as I explore the facility further. Doors open freely, alarms fail to sound.

I start to feel like a character in a children's book: Audie goes in. Audie goes out. See Audie go upstairs? Go downstairs, Audie, go down!

I test my limits *here*. I test my limits *there*. I am (apparently) allowed to go damn near *anywhere*.

This seems like very bad judgment on their part.

How fucking crazy do you have to be before they actually lock you up?

Only once is my freedom challenged. Several steps out one set of doors that open to within sprinting distance of the outside world—an unfenced, unchained outside world, no less—a frizzy-haired nurse wearing mismatched pastel scrubs chases me down. I'm sure I've been caught and I'm about to be reeled back inside, but she only wants me to sign out if I'm planning to leave the grounds at any point. She tsk-tsks mildly and hands the clipboard back to me when she sees that I've signed as Charlotte.

It surprises me, too, that I did that. Habit, I guess.

Even with my freedom granted I don't roam far, and I don't attempt to leave the grounds just yet. A clock on the wall tells me I only have another hour to kill before meeting Jameson.

As I explore, I take note of the studious demedicalization of certain areas of the facility. Prefabricated tranquility abounds, from the carefully curated art studio (nary a decapitation or animate phallus depicted in any of the artwork hanging on the wall) to the obsessively weed-free community garden, and right down to the belligerently peaceful scent of the eucalyptus/lavender air freshener permeating the building like olfactory Haldol.

The pretense fades gradually toward the west, however—westward being the direction of the main hospital. The *real* hospital, that is. The one that doesn't pretend to be anything but a hospital. The hospital not suffering from delusions, one could argue. (Sense of humor: intact, but hanging on by a thread.)

I feel more comfortable in these westward, nondelusional corridors, with their wafts of unapologetically alcohol-swab-scented air and the percussive rattles of unmuffled metal trays against unmuted metal bed rails. I peek into one room and see a young doctor irrigating a wound—an angry, open slash across the bicep of an uncomplaining man with a matted beard—and the sight actually soothes me.

I guess I prefer the kind of treatment where the pain comes up front.

It's only when I follow a hedge-lined walkway to its end and enter the lobby of a separate building, shiny-new and clearly more modern than the others, that I encounter any real obstacles—this time in the form of a receptionist who intercepts me apologetically. She's as wide across as three of me standing side by side, but she's skittish as she blocks me, and when she speaks it's in that high-pitched, saccharine-sweet voice that people save for babies, old people, and imbeciles.

"Now, Audie," she coos. "I don't think you have an appointment with Dr. O'Brien today. If you need to speak with him, you'll probably be able to find him out wandering the halls, though. He has to be the most dedicated doctor I've ever worked with; we just love him around here. I'm sure you must know how lucky you are that he's taken such a shine to you."

I half expect her to reach out and pinch my cheeks, the way she's simpering at me.

I ignore her and peer over her shoulder. The smile fades a few degrees, replaced by a tiny, nervous laugh that makes her fleshy face jiggle slightly.

It's an impressive building. The lobby is a soaring atrium with huge glass panes angled in such a way that it almost feels like you're standing in the middle of a well-cut diamond. Deep-set, overcushioned chairs engulf slack-faced patients in this jewel of a waiting room, many of whom are accompanied by watchful attendants, and the amplified sound of an artificial waterfall flowing through the center of the room drowns out any possibility of meaningful conversation. The lobby is ringed by offices with closed wooden doors, each bearing the name of the doctor holding court inside. I can't be positive, since I'm standing too far away, but if I squint I think I can just make out Dr. O'Brien's name on the third door from the left.

The first thought that jumps to mind is that old saying about people who live in glass houses. "Shouldn't throw stones," I whisper, making the nervous receptionist jiggle and giggle even more.

Then, as I stand there, squinting against the almost intolerably sunny brightness of the atrium, another quote comes to mind—one that fits even better. The one the Professor—Dr. O'Brien—underlined in the copy of 1984 he left for me. *We shall meet in the place where there is no darkness.*

Something about making this connection makes me shiver violently, and I wrap my arms around myself to quell my shaking.

My sudden(ish) movement pushes the nervous receptionist too far, and she springs surprisingly fast back to her desk and picks up a phone. "Audie, dear, I'm just going to call someone to come get you. Is that okay? Hmmm, dear?" Her voice is still sugar-pitched, but her pink-painted fingernails drum a staccato beat on the desk as she waits for someone on the other end to pick up. "Just stay right where you are, okay, sweetie?"

I do as instructed. Now that she's moved out of my way, I can see one more door, this one different from the rest. This one is metal and secure—I see both a keypad and a card reader controlling access—and instead of a fancy brass nameplate, this one bears only a small institutional plaque. White letters on a dark-green background: LOCKED WARD.

There's no reason this should trigger anything at all in my head. I mean, the presence of a locked ward in a mental health facility is hardly surprising, but trigger something it does. One last quote—this one more clichéd, less literary, and straight out of Jameson's mouth.

"She's in a better place," he'd said of Charlotte.

At the same time, it occurs to me what Jameson has never said, not once: *Dead.*

The receptionist is still on the phone. She's huffing and puffing from being put on hold, as far as I can tell, and my presence has her skittish as a horse. I'm not interested in staying there any longer, though. I've seen enough.

I arrange my face into its most wholesome configuration— wide, smiling eyes, deferential tilt to the head—and reassure her in a voice almost as syrupy as her own. "Oh, I'm okay, really. I just got my appointment dates confused. I'm such a space cadet!"

She looks at me for a long moment, then replaces the receiver. "That's okay, honey. It's no problem at all," she says, but her hand stays close to the phone and her eyes follow me out the door.

CHAPTER 42

fact: a thing that is indisputably true
indisputable: impossible to question or doubt

It's a problematic definition, if you stop to think about it. I mean, how many things in life are truly impossible to question or doubt?

Your health? Your wealth? Your relationships? Your safety?

Your hairline, your waistline, your paycheck, your plans? I'll shut up about it now—you get the picture. The list is endless.

I, for one, am capable of questioning anything and everything.

Here is how I know I am not yet "well," by any stretch of the imagination: The whole time I'm walking around the hospital, I'm looking for Dylan. I can't help it—it's like a reflex. A habit. I'm a goddamn placebo junkie, addicted to the fake-out cure of my factless, delusional world.

Just close your eyes and click your heels together three times . . .

And now on top of all the rest of it, I'm also questioning everything I thought I knew about Charlotte. Is she really dead, my bright-light, hot-sauce, scheming-twirling-singing friend, or is she just locked away in the hospital equivalent of an attic somewhere?

But I entertain these questions without any real sense of hope. If she's locked away, there's a high likelihood that she's functionally, if not factually, dead. Charlotte would never consent to life in a cage.

But then again, nothing is truly indisputable.

It makes my head hurt just thinking about it. Or maybe my head was already hurting. Things are still a bit jumbled in the wasteland north of my shoulders.

I make my way to the back parking lot, still surprised not to be stopped or even questioned. Jameson is already there, waiting in his car—something shitty and dented and red. I use it as a test. *Have I ever ridden in this car with Jameson?* I ask the newly awakened part of my brain. *No,* says the less crazy part. It sounds reasonably confident.

"Have I ever driven anywhere with you?" I ask Jameson when I slide into the passenger seat.

"No," he says. "Can't say that I've had the pleasure."

Score one for a correct answer. I need to learn which sectors of my memories I can rely on, particularly before I start asking Jameson the important questions. I need to be able to judge whether he's lying to me.

He looks me over, head to toe, before he starts to drive. He nods, satisfied, like he knows exactly what he's looking at.

"Mm-hmm, I thought so. You're pulling out of it again. Good for you."

"How can you tell?" I ask him.

He grins. "Audie, I know you better than just about anyone. Definitely better than fucking Dr. O'Brien, that quack, knows you. Who do you think watches out for you when you're deep in it?"

"Deep in *what* exactly?" I'm hoping he has a word for it— something to call what I'm going through. Something to call what I *am*. I need an anchor.

He shakes his head. "Nuh-uh. You're not going to get me with that. Every new doc who comes through this place has a different diagnosis for you. Conveniently enough, it usually coincides with whatever drug their pharmaceutical sponsor of choice is hawking. But you're a bit of a moving target. There's no one obvious thing, like there is for most of the people here. But, hey, that's what makes you interesting, right?" He winks at me.

"What's wrong with Scratch?"

Jameson honks at someone who cuts him off, swearing softly. "Oh, he's a kick, isn't he? Morgellons. Delusional parasitosis. He thinks he's infested with alien fibers. Like, fully convinced of it. You wouldn't believe what that poor guy has done to try to get the imaginary critters out of his skin—the dude'll use anything he can get his hands on to pick, or scrape, or worse. Have you seen the scars on his back? He tried to burn the fibers out with acid. That particular stunt is what finally earned him his entrance ticket here."

"He did all that to himself?" My stomach turns just thinking of the peeling skin, the oozing sores, the pockmarks. The fact that it's self-mutilation just makes it all so much worse.

But then my mind zip-lines back to the magazine I found in Dr. O'Brien's briefcase—the piercing and stitching and impaling I saw in the photo spreads, and how much it upset me to be compared to the people who chose to do those things to their bodies—and all of a sudden I see it differently.

Now I see poor, altered souls in search of just the right adjustment. A prescription, a doctrine, a nose ring, a diploma, a plane ticket. We're *all* always a step or two away from being a finished product.

"Sure did. But his new meds are working pretty well, so he may get out soon. Hey . . ." Jameson turns and looks sharply at me. "Now that you're lucid again, or whatever you want to call it, you know you can't tell anyone that I talk to you about the other patients, right? I'm one more write-up away from a suspension as it is."

"I won't tell anyone," I say. Who would believe me, anyway? I sure as hell wouldn't. "Where are we going, incidentally?"

"We have a few stops to make before we get to the testing center."

It's a nonanswer, but I don't push for more. I don't really care where we're going, or how long it takes to get there—it's not as if I have anywhere better to be. I lean my seat back and stare at a star-shaped chip in the windshield. But then I sit up straight again, only to be practically garroted by the seat belt. My muscles twitch, fighting involuntarily against the familiar feeling of restraint.

"Wait a minute—you said the testing center. Are you telling me that testing is real? That's really how I make money? I mean, it's actually a thing, getting paid to take meds?" I had convinced myself that this was another Dylan. A distortion of reality designed to make my shitty life more palatable.

Jameson sighs. "I'm just going to write this down for you one of these days. Save me the trouble of having to explain it every time."

"Tell me again. Please."

So he explains. Again.

The guinea pig thing, bills for pills, is real. Sort of. It's another one of those facts-braided-with-lies things. Sometimes I get paid to take medicine. Sometimes I just think I do.

He laughs when he describes it. "Girl, you know I love you, but you can be a real pain in the ass sometimes when you don't want to take your meds. And just try to drag your ass into a treatment room when you don't want to go—you've given me more than one black eye." He turns and winks at me. "So, you can't really blame me if sometimes I let you believe you're getting paid for it. I mean, I don't out-and-out *lie* to you about it. You do all that yourself. But maybe I do encourage you a little more than I should. Like your fake blog thing. I like reading it, though. And you *are* a good writer."

I feel myself shrinking in the seat. "But sometimes I do get paid. Right? At least something?"

"Oh, sure. You all do it—I think the whole system would implode if you didn't, since the university would be shit out of luck for getting human subjects for their research. And no research results would mean no more corporate funding. No more corporate funding, no more fancy new hospital wings. So it doesn't really matter if O'Brien doesn't like it," Jameson says. "The hospital makes the rules, not him, and they sure as hell don't want to lose their handy-dandy stable of in-house volunteers. Plus, he can't really stop you unless he restricts you to the ward."

He honks as another car cuts him off, and then his voice turns catty. "And if he restricts you to the ward, your file automatically comes up before the quarterly review panel. He definitely doesn't want *that*. You want to talk about some seriously shady experimental methods . . ." He winks at me again, like I'm in on the joke. Which, of course, I'm not. "Anyway, since you're already right there on the hospital grounds, then it's easy enough for you to sign up for studies. And Lord knows, they're not picky about who they get. Case in point . . ." He puts the car in park and points at the line of people snaking around a building.

It's a thready, undisciplined queue—the type of line formed by people who *have* to wait, not by people who want to wait. There are four men to every woman, most of them hiding underneath pulled-up hoods or pulled-down hats. I'm not surprised in the least when I finally spot the sign and see that we're parked outside a methadone clinic.

"Here, help me out, would you? You start at the back of the line, I'll start from the front, and we'll meet in the middle." He shoves a handful of flyers at me. "Just make sure they understand they need to hand in this paper when they get to the testing center. Look, it's coded, see? Otherwise, we don't get our referral fee." He points to a tiny string of numbers printed at the bottom of every page.

On the flyers are short, simple words—an easy-reader message for the quasi-literate. More space is dedicated to the address and directions than the actual point of the flyers: New Drug Study Seeks Volunteers. "Cash Compensation" is advertised in bold colorful print—once at the top of the page, then again at the bottom.

It takes several more stops until I fully appreciate the scope of our task: we're passing out invitations to the world's least exclusive party.

Jameson's route takes us to all the wrong parts of town. Homeless shelters. The city bus terminal. A shabby medical clinic. It's a tour of the down-and-out; add in a mental institution and you'll have a royal flush.

Oh, wait . . .

We'll split the finder's fee seventy-five/twenty-five, Jameson tells me. The more people we get to sign up, the more money we get.

It's a good deal for them, Jameson tells me. They get the meds they need, plus more cash than they've seen in a long time.

We're doing a good thing, he says.

All the doctors do it, he says, even the ones who don't like to talk about it. "Just look at Dr. O'Brien. That smug bastard acts like he's above all this, but he's raking in the grant money left and right. Where do you think that comes from? Who do you think puts up the money for those big research projects? You think his regular salary bought him that shiny new Lexus?"

The pharmaceutical companies need to test their new

medications on *someone,* he says. And this is a big one. A big study. It could do a lot of good for a lot of people someday. There's only one way to know.

It makes my veins tingle, just listening to him. A buzzing sound low in my brain hums along with his words.

Our last stop, an underpass just outside the city center, is the worst of the bunch. It's the tail end of the tent city that meanders around the wrong side of the tracks—a post-apocalyptic stomping ground for people barely hanging on. We park next to a scrubby bush that's been decorated Christmas-tree-style with empty plastic bags and used condoms.

As we step out of the car, a bedraggled gray-haired woman shuffles up to us with a lopsided grin. The left side of her face droops uselessly as she greets Jameson.

"Mary!" Jameson calls out, like he's genuinely pleased to see her. "How're you doing? Up for another round? Same pay, as long as you've waited the thirty days." He winks at her when he says this—*has he always been such a big winker?*—and I get the impression that whatever rules govern this system are loose at best.

She grabs one of the flyers with a clawed hand and walks away. "Oh God. Jameson, look." My hand flies involuntarily up to my mouth. She's wearing only a bathrobe, and she's wearing it backward. It trails open behind her, revealing filthy bare skin and evidence that she's soiled herself, probably more than once. Slept in it, too, it looks like. "Oh God," I say again.

"I have a few blankets in my trunk," Jameson says to me, handing me the keys to his car. "I gave her some clothes last time, but what're you going to do? We can't force her in off the streets. She's been in and out of the system for years—she's a tough old bird. Talk about a survivor."

I run to his car, grab a stack of blankets, then hurry after Mary. She's easy to catch—she doesn't seem to move very quickly. Plus, she's only wearing one shoe—a man's boot. Her other foot is protected by a thick layering of dirty socks.

"Just one, honey. Weather's getting warmer. It'll be hot as fire soon enough, you'll see," she says to me with her slanted grin as she pulls a single blanket off the pile I offer her. "Keep the rest for yourself. Least I got me some padding—you're just skin and bones. Heat's coming, but that don't always stop the cold. I know you know what I mean."

She cackles softly, then spits, and when she turns and walks away from me I see the tattoos crawling up her back. Circles made from snakes, four of them, rising above the dried shit caking her skin. Four serpents destroying themselves atop her knobby, bruised spine.

They're the same tattoos I saw on Charlotte's back just before she died.

If, in fact, she died. Neither side of my brain feels certain about that yet.

"Mary?" I want to ask her about the snakes, but she waves me off without even turning around. She's muttering to herself about the weather, and she can't be bothered with the likes of me. "Hot as fire," she's saying again as she walks away. "I know you know."

CHAPTER 43

IN VALEDICTION

Well, hello there, faithful readers.

Or shall I address you simply as the voices in my head?

No, no, you're right. Let's not drop the charade just yet. It's a productive conversation, in any event, regardless of how you classify our relationship here.

If a blogger shits on the Web and nobody clicks on it . . . ?

Anyway. For today's topic, let's move outside ourselves for a moment. It's so easy to get focused on our own bottom line, on the *me, me, me* of it all, that sometimes we forget to examine the motives of people around us. People whose behavior and decisions may be controlling *our* behavior and decisions.

People who hold invisible keys.

When you don't even know you're locked in a cage, you don't realize how limited your options are. And then you just end up chasing your own tail.

Ha ha—see what I did there? Oh, sorry. Inside joke. I'll explain some other time.

Moving on.

Up until now we've been focused on the microeconomics of the testing world. *Who* will pay *how much* for *which* study. Oh, and how much each of those pills or procedures is going to hurt, of course. We've been distracted by all the talk about *this* scalpel, and *that* side effect. How am I going to feel *today*? Will I still have that rash *tomorrow*? *Which* of my friends will end up in a morgue, and *which* one will stick a knife in my back?

The shitty nitty-gritty.

Because that's all you can see when you're locked in a cage.

But when you get out of that cage, escape even for a moment, all of a sudden you see the big picture. The macroeconomics, you could say.

Do you remember anything from your econ class? If you even made it that far in school, obviously. Does GDP ring a bell? Gross domestic product? It's the total value of all the crap a country produces in a year.

Yeah, snoozefest, I know. But let's talk about the guinea pig version, which I think is a little more interesting:

Gross Domestic Pain (GDP): The total value of all the things you've ever taken. Pills and kicks and slaps. Insults you've sucked up, bullshit you've tolerated. Electrodes on your skull, a stranger's hands on you, in you, holding you down, holding you back. An experimental cough syrup. A prison sentence. A needle in your spine. The endless grief of everyday life.

Because, really, isn't it all the same?

Gross Domestic Pain: the value of everything you've ever absorbed.

So what?

What's the fucking point?

To be honest, chickadee(s), I'm not really sure. But I guess if I've learned anything, anything at all from this lab-rat life, it's the importance of control. The importance of taking all the crap life has thrown at you all these years, and turning it back on the crap flingers.

So use your GDP, my silent, invisible friends. Add up all the pain you've accrued over the course of your lifetime. And once you're sure there's enough—that is, once you're certain you've had enough—then cash out and spend it wisely.

And never look back.

CHAPTER 44

Once our stack of flyers is exhausted, we drive in Jameson's shitty, dented car to a shitty, dented strip mall in a shitty, dented part of town, where a testing center sits between two vacant storefronts. CLINIC says the sign masking-taped to the door.

This is not a place for healing, says everything in sight.

Jameson tucks his shirt into his pants before we walk in. Smooths his hair. Stands a little taller.

We go inside and he cuts through the crowded waiting room to an office door in the back. He knocks once, then opens the door without waiting for an answer.

I know without being told that I'm to wait out here, so I sit down in an empty chair in the back of the room. I can still hear him from here. He's talking in a different voice than he uses with me, a little deeper and maybe a little louder, and he's using words like *clinical assessment* and *population* and *inclusion criteria*. He doesn't do his throat-clearing thing, not even once, and he doesn't sound like an orderly anymore.

Here, he sounds like a guy with a well-tucked-in shirt who's read lots of medical journals. Here, he looks like a man who's in control of his life.

Naughty little schemer.

I can't see the person he's speaking to inside the office, but I can hear a woman's voice murmuring sounds of agreement and appreciation. It makes me feel better to know I'm not the only one who's been tricked into believing in a fictional version of Jameson.

He looks over his shoulder, then closes the door so I can't hear what's being said anymore. Denied, I focus instead on the people sitting around me in various states of quiet agitation. It's depressing as hell, the view from here, and I wish I had waited in the car.

This is not a smartphone-checking kind of crowd.

This is not a magazines-and-bottled-water type of waiting room.

These are not sick people in search of a cure.

All around me, I see my future. It's like a Benetton ad turned inside out in here—a grayscale cross-section of the indigent and the addicted. Labor-dirtied men whose spring-loaded postures and darting eyes telegraph their questionable immigration status sit next to pierced and green-haired teenagers carrying their world's worth of possessions in backpacks covered in Sharpie-drawn anarchy symbols. A woman with trembling hands sits next to a man with a trembling jaw.

The destitute. The down-and-out. This is a no-other-options kind of crowd—each and every one of us.

Because, let's be honest. I'm one of them, aren't I?

Like its occupants, the room itself is filthy, the patchy carpet tarred over with a decade's worth of grime, the walls covered with scuffs and smears and graffiti. An overflowing trash can sits on its side in the corner.

Back at the hospital, there is at least the comfort of procedure and the pretense of a cure. There is protocol. Basic sanitation, at a minimum. Even when they're torturing you—tearing your flesh, or scrambling your brain—at least they practice good hygiene while they do it. They steal your thoughts in sterile conditions. They document your screams in triplicate.

Not here. This is a place where hopes curdle and options wither. This is the clinic at the end of the world.

Have I been here before?

I double over, head on my knees, trying to stop the panic that's fluttering and expanding inside my chest like a trap-frenzied bird. I try to slow my breathing, but I can hear the animal sounds of my panting and I know I'm already too far gone.

Have I been here before?

"Jameson!" His name tears out of my throat in a shrieky roar. Downturned faces swivel up in concern, and even in my panic it's not lost on me that *I* am the spectacle in this roomful of castoffs. *I* am the down-est and the out-est.

I am the crazy one.

Jameson comes running and now he's an orderly again, whisking me up and out by my arm, gripping hard enough that I know it's going to leave a bruise. By the apologies he offers over his shoulder as he steers me through the door, it's clear he's more embarrassed than concerned.

"Audie, what the fuck?" he asks once we're back in his car. "I was in the middle of a business conversation in there." His voice is whiny, like a child who wants what he can't have.

"What the hell is that place?"

He sighs. "It's called a CRO. A contract research organization."

He tries to stop there, as if that answered anything at all, but he sees me glaring at him and heaves another big sigh, like I'm torturing the answer out of him.

"It's capitalism. That's what it is." He puts a hand up in the air. "I know, I know—don't look at me like that. It's fucking disgusting in there. They run clinical trials for whoever's willing to pay for it. Some of the big pharmaceutical and biotech companies like to outsource the grunt work, so they pay places like this to do it for them."

"They do medical research in that dump? I felt like I was about to audition for a goddamn snuff film in there. Incidentally, can we get out of here? This place gives me the creeps."

Jameson tells me I'm being melodramatic, then puts the car in reverse. Halfway out of the parking space, he slams on the brakes. "Damn it!" he swears, and jumps out of the car. "I didn't hit you, did I?" I hear him asking the person standing behind his car.

I climb out, too, just in time to see the look of unhappy recognition flit across Jameson's face. The dark-haired young man staring at the bumper that's stopped a centimeter from his kneecaps, on the other hand, shows no sign that he's even registered our presence. "Oh, hello there," Jameson says. "Uh, how are things going? Well, I hope? I thought you were long gone by now." He's trying to use the formal, tucked-in-shirt voice he'd been using inside, but I can hear his nervous stammer jitterbugging underneath his words.

The man hitches one bony shoulder up in response, a vague semblance of a shrug, but keeps his eyes on the car's bumper. I have to fight the urge not to reach out and rip off the grimy hospital bracelet I see looped around his wrist; it looks like it's been there a very long time.

Jameson lets out a phony laugh sound and gestures over to the guy, who shows no signs of moving. "This is the hardest-working guy I've ever met," he says to me in a loud voice. He turns back to the man with an overbright smile. "You're saving up for your wedding or something back home, isn't that right? Or was it law school? I remember it was something important."

The young man turns his glassy, unfocused eyes to Jameson, but still doesn't answer.

Heh heh. Jameson's nervous throat-clearing habit comes back before he can fill the awkward silence. "See, I told you this was a good gig," he says to me. "Guys like this come over here for a month or two and make ten times what they can in a year back home. Free medical care, too. Right?" he prompts the man, who does not look like he's been on the receiving end of anything remotely resembling proper medical care.

Finally, the guy seems to hear what Jameson's saying, and a huge grin splits his face. "Ka-ching," I think he says, though his accent makes it hard to be sure. "I got one. A side effect—one of the big, good-bad ones. I just gotta check for my check, see if it's here yet, then I'll go home." This seems to amuse him, and the smile across his face goes even bigger. "Check for my check for my check," he says, then giggles in a high-pitched voice.

"Ka-ching," he sings out one more time, and then turns around to resume his shuffling, crooked path across the parking lot toward the clinic.

"Holy fuck, Jameson" is all I can think to say as we slide back into his car.

He shakes his head to stop me from saying anything else. "They're not all like that. That guy . . . this study is . . ." He sounds rattled. "This study is more concerned with maximizing profit than most of the others I've worked with. The lower the overhead costs, the more money they get to keep at the end of the trial period, so some places cut corners anywhere they can. The testing you've been doing has all been at a university hospital. It's just a totally different business model."

I try to ask him in the nicest possible way how a loony-bin orderly got so involved with whatever it is he's talking about, but it doesn't come out as tactfully as I hoped, and Jameson clamps his mouth shut and sulks in silence for almost the entire car ride back home.

Back to the hospital, I mean.

To the Cedar Fucking Hill Center for the Reality-Challenged.

A few blocks out, though, he finally answers. "I help out with the recruiting. They need bodies through the door, as many as they can get. They have a tight deadline, and they get a bonus if they meet it. It's big money, Audie. For them, for me, and for *you* if you'll help me." He gives me a pointed look. "And for the volunteers, too. Most of whom, I should add, wouldn't be getting any medical treatment at all if it weren't for this study. So it's not as bad as it looks, I swear." He sounds like he's trying to convince himself.

Dirty rotten liar.

"I can't get caught recruiting anyone from Cedar Hill. I told you, O'Brien's been breathing down my neck. But *you* can talk to people there. Spread the word. I'll even go up to a sixty-forty split for anyone you recruit."

"What are they testing?" I don't look at him when I ask. I don't want him to know what I'm thinking. Which dots I'm connecting.

He perks up a little. "Long-acting antipsychotics. It's pretty cool, actually. You take a bunch of people like the ones we saw today, it's obvious they're never going to comply with regular treatment, which basically consists of shoving jarfuls of pills with unpleasant side effects down their throats. We send people like that out in the world with a handful of prescriptions they're never going to fill, and then we wonder why so many mentally ill people are homeless or in prison."

He's animated now, the sulking already forgotten. It actually makes him happy, talking about this stuff. I think about all the times I've seen him playing armchair doctor, reading medical journals he probably swiped out of the offices of the real doctors. This is who Jameson wants to be—a scientist, or a businessman, or some twisted hybrid of the two, instead of a lowly peon in a nuthouse, a half step up in rank from janitor.

We all have our fantasy lives, don't we? There's a fine line between delusional and ambitious, it occurs to me. We're all just hoping for a better reality.

He's still going on about the trials. "If this stuff works, it could really make a difference. Get this—instead of pills, it's an injectable, which gets rid of the whole compliance problem. It goes right in the spine, and lasts for months. They already know the stuff works; now they're just focusing on administration issues, trying to figure out if placement or frequency changes the outcome."

I go cold when he says this. "Spinal injections, hmm? Let me guess: they make a little tattoo at the injection site?"

Jameson nods, too busy accelerating through a yellow light to notice my reaction. "Yeah, they rotate the injection location, so the tats are to make sure they don't accidentally repeat the same location."

I picture Charlotte's back.

I picture Mary's back.

My lips feel numb and my spine tingles in the most literal way—like someone is brushing against it with the tip of a needle. It's funny how sometimes your body remembers things your mind doesn't.

Or perhaps I just have an overactive imagination.

I know without him saying so that some sick bastard in that fly-by-night craphole of a clinic likes to get creative with their markings. Why ink up your nut-job test subjects with a boring old X-marks-the-spot when you could have fun? With little snakes eating their own tails, perhaps?

"Jameson, did you send Charlotte there? Is that what happened—you sold her out, and something went wrong?"

His hands go tight on the steering wheel, and he doesn't answer.

But his silence *is* an answer. "Is that why she had all that cash? Was that some kind of giant payday for both of you?"

He pulls into the hospital parking lot too fast, car tires squealing, and then brakes hard enough that I slam forward against my seat belt. It locks into place and restrains me, just as it's supposed to do. Just as he's supposed to do.

It's for my own good.

" 'She's in a better place.' Isn't that what you said? And where exactly is that better place, Jameson? Did you fucking kill Charlotte?" I'm getting louder with every word. Shriller. Angrier. "Or did you just turn her into a vegetable with your little not-such-a-fucking-miracle cure?" I need to be calmer than this; I need to be more lucid than this when I ask him these questions. This is too important for crazy, I know it is, but I can't seem to control what's coming out anymore.

"How much did they pay you for her? How much was Charlotte worth?" I scream. "A new pair of shoes, maybe? A set of tires for this shitty car? I hope they're really great fucking tires, Jameson!"

He reaches over me and flings open my door. His mouth is clamped shut—he's done talking.

He looks around. To make sure no one else heard me? Or maybe for help.

My head is buzzing again, and I know that I've just spoiled everything. My anger sounds like a hive of bees inside my skull.

Orderly-quick, Jameson hops out and comes around to my

side, scoops me out, and hustles me away from his car before I even realize what he's doing. "This was a mistake," he says. "You're still fucking crazy. Go check yourself back in. Do it now, and I won't report this to O'Brien."

He gets in his car, watches me with his doors locked and windows up.

We stay like this, staring at each other, for another minute, then he roars out of the lot, his tires nearly rolling over my foot.

"*Still* crazy?" I call out after his car. The braying sound of my laughter surprises me—it's not because anything is funny, but because my brain is spinning with the ticklish, kaleidoscope feeling of déjà vu. "Oh no, my friend. I'm just getting started!" It doesn't even make sense, really, but I don't care. It feels good to say it, like a satisfying line straight out of the end of some cheesy action movie.

It sounds like something that you say just before you take back control. It sounds like a decision.

I say it again, louder, grinning at the way it makes a group of women walking back to their car stare at me like I'm insane. Because that's kind of the whole fucking point, right?

TransiGatory

Dr. O'Brien does not like it when I challenge him. Oh no sirree.
He does not like it one little bit. Nor does he approve of my extra-
curricular activities.

"Audie, when it comes down to it, you are a minor, and you've
been placed under my medical guardianship. So when I discover
that you haven't been complying with treatment, then I have an
obligation to take certain steps that are in your best interest. I'm
just sorry we've come to this point again. You were doing so well."

He sounds so sure of himself when he talks like this. He thinks
he's safe, hiding behind his medical-legal jargon and his mountain
range of a desk, with all those snowy paperwork peaks.

But I know his secrets.

The snakes are talking to me again, telling me things I can
use against him. Even now they're twisting and shining atop his
fancy silver pen, only he's too fucking blind to see it. Is it one snake
with two heads? Or is it two snakes conjoined? It doesn't matter.
One is clearly stronger than the other. I smile as it begins to eat its
twin—I do so admire a strong survival instinct.

You get hungry enough, eventually you're willing to do what-
ever it takes to save yourself.

I turn my snake-charmer smile on the doctor.

"And do you also have an obligation *to take money for force-*
feeding me all those pills? Are you also obligated *to keep the bonus*
you get for hooking me up to your machines?"

His hand freezes in his beard, midstroke.

He doesn't take many notes anymore. Hasn't for days and
days. Instead, he just taps his pen on my stagnant file.

tap tap tap tap

The silver caduceus atop the pen catches the light. It's such an
appropriate symbol for doctors, don't you think? It's from Greek
mythology—from the staff carried by Hermes. Hermes, the god of
thieves and commerce.

Oh yes, I've done my homework. This is one test I'm deter-
mined to pass.

tap tap tap tap

"I've been perfectly clear all along that you're part of an ex-
perimental protocol, Audie. Yes, my study is being funded, in
part, by grants from the pharmaceutical industry, but in no way
does that influence my clinical judgment."

He flinches when I hiss at him.

I've grown much stronger lately. I'm getting stronger every day.

"Your tan is fading," I tell him. "Remind me—where was this
year's conference? Hawaii? How nice that they paid your way.
And a little bird told me you were even the keynote speaker. How
much do they pay keynote speakers at medical conferences in lux-
ury hotels in Hawaii these days?"

I wink at the dominant snake atop Dr. O'Brien's pen. You could almost forget the weaker twin was ever there in the first place.

Dr. O'Brien sighs and closes my file, sets the pen on top of it. He's conceding his defeat: he has nothing left to write. "Audie," he says after a long silence. "Your mind is tricking you right now, offering you false solutions. Is there any part of you that can understand that?"

"I promise you that my solution is a hell of a lot better than what you're peddling, doc." I say it gently, since I've obviously already won the battle. No sense being a poor sport.

He just nods slowly and sort of wilts into his chair. Even his beard looks limp and defeated.

It's survival of the fittest. I am the dominant snake in the room now. I am consuming him, consuming his research, consuming his career.

I control the cycle.

He is so cowed that he doesn't even notice when I slide his pen into my pocket as I stand up and walk out of the office. Outside, in the hallway, I celebrate my victory with my hand wrapped around my prize, glorying in the heavy silver sharpness now in my palm. It's beautiful and dangerous, and I very much want to keep it.

I toss it into a trash bin as I leave the building, just to prove to myself that I can.

CHAPTER 45

I'm catching up on some reading when Jameson comes in a few hours later full of bullshit excuses. "I forgot my lucky sweatshirt," I hear him say to the nurses in the little office where they congregate, isolating themselves from the "residents" (ha) in their care [avoidant personality disorder, diagnostic code 301.82]. "It's a game night, so I have to have it. You know how it is."

They accept his ridiculous explanation [ritualized behavior indicative of obsessive-compulsive personality disorder, diagnostic code 301.4] without comment. He's just an orderly (excuse me, a psychiatric technician) here—almost as invisible to them as I am.

I'm sitting in the common area, a sad little lounge where crazy people can blend into ugly upholstery as they ignore one another. It's the same place where I remember a party happening. The guinea pig blowout where I last saw Charlotte.

The strong stench of urine bridges both versions of the room.

The befores and afters are clicking into place, though

sometimes they hop around and switch positions on me mid-thought. Often the facts and the faces are exactly the same. The only thing that changes is my interpretation.

Before: Party!

Now: Purgatory. A place where the already dead wait for whatever comes next.

Ain't reality grand?

Jameson walks up behind me and drops down to one knee, sneaky casual, acting like he's just stopping to tie his shoe. I don't turn around, not even when he does his little throat-clearing thing extra loud [persistent vocal tic disorder, diagnostic code 307.22]. "I'm sorry I freaked out on you, Audie. I think of you as a friend, and sometimes I forget that you're . . ."

I fill in some possible words for him. I hold up the heavy diagnostic manual I've been reading, show him that he's not the only one who can swipe things from doctors' offices.

It's actually sort of fun to flip through the pages and pick out labels for people. If you get to know someone well enough, I guarantee you can find a diagnosis or ten for them in here. Everyone's got at least a little crazy going on just below the surface.

"No." He shakes his head. "I was just going to say that sometimes I forget how sick you are. I shouldn't have brought you today. It was unprofessional."

He hangs his head, puts on his best shame-faced expression. He knows what it looked like over there, he says. But it's really not that much different from what the doctors are doing here. "It's just the way the system works." He shrugs and makes his eyes go round and blameless.

He doesn't want to leave me with the wrong impression, he

says. He has big plans. He's going to open up his own CRO, do things the right way. "You don't have to have a degree or anything. Only a doctor's name somewhere on the letterhead, someone willing to act as a silent partner. It's just a matter of running a good business," he says. He's going to run studies the right way, he says. Maybe I can work for him (awkward pause, foot shuffle). When I get out.

Now look who's delusional [diagnostic code 297.1].

As if this were only some sort of temporary psychosis [diagnostic code 298.8].

What's that old saying we were talking about earlier? Sometimes paranoia [former diagnostic code 295.30; current manual no longer distinguishes a paranoid subtype of schizophrenia] is just having all the facts.

"Funny thing," I tell him. "There's no diagnostic code for a compulsive liar. Why do you think that is, Jameson?"

He doesn't answer. Shocker.

"Maybe because you'd all have to diagnose each other. Every single person working here who's making a living putting poison in my veins."

His skin flushes pink, and he stands up and stops pretending to tie his shoe. "You've gone off your meds again, Audie. Haven't you?" He shakes his head, tries on a few different expressions, and settles on sad. "I hate that it has to be this way," he says, and then turns and walks away.

I start to laugh. "Oh, don't be like that. I'm just messing with you, Jameson. Come back."

He doesn't.

CHAPTER 46

The nurse brings a paper cup of pills to my room as I'm getting ready for bed. I thank her automatically, like she just delivered late-night pizza, double-pepperoni mushroom, instead of a cup full of poison.

Because, what was Jameson *really* doing here?

Lucky sweatshirt, my ass.

I can't take the chance that his off-schedule visit, his casual swing through the nurses' station, was a coincidence. I can close my eyes and picture it: him floating past the nurses who ignore him anyway, leaning in to spike my nightly dose with something a little stronger. Something a little more deadly, perhaps.

I've seen him with the books. I know about his special interest in certain controversial pharmaceuticals. I know about his secret stash.

I know quite a few things about him, really. Things he probably wishes I didn't know.

I stare at the pills, poke through them with my index finger.

How many *should* there be? In which sizes and colors? My memories aren't clear enough to answer these questions.

I have no way of knowing whether these pills are the cause or the cure.

Taking them would be an act of faith.

Not taking them would be a very different act of faith.

Who to believe? Who to choose?

The longer I stare at the pills, the more the lines between everything blur together. I'm afraid to blink, afraid everything around me will blend together into a gooey mess, the way my memories do. I swat away the buzzing sound in and around my thoughts to give myself a second to figure this one out. I've been down this road before; I've raced this same track a time or two. Surely I've learned from my mistakes.

Through it all, the buzzing and the blurring, only one thing remains clear: how very, very alone I am in all of this. Without Dylan, without the people I thought of as my friends, my life is a permanent experiment on the long-term effects of total isolation. I might as well be still locked in the sensory deprivation tank.

Or maybe I'm not quite as alone as I think, because when I close my eyes I can hear Charlotte's voice singing. *Oh, which came first, the crazy or the pill . . .*

I stand up. I've made a decision.

I race out of my room. This is no time to be selfish. As I run, my progress down the long hallway is marked in units of Plexiglas-framed motivational posters bearing aggressively capitalized advice:

COMMIT TO YOUR CHOSEN PATH

EVERY ACCOMPLISHMENT STARTS WITH THE DECISION TO TRY

BE THE BEST VERSION OF YOU THAT YOU CAN POSSIBLY BE

WE DO NOT REMEMBER DAYS; WE REMEMBER MOMENTS

COURAGE IS A CHOICE

It's a long fucking hallway. It's a lot of fucking advice.

Here's my advice—capitalize it however you'd like: Don't mistake consent for surrender.

I burst through closed doors into other rooms at random, slapping pill cups out of hands, sticking my fingers in people's mouths if I have to, ignoring their protests as I fish out the toxins. Because how would Jameson have known which medicine cup was mine?

If he wanted to be sure, he would have spiked them all with his poison.

That's what I would've done.

I'm on a roll. I run down the hall, screaming my warnings. I feel powerful and unafraid, because now I finally understand: I am the hero of this story. I can save us all—myself and all these other poor, gullible bastards locked in here with invisible keys. I smash and I grab at anything dangerous. Even if Jameson didn't do anything to our medicine, the pills are killing us just the same, with their broken promises and profit margins and bogus hopes. They're false idols in capsule form; they're sugar mixed with cyanide. They've turned us all into addicts and zombies—we're broken-down junkies, drooling and shuffling our way through the years, waiting for something outside of us to change what's wrong inside.

But not anymore.

I am finally in control.

I ignore the footsteps and shouts behind me; I ignore everything until I hear the sound of Dr. O'Brien barking out commands, and then I know it's too late to save myself, so I go even further. I *will* be the hero of this story, even if it kills me. I shove the pills I've collected into my mouth and swallow until I choke. My pills, everyone else's pills, the nurses' pills, tucked discreetly away into purses and taken when no one is looking. The pills under my bed, the pills in Jameson's secret stockpile in the back of the supply closet. I swallow them all, and by the time anyone catches up to me, before they can restrain me, hook me up to their machines, plunge their needles into my veins, it's too late for them to change what I've done.

I am the Ouroboros, choosing my own fate. This may look like an act of self-destruction, but it's not. It's an act of salvation. Of self-preservation. No one else will ever nourish themselves from my body again.

I stop as the blur of white coats descends—a feathered flock closing ranks, wings flapping around me until I am overcome. I feel a prick, and then the sting of snake oil coursing through my veins, and the words of one last motivational poster start to dance and blur overhead: It Is Never Too Late to Be What You Might Have Been.

I am the warning label. I am the list of side effects. I am the guinea pig; I am the safety net.

I am the probable outcome. I am the cure.

I am in control.

I close my eyes against the bright lights and the faces, and soon enough the hissing of the snake becomes the gentle shush of icy ocean waves as I drift off to sleep dreaming about a castle at the end of the world.

CHAPTER 47

"Really? Audie, are you serious? Are you completely serious?"

The look on Dylan's face is priceless—this is all turning out even better than I'd imagined.

He's so handsome, but the last few weeks have been hard on him. Really hard. You almost wouldn't recognize him, the way his cheekbones stand out now and the way his eyes almost look like they've changed color. They're darker now, a stormy shade that's hard to pin down. It's because of the pain, I think. It can change a person, it really can.

Trust me, I'd know.

It makes me so happy to do this for him, after all he's been through. After all he's done for me.

I tell him all about the trip. "I'm taking care of every detail," I say. "No luxury spared." I tell him all about Castillo Finisterre, since his memory isn't what it used to be and he doesn't quite remember seeing it that night on TV—the spa, the guided kayak tours through meandering glaciers, the unbelievable views. "I mean, it's the end of the freaking world. How amazing is that?"

Nothing compares to the look on his face. The way he's looking at me right now, almost overwhelmed with happiness and surprise. Nothing beats feeling *loved* like this. Good and fully and finally fucking loved.

I wouldn't trade it for anything.

Moments like this make me feel sorry for those poor fools who get so caught up in the day-to-day bullshit that they never take the time to unplug and just *escape* now and then.

The sad thing is, most people don't know how. They don't realize that the paralysis they feel is in their minds.

And so is the cure.

All our lives we're told what to do, what to strive for. Two plus two equals four, they tell us. If you can just get to four, then you'll be complete/correct/balanced/approved. Aim for four, then pat yourself on the back for a job well done once you get there.

Fuck that. I want more. I reject the restraints and the crutches. I reject anything that numbs or sedates or embalms.

I choose five. I choose the castle at the end of the world.

Have I shown you the pictures?

It's kind of hard to see it, the way it's carved into the cliffs the way it is. But take another look. Give yourself a minute to get into the right frame of mind. Now look again, there, between the ice floes.

No?

The thing is, you have to make a choice. You can look at the picture and choose to see icebergs crashing, melting, and careening into cruel, dark waves below. The only thing you'll see, then, is the end. Or you can look again, and this time you can choose to see the castle carved into the ice, so high and precarious it almost seems like it's floating. So pure and dream-like you could almost mistake it for a cloud.

Choose to look at it like this, and instead of the end of the world, you'll see the ultimate *what next*.

Sometimes you have to retrain your brain to see what's possible instead of what's obvious.

The trip isn't completely finalized, not quite yet. But do you see the way Dylan has his arms around me? Do you see the way he kisses me? The way his lips dance over every inch of my flesh, the way they *know* me in the best possible way? Watch how he's careful of the tender spots along my spine, the old ones and the new; see how his fingertips draw gentle little circles, tracing the lines of the tattoos hidden beneath my clothes.

It's hard to break away from something as perfect as this, sometimes.

Once I'm back on my feet, I'll finally have enough to pay for the whole trip. It may hurt a bit, but that's okay. Because this is a love story.

The IV piercing my arm is Cupid's arrow.

The hum and the beep of the life support are the priest reciting the vows.

Watch how my heartbeat responds when you give it a little poke: *I do. I do. I do.*

It doesn't matter that I'm in pretty rough shape, or that I'm alone. I'm doing this for him, so he is in the room with me, even if he's not. My eyes don't need to be open to know he's by my side.

I choose five. I choose the castle at the end of the world. I choose love. I've found what I was looking for, and I've written my own perfect, happy ending.

Because this is a love story. If you can't see that, maybe you're just not trying hard enough.

AUTHOR'S NOTE

In late June 2013, I crawled out of bed at 3:30 a.m. and wrote what is now the prologue and first chapter of *Placebo Junkies*. This fact is remarkable for several reasons. First, because I was traveling with an infant at the time and was so jet-lagged and sleep-deprived that it's amazing that *anything* could compel me to get up at such an early hour. And second, because never before in my writing career have words come so fast and furious—as if several entire chapters had been gifted to me by some character in a dream I could no longer remember.

It may have felt like it at 3:30 in the morning, but the concept definitely did not materialize out of thin air. Instead, it was inspired by two very brief and totally unrelated experiences from the day before; it just took a short night's restless sleep for the ideas to loop and coil and, ultimately, converge in my travel-fatigued mind.

1.

I spent the day before my 3:30 a.m. writing session in a section of Seattle with a large homeless-youth population. I'd worked in this neighborhood for several summers back when I was in college, and at first glance, not much seemed to have changed over the years. But unlike when I was nineteen and passing through the occasional cluster of homeless teens as I made my way home on public transportation, this time I reacted as an adult and as a mother. These were *kids,* I now saw. That day, with my own children in tow, the thought of the circumstances that must have led to these young people living on the streets struck me as particularly heartbreaking.

2.

A few hours later, I woke up from the nap I was taking in the car en route to my in-laws' house, where we were staying. I opened my eyes as we pulled up to a red light and stared groggily at a small, handwritten sign staked into the ground. "I made hundreds of dollars losing weight and so can you!" the sloppy writing said. "Get paid to try an amazing new weight-loss drug." Two digits of the phone number provided had been scribbled out and corrected with a different-colored marker.

Does anyone, ever, actually believe signs like that are legit? Who would possibly think it a good idea to swallow pills provided by a random stranger who stuck a homemade sign at an intersection? I wondered about the sign until our light turned green, and then promptly forgot all about it.

That night, the two elements came together while I slept: the characters, as viewed on the streets of Seattle; and the premise, inspired by a dubious claim on a roadside sign.

When I sent the initial chapters to my literary agent, semi-apologetically since they were "kind of crazy," I thought that the concept was perhaps a little too outlandish. I mean, come on—people actually trying to make a living by participating in paid drug studies? No way.

But once I started to research, I was amazed to learn that my concept wasn't outlandish at all, and that the practice of making a living via paid medical trials has a long and well-documented history.

In the course of conducting research for this book, I spoke to numerous people on each side of the testing equation. I even interviewed several people who had personal experience as both a subject and as a researcher. One, a physician who now runs clinical trials, regularly "volunteered" for drug studies while he was in medical school in order to earn extra money. Another source, who is employed by a contract research organization (CRO), had enrolled in a clinical trial of birth control pills along with several other coworkers, because, hey—free birth control!

The people I spoke to had had wildly varying experiences. One source on the research side told me horror stories of some of the studies she had facilitated; she had personally witnessed the recruitment of obviously mentally ill "volunteers" from a New Orleans bus station. Another source employed by a research organization in Mexico, on the other hand, described scrupulously designed and controlled studies with both ethics and safety considerations paramount.

Many of the paid test subjects thought it was a great way to earn easy money. Others swore they'd never make that same mistake again.

My book is not intended to condemn clinical trials. Personally, I like having the latest and greatest medicine available when I'm sick, and human-subject testing is a critical part of getting drugs onto pharmacy shelves. Furthermore, the overwhelming majority of the men and women who are a part of the discovery process are dedicated to ethical and safe practices. There are, of course, exceptions—on both sides. But in this book, I specifically wanted to avoid the traditional medical-thriller pattern of having "Big Bad Pharma" at the root of the evil. Instead, I wanted to turn things upside down a little. I wanted to create a spin on a medical thriller, in which Big Pharma did not play the typical villain's role. This gave me a joyride of an opportunity to explore a number of themes that I find fascinating: control, ideological versus physical threats, perspective, causation, and intent.

One of the biggest challenges I faced while writing *Placebo Junkies* was achieving the right balance between certain scenes that are (I hope) quite funny and certain topics that are not at all funny. I have a sense of humor that veers sharply toward dark and a solid appreciation for the poetically grotesque, but I absolutely did not want to make light of any of the very serious subjects touched upon in the book: mental illness, drug addiction, medical ethics, or human-subject testing, among others. My goal, then, was to craft a story that simultaneously thrills and challenges readers. *Placebo Junkies* is intended to spin assumptions and prompt questions and discussions, and it is my sincere hope that it does.

ACKNOWLEDGMENTS

Writing *Placebo Junkies* involved some of the most extensive and most outlandish research that I have ever conducted for a book; I remain surprised that my Internet search history alone didn't trigger some sort of legal intervention. Due to the subject matter, I can't name or properly thank most of those who provided me with data, insight, and personal stories. From the CRO employees who provided inside information both damning and exculpatory, to the physicians who answered my bizarre questions with only a mild eyebrow raise, to the individuals who told me about their own volunteer experiences, to the heavily inked and pierced cashier at the grocery store who cheerfully answered my questions about body modification every time I shopped—please know that you are appreciated! I'll break my policy of source discretion only to thank my retired-radiologist father—mostly for not calling the authorities on any of the many occasions when I asked questions about how one might go about tampering with an MRI machine or the mechanics of spinal injections gone wrong. . . .

I can, however, name some of the good people who helped this book come into existence on the publishing side. Many thanks to my agent, Jessica Regel, and my editor, Katherine Harrison, for taking a chance and championing the strange little nugget of an idea and a voice that only later grew into a proper book. Thank you to Ray Shappell for noticing that my title had just the right number of letters to fit on a couple of pillboxes and designing an amazing cover around that concept. Much appreciation to Iris Broudy, Artie Bennett, and Alison Kolani for saving me many times over with their copyediting magic. (Was it terribly immature of me to snicker a little whenever I read your utterly professional corrections of things like my improper habit of writing *douche bag* as one word?) Thanks also to Heather Kelly for tackling some complex interior design issues, and to managing editor Dawn Ryan for her support!